MAIA

– PETER LATHE –

Best Wishes

Peter Lathe

An environmentally friendly book printed and bound in England by
www.printondemand-worldwide.com

Mixed Sources
Product group from well-managed
forests, and other controlled sources
www.fsc.org Cert no. TT-COC-002641
FSC © 1996 Forest Stewardship Council

PEFC Certified
This product is
from sustainably
managed forests
and controlled
sources
PEFC
www.pefc.org
PEFC/16-33-415

This book is made entirely of chain-of-custody materials

i

www.fast-print.net/store.php

MAIA
Copyright © Peter Lathe 2012

ISBN 978-178035-289-3

First published 2012 by
FASTPRINT PUBLISHING
Peterborough, England.

About The Author

Peter studied with the late author and broadcaster Archie Hill. With several articles published in the UK and a travel book in Cyprus, this is his first novel. Born in the Midlands the author now lives in Cumbria.

Author's Note

Roman legions began the construction of Hadrian's Wall in AD 122. Almost 2000 years later this ancient frontier stands as a prime example of Roman engineering. Given their incredible skills we can be sure that every fort and settlement along the Wall was supplied with fresh water. This came directly from natural springs and streams or via Roman aqueducts. As remains of these aqueducts are visible today near the Cumbria - Northumberland border, in all probability they also served the Wall's western terminus. Here, on the Solway Estuary, once stood Hadrian's second largest fort... *MAIA*.

Now buried beneath the village of Bowness-on-Solway these ancient grounds hide untold mysteries, but visitors to its church can still see the stone blocks carved by Roman hands. They might also notice something quite unusual; for on the stone floor at the foot of the west wall stand two large bells.

Legend has it that in the 17th century the original bells were stolen from this church by Scottish raiders.

But they heaved them overboard into the Solway as their boat was chased by the villagers.. In turn, Bowness men 'acquired' from Scotland the bells now on display. A plaque on the wall nearby tells this tale… and yet, older residents here know these bells have another, more poignant meaning. They are a silent tribute to one man. He was a stranger to the village, but his courage, dedication and generosity will never be forgotten.

This book endeavours to tell his story… and how he uncovered *MAIA*'s greatest secrets.

Peter Lathe 2012

For my wife Joanna… and my brother Derek

★ ★ ★

I would like to thank Lyn and Andy Lewis, Richard Wills and the people of Bowness-on-Solway for their help and advice. My 'reconfiguration' of their village, its church, the old rectory and the characters within are pure imagery.

Peter Lathe

CUMBRIA

LONDON
1987

Chapter I

He saw a light down in the churchyard, and then came a thud of metal striking the soft earth. He listened in disbelief… it was after midnight, yet someone was still out there digging a grave. Ben Miller remembered this because it set the scene for almost everything that followed.

He paused at the lych-gate with a rueful smile; it seemed a long time since he'd buried his own past. As a high-flying journalist on Fleet Street, his career and bank balance had vanished in a haze of drunken notoriety. It seems a lifetime ago, he mused, but this is me now… investigating some strange place where they bury their dead at night!

Being in this remote coastal village wasn't his idea, yet as reputations go Miller could hardly refuse the offer of freelance work. To report on an archaeological dig for a local rag would hardly test his journalistic skills, but he was strapped for cash and his rent was due. The irony of it all was in a damning article he'd once written, shaming a politician's weakness for drugs and drink. But soon these same words echoed his own demise from a swish apartment overlooking the Thames to a freezing, run-down cottage in Cumbria. Miller shrugged, and turning his collar against a chill wind from the sea, he moved on.

The cobbled street climbed steeply to the village pub, and within the confines of his walk he made out a mixture of traditional cottages, sandstone houses and modern bungalows. A power cut had cast the village in shadow... nothing stirred in the darkness. Now the rain added to its desolation, whispering in the wind as though some ancient ghost followed in his footsteps. He shivered, tightened the belt of his raincoat and turned back.

All this was in stark contrast to his arrival that afternoon. To meet Lucy again after all this time was incredible. He'd lost count of the years since their relationship ended, and how she'd chosen to marry some college lecturer. Miller's life began to crumble after this. Sure he'd dated other women, but only for sex. Lucy was different... he could never truly love anyone else. Then suddenly there she was, as beautiful as ever...

Miller grinned as he recalled parking his car, only to hear her call: "Excuse me! I'm afraid you can't leave it there it's..."

Lucy was walking from a nearby driveway towards him. "Ben? My god, it's really you!" she cried, throwing her arms around him. He smiled. "It's so good to see you, Lucy."

She looked amazing. Her slim body, flawless skin and those soft green eyes made him realise how washed-out he appeared himself. Unshaven for days, he wore frayed jeans and a sweater which hung loosely on his skinny frame. At thirty-eight, he was only two years older... no wonder Lucy barely recognised him. But within minutes she was holding his arm, walking him to the house.

Over coffee he explained the purpose of his visit and without hesitation, Lucy offered him a room.

"Most of the year," she said, "the village guest houses are full. They're walkers mainly, either starting out or just completing the journey along Hadrian's Wall. But I can offer a bird's-eye view right here." She laughed at his quizzical expression. "Come on, I'll show you."

It was an impressive house: double-fronted with two spacious reception rooms, a study and large kitchen. The oak-panelled walls through the hallway continued up a matching oak staircase rising to a wide landing. There were four bedrooms, and his single room was at the front with a sea view.

At the window, Lucy pointed to a field directly opposite. "That's where the archaeologists will be working on Monday," she smiled.

Ben could see that beyond the field a strip of marsh-land edged the Solway Firth. The estuary narrowed dramatically at this point as it curved in an S-bend around the headland.

"It's perfect, Lucy, but are you sure your husband won't mind? Charles, isn't it?"

Lucy brushed a wisp of blonde hair from her face. "It *was* his name… but he's gone now."

"I'm sorry. Can I ask what happened?"

"His secretary… she's what happened! Even my daughter, Sarah, won't have anything to do with him now."

Ben saw the anger in her eyes, but said nothing.

"I was carrying our child when I found out. I rushed to the college to have it out with them, but…" Lucy paused, and Ben touched her hand, reassuringly.

"I fell down some steps there... and lost my baby."

He'd put his arms around her then, and she'd cried... the years of emotion and regret touching them both.

Miller's return to Lucy's house that night was delayed. When he reached the church he stopped... the light was still there. He entered the churchyard. At least, he thought, a chat with the gravedigger for some more local opinion on the arrival of archaeologists would help his article. So he followed a path from the lych-gate which led to the church's south entrance through a porch. Beneath the branches of a cypress tree he saw a man working in the pale glow of a lantern.

His steel-grey hair was cropped almost as short as the stubble on his face. He was solidly built with a fearsome look about him, but Miller's greeting startled him. The man cursed softly as the raincoat draped around his shoulders fell to the ground.

"I'm sorry, but I saw your lamp from the street. My name's Miller... Ben Miller. "

The man stared at him suspiciously, ignoring his outstretched hand. "George," he mumbled. "You're not from these parts, eh?"

"No. Near to London, but now I... "

"So what brings you 'round here then?" The gravedigger had already turned back to his spade.

Purely on instinct, Ben chose not to reveal the true purpose of his visit. "Well I'm interested in Roman history and thought of walking the trail along Hadrian's Wall. Do you know anything about ancient *Maia*, George?"

The old man said nothing, merely a grunt as he lifted another spade of earth.

Miller could see now it was a small grave. He tried again. "A tragic loss for someone in the village, I suppose?"

George sniffed against the back of his hand. "What you say?"

"The grave… is it for a local child?"

"Ah, I… I guess you could say that. I'm just doin' my job before they find…." The old man stopped abruptly, unable to hide his annoyance. "Anyways… that's me done," he added quickly. "I should be getting back to the wife. Can't be helping you none."

Miller watched him cover the grave with a tarpaulin sheet. He knew George was anxious about something, and what he'd said didn't make sense. Who were 'they'… and before they 'find' what? Miller's years of experience told him to question the old man further, but he let it go. "That's okay, George. Perhaps we can meet again sometime before I leave?"

The gravedigger smiled weakly. He collected his tools in silence, and then trudged away down the path. As Miller stood there in the darkness again, he noticed another glimmer of light through a window in the church. He tried the door and finding it open, entered the porch. A second door facing him was ajar and he stepped inside.

Within a few paces Miller was standing in the centre aisle. To his left a solitary candle shed light on a wooden unit, containing hymn books and magazines. A short distance away was a font, carved in stone and mounted on a dais. Beyond this, two ancient-looking bells stood on the floor. He turned right, walking slowly towards the flickering candles in the chancel.

There was a fragrance of lavender, and rose petals were falling from a large basket of flowers beside the altar. As he paused at the lectern to admire its wood-carved eagle, a figure moved from the shadows of the transept behind him.

"A symbol of John, the Apostle, or rather the height he rose to in the first chapter of his Gospel. Those figures at the base are Mark, Mathew and Luke."

The richness of his voice belied the man in front of Miller. He was frail and unsteady, leaning heavily on a stick.

"You must excuse our primitive lighting," said the vicar. "The loss of power is a typical village problem, I'm afraid. We don't normally have visitors at night," he smiled, "but you're most welcome. I'm Reverend Thomas; can I help you at all?"

Miller introduced himself, and apologised for the lateness of the hour before playing the role of a tourist again. "Well I'm interested in the ancient Romans, especially Hadrian's Wall. I wonder if you might know of any ruins here."

The vicar shook his head. "I moved to this parish about thirty years ago, and to my knowledge only a few coins have been found. However, there's Roman-cut stone all around you in these walls. But sadly, there's nothing left of Maia, the Roman fort."

Miller knew this from his research, but said: "What about the Roman thought to be buried here?"

It was meant as a casual remark, a ploy he sometimes used to prompt a reaction. It worked; the vicar seemed taken aback.

"Do you know his name?" he asked, in a more serious tone.

Miller said the first thing that came to mind: "Prator, I believe."

Reverend Thomas smiled again. "So, it seems you are more interested in dead Romans than pottery. That's a pity because we have some nice pieces around the church."

He pointed his staff at the darkened shapes of pottery set in the wall niches behind his visitor. "Not Roman, but very old. I managed to salvage some fragments from the sand and marshes. But that was long ago," he sighed. "I can't get down there anymore."

"Perhaps I can see them another time, Reverend?"

"Yes, of course… and I'm sorry about your Roman. I think you must be mistaken, my friend."

There was something in his voice which prompted Miller to pursue the subject. "Are you saying that despite the thousands of Romans who once lived around these parts, no-one could be named Prator?"

The vicar sat down in the nearest pew, his white hair gleaming in the candlelight. "Forgive me; I tire so easily these days. Here… sit with me for a while. I should explain."

He looked weary; his eyes avoiding Miller to gaze at the sombre figures portrayed in the stained-glass windows above them. They stared back at him without emotion.

"Prator seems an unlikely name for a Roman," he began, "it's more of a title. We know that the Roman consuls held overall military power, but 'praetors' were highly ranked officers.

"Roman leaders ruled in various ways: some by valour on the battlefield, while others were driven by corruption, greed and depravity. Yet the likes of Hadrian and Cicero were highly intelligent scholars. Although Cicero was a consul he's remembered as Rome's finest orator, not a military man. Cicero's prowess was in the Senate House and the courts of Rome."

"I don't imagine he ever aspired to match the conquests of Julius Caesar," said Miller.

The vicar appreciated his comment. "No, you're absolutely right. Caesar was a great leader and a tactical genius on the battlefield. He would fight on the spur of the moment; his opponents never knowing when he would attack. Caesar favoured the element of surprise: in atrocious weather or at the end of a long march. The man had a remarkable instinct for caution or daring…"

The reverend stopped for a moment, the pain in his leg causing him to shift uneasily. But Miller's reference to Caesar now encouraged a ten-minute historical sermon on the Roman's life.

Miller listened with interest to this learned man, whose words flowed without thought. Finally, he said: "Well, maybe that Prator fellow never existed after all."

Reverend Thomas was already rising to his feet as Miller thanked him for his time. "You're most welcome," he said. "My church is always open to you."

In closing the heavy porch door behind him, Miller glanced towards the shallow grave. He wondered why both the vicar and his gravedigger failed to mention one important issue: the imminent excavations. In such a small community as this strong opinions and protests would be foremost in any conversation, as it was with Lucy earlier. Yet with a team of archaeologists, their vehicles and equipment disrupting their village, neither man had spoken of it.

Miller smiled at an old familiar feeling… there could be a story here after all.

By the time he reached Lucy's house the power supply was restored. He let himself in with the key she'd given him, and locking the door he quietly went upstairs.

Lucy was awake, worrying over him. His absence so late at night used to happen frequently when they were together. The tragic death of his younger brother was a recurring nightmare to Ben. He was twelve years old, and almost died himself trying to save his brother from drowning.

Now his loss of weight also concerned Lucy. It looked as though he hadn't eaten properly for months. But then she smiled, reminding herself how handsome he still was, and the special way he looked at her hadn't changed at all. She remembered the crazy things they did together at university; his outspoken manner; the self-assurance; their unbridled passion... and the tenderness of his undying love. Yet he was always restless, hell-bent on making the big time as a journalist. Well he did, and with great success.

Lucy sat up in bed. "I know what really happened, Ben, but I want you to tell me," she whispered... as if he was lying beside her.

Miller's room was spacious, with pine furniture and a luxury en-suite bathroom. On a small table under the window was a courtesy tray. He undressed for bed, made some tea and settled down to read a book about Roman Britain he'd borrowed earlier from the study. The pages were still crisp and unread. Inside was a gift card bearing the words:

'Happy Birthday, Charles.
With all our love. Lucy, Sarah and baby?'

Apart from this, he thoroughly enjoyed the author's study of Roman architecture, their incredible feats of engineering and the two chapters given to Hadrian's

Wall. Even so, as interesting as these fragments of history appeared he eventually closed his eyes.

Ben Miller slept without ever dreaming that he would experience the most astonishing day of his life.

Whatever it was that disturbed Miller came from outside and he moved to the window. A faint glimpse of daylight touched the skies, but the sea was still dark and silent. A veil of mist crept across the field, pausing then drifting on as if searching for the lost souls of *Maia.*

Miller was about to draw the curtain again when he noticed someone. A man stood under a street lamp near the track at the side of the field. He wore a long dark coat and supported himself on a walking stick… it was the Reverend Thomas. He seemed to be urging someone down the track. Then Miller saw a second man struggling to push a wheelbarrow. When he reached the vicar he stopped to rest. The burden old George carried in his wheelbarrow was heavy, and covered with sacking.

Miller dressed in a hurry with trousers and sweater over his pyjamas. He left the house, keeping a safe distance behind the two men. It must have been a hundred yards to the church, and George was forced to stop several more times; the weight in his wheelbarrow increasing ten-fold up the hill. Miller waited for them to go inside the lych-gate before scaling a stone wall into the graveyard.

Near the church he saw the lantern being lit. He guessed their destination, and keeping the lantern in sight he moved slowly between the tall headstones. Miller was close enough now to hear the vicar.

"You can't work with your hand bleeding like that. Come inside and I'll dress it for you."

"But we don't have the time," protested the younger man.

"That's okay, George. It will only take a few more minutes."

When the door closed behind them and a light came on in the church, Miller approached the freshly dug grave. There were no human remains inside… only a slab of stone some eight inches thick.

In the glow from the lantern he could see where the dirt and moss had scraped away in transit. Something was etched on its surface.

Miller whispered: "Why on earth bury a broken slab of stone?" But then he saw the inscription and realised the words were different: it was Latin… a Roman stone. Where the grime had peeled away there was an unusual message… and a familiar name.

He crouched down closer, his fingers trembling as they brushed over the nine words. They were so faint some letters were indiscernible and others missing, but Miller pieced together the text as best he could and memorised it. He checked the name again but there was no mistake… it read:

'… *CAESAR OCTAVIANUS DAMON*…'

He stared in bewilderment, unable to take in the enormity of its meaning. Miller could hardly recall finding his way back to Lucy's house, or even climbing into bed again. It was 8 am when Lucy knocked on his door to announce his breakfast would be ready in thirty minutes.

Miller showered and shaved, trying to reason why someone like the vicar would break the law? The field was part of *Maia's* Roman settlement and was listed as a Scheduled Monument… so why remove the stone?

More to the point how did he and George know its location in the field?

There were so many questions to find answers to, but they would have to wait. He dressed in some decent trousers and sports shirt, before greeting Lucy in the kitchen. He noticed her look of approval… and over breakfast, even a hint of flirtation in her wonderful eyes.

"Be sure you eat every scrap, Ben Miller," she told him. "You need to look after yourself… or at least someone should."

"Is that a threat or a promise?"

"It could be either… or both," she laughed. "So, do you plan on working today?"

For now, Miller thought it best not to tell Lucy about the previous night. He wanted to find out more. "I just need to visit an old friend in Allonby. He's Greek, but good with archaeology and stuff about the Romans. I won't be long because I don't want to miss seeing your lovely daughter, Sarah."

Lucy smiled at him. "I spoke with her earlier. She's dying to meet you."

Thirty minutes later Miller was well on his way down the Solway Coast. He had concluded that with little knowledge of Latin his first priority was to find someone who could translate the stone's complete text. The only thing he could be sure of was that the stone must be rare indeed to carry the name of 'Caesar'.

It was just before ten when Miller reached Allonby, another village on the estuary. The man he had come to see was reading his newspaper in a small café on the seafront. Andreas had studied archaeology, and his interest in all things Roman made him a logical choice.

Miller approached his old friend. "Kalimera, Andreas."

A small, wiry man raised his eyes, squinting at him. Miller offered a few more words in Greek.

"There's no need to struggle," Andreas cut in. "I can understand your English better." Then a broad smile lit up his face as he recognised Miller.

They sat there together, catching up on old times over a fresh pot of tea. After a while, Miller mentioned his assignment in Bowness. "Have you any idea what this means?" he asked, passing Andreas his note-book.

In one comical movement the Greek took another pair of spectacles from his waistcoat pocket; rubbed the lenses vigorously on his sleeve and perched them on the end of his nose.

"It's some dedication or other," he said. "The kind you see on memorial stones… it's certainly Roman." He pointed to the words. "Here it says: *'The Second Augustan Legion made this…'* But the other part is much more interesting… *'Caesar Octavianus Damon'*," he read aloud. Andreas scratched his head, looking vacant until Miller took out his wallet. He gave him five pounds. "For the tea," he said.

"But of course," Andreas grinned, slipping the note into his pocket. "Now, my friend, this is quite unique…. some great Roman names with a Greek."

Miller looked at him. "Are you sure?"

Andreas nodded, and asking for his friend's pen he began making notes while he explained: "The full name on the stone would have been *'Gaius Julius Caesar Octavianus Damon'*. It's quite a mouthful, but it is the Roman way and tells us your man was alive after 44 BC, but died before 27 BC."

"How can you possibly know this, Andreas?"

"Well… to begin with, Octavianus - whom we know better as Octavian - took his adoptive father's name,

Caesar, after the Roman leader died in 44 BC. And even though Octavian never had a son called Damon, we can still determine other important facts. The first is that in 27BC the Roman Senate honoured Octavian. They made him the first emperor of Rome, and his name was officially changed to Augustus. So, Damon had died before then."

"But how can a Greek have such an important title as this?"

Andreas handed back the pen and note-book, then slowly removed his spectacles and smiled. "We can still establish his true identity. But for him to be remembered this way by the Second Augustan Legion after more than 150 years is truly remarkable. This honour is normally reserved for Roman gods and emperors, so whatever he did the Greek must have been a very special man.

"I would imagine he was granted manumission: his freedom," he said, quietly. "Yes… there's no doubt in my mind… Damon was once Octavian's slave."

When Miller returned to Bowness, Lucy and Sarah came down the driveway to greet him. Even at the age of fourteen, Sarah already displayed the poise and self-confidence of her mother. Aspiring to be a journalist herself, she was in awe of what Lucy had told her about his rise to fame with the national press. Yet from the content of Sarah's questions Miller seemed to think that Lucy knew nothing of his downfall.

"Mum says you're over here now on a special assignment. Can I help, Mister Miller?"

"Only if you call me Ben," he grinned.

Sarah was showing him the gardens while Lucy prepared Sunday lunch. There was a huge lawned area which swept around the house under a canopy of pine and yew trees, and at the far end was a pool where an old rectory house once stood. The whole plot seemed well over an acre.

Miller noted with interest how informative the teenager was about the variety of plants, shrubs and trees. "Did your father landscape the gardens, Sarah?" he asked.

"Oh, 'destroy' is a better word!" the girl replied, frostily. "There were some nice features here: broken statues, stone animals and things. Over there by that rhododendron, for example, were the remains of a concrete dog kennel. Well, not really a kennel, but it looked the same. There was something similar in our church cellar. I think it used to be an old well."

Sarah pointed at a metal drain cover set in the lawn. "Under there is a shaft and he was going to fill it in... but he never did. Everything else was thrown away!"

She turned to look at Miller. "Would you have kept the dog kennel, Ben?"

"Sure... if you liked it so much, why not?"

"If I tell you something, promise you won't tell Mum?"

Miller sighed. "Oh, okay... just this once. What have you been up to, then?"

Even though Lucy was in the kitchen, some twenty yards away, Sarah's voice fell to a whisper. "Some time ago my friend Alice and me... you know, the friend where I stayed last night?"

Miller nodded, feigning a worrying glance in Lucy's direction.

"Well, we sort of explored under that cover. I managed to open it, and we climbed down there."

"So, what did you find," smiled Miller, "some coal?"

Sarah laughed, giving him a playful push. "If you must know, we found... absolutely nothing. It was dry but too dark to see anything, and very cold."

"Oh, no!" gasped Miller, his eyes open wide in mock horror. "I knew it. Those graves next door... there's a ghost down there!"

He dodged Sarah's swipe, and ran towards the house with Sarah right on his heels. Ben tripped in the hallway and went crashing to the floor. He sat on his haunches, rubbing his knee while Sarah stood over him in fits of laughter.

What a lovely man, she thought. He's a little crazy, but in a nice way. How different from my dull, serious father. Yes, I like Ben... and my Mum certainly does. Yet even when Miller smiled up at her, Sarah noticed the sadness in his eyes. It puzzled her.

Lucy, rushing in from the kitchen, disturbed her thoughts.

"What's all this noise, then?" smiled Lucy.

They both looked at her, and with more laughter, simultaneously blamed each other.

The light-hearted mood continued through lunch, and Lucy was content to listen to Ben and Sarah chat away while they washed the dishes. His interest in Sarah's ambitions was genuine, and Lucy was pleased when Ben promised to involve her with his work.

In the evening, as they all sat together in the lounge, Ben gave Sarah a little project to do on the church. "It's essential with something like this that journalists collect all the background information they can." He smiled at Sarah, handing her some notes. "Here's what I'm looking for. Are you in with me?"

Sarah glanced down the list. "Gosh...do you really want ME to do this for you?"

"That's the idea, partner. Oh, and feel free to add some more information, if you like? No make-believe, Sarah... they have to be facts, you understand?"

Sarah nodded, jumped up from her armchair and planted a kiss on his cheek. "Thank you so much, Mister Mi... I mean, Ben. I... I won't let you down."

"I know you'll do your best, Sarah, and that's all that matters."

The girl kissed her mother goodnight, and Lucy had rarely seen her happier. She realised then the difference Ben was making to them both. The change in him was obvious, yet also confusing. The young man she once knew was fiercely independent, but now his whole demeanour almost cried out for someone to love him. It was this vulnerability and shyness which now made him even more attractive. She was smiling to herself when she heard her name.

"Lucy..." He was touching her hand. "Is everything alright? I really should have asked your permission first."

"What? I... I'm sorry," she stammered.

"The work I wanted Sarah to do. I hope it was okay to..."

"Ben. You saw her face, how excited she is. I think it's a wonderful idea." Lucy kissed him. "Thank you," she whispered. "I'm so glad you're here."

Miller slowly shook his head. "Maybe when I've told you about the last fifteen years you'll think differently?"

He expected the worst. Although it was all behind him... his drinking, gambling and womanising was enough to deter any woman. But Lucy had to know.

They were holding hands when he began: "The real reason I'm here is that the Fleet Street Press kicked me out. Everything I owned in London: my apartment, the flash cars and money… a lifetime's work has gone. I became an alcoholic of the lowest order. The…"

Lucy squeezed his hand. "I know, Ben. I heard all about it. Charles took great pleasure in reading it to me from one of his magazines. There was an article all about you. He skipped the praise, like your two 'Journalist of the Year' awards, the sorrow felt by some reporters and ex-colleagues. All I remember was his cynical voice, saying he always knew you were a loser."

"He was right, Lucy… there's no way back for me."

"That's nonsense! There are two people in this house who believe in you. You're a kind and wonderful man, Ben Miller." She snuggled closer to him. "Now… change the subject. Tell me what a smart journalist like you is looking for at Bowness in the very early hours?"

Miller laughed. "I was just coming to that, Miss Maples!"

Lucy listened in amazement to Ben's story. From the misdeeds of Reverend Thomas to the name on the Roman stone was staggering. She had no idea anything like this existed, least of all in her own village.

"The vicar and old George never saw me, and the stone's safely buried by now," concluded Miller.

"What about the archaeologists? Is this what they're looking for?"

"It could be… but they'll be wasting their time now."

Lucy looked at him, a little concerned. "What will you do, Ben?"

"Stay another day or so, if that's okay, Lucy? I'll see if I can claim some more expenses to do my research in London. I think my editor will agree to it, as long as he gets some kind of a story."

"Where will you go?"

"Well, the British Library has all the books and information I'll need."

"Oh, does this mean Sarah's not really wanted?"

"Of course she is, Lucy. I promised her. However, I don't think we should tell her yet what's happened here, do you?"

"I agree. It can wait until you're ready," she said, placing their coffee cups on a tray. "Now, if you'd like to stay with me a bit longer, you can earn your keep. To the kitchen, Mister Miller, there's work to be done before you go roaming any more churchyards tonight!"

Fortunately, the local editor had taken a liking to Miller's work, and although the journalist's phone call sounded rather vague, his previous articles were well received by his readers. With a promise of an 'unusual story', therefore, he was happy to fund Miller's trip to London.

The night before he was due to leave Miller sat with Lucy in the lounge. They spoke of another disappointing day for the archaeologists as Sarah came in with her report on the church. She watched Miller carefully read the type-written pages, waiting anxiously for his response.

Miler eventually looked up at her, slowly shaking his head. "In all honesty, this is not what I expected from you, Sarah," he said.

Her heart sank.

"The truth is, young lady... this is very good indeed!"

Both Sarah and Lucy breathed a sigh of relief, and after her ecstatic daughter had gone to bed, Miller gave reason for his praise.

"I purposely listed routine things for her, most of which I already knew; yet look at this: two pages of her own additional work. There's also a detailed plan of the church attached, and here she marked a cover in the cellar floor, apparently an old well once upon a time.

"It may all seem irrelevant, but this is what I was hoping she'd produce. Sarah has used her initiative, she investigated… and unknowingly, she's found it. See what I mean?" smiled Miller, pointing to the last paragraph.

Lucy saw that it listed some of the oldest graves, including the headstone of a raider from the Isle of Man, named Thomas Stoal. It ended with her discovery of a new, unmarked grave.

Lucy suddenly felt so happy and relaxed beside him. When she looked up into his eyes, her own were full of longing and passion. She took his hand and they quietly climbed the stairs to her bedroom.

Afterwards, as they lay in each others arms, Ben said: "It must have been terrible losing the baby, but you must be so proud of Sarah. She's a great girl." He ran his fingers over the sweet curve of her breast. "My deepest regret is not being a father."

Lucy put her lips to his ear, whispering: "But you are, Ben. Sarah is your daughter…"

Time seemed to stand still… "But when… how do you know?" he said.

"I was already pregnant when I married Charles."

"Did he know? Does Sarah know?"

Lucy kissed him lightly. "If he knew, he never said anything. And Sarah doesn't know yet. I was hoping when you come back from London we could tell her together. Is that okay?"

"Is it okay? Lucy, those are the most beautiful words I've ever heard."

It was 5 am when Sarah raised her head from the pillow. A floorboard creaked outside her door. She smiled, turned over and went back to sleep.

Chapter II

When Ben Miller arrived in London he knew the area near Euston Station provided ample accommodation for visitors. He found a small guest house just a few minutes walk from the British Library, and quickly settled into a daily routine. But despite his long and intensive studies the most vital piece of information still eluded him.

It had started well enough. He knew the British Library from numerous visits there in the past. Regulations changed over the years, but by producing the necessary documents Miller acquired the pass allowing him access to the Reading Room. As only general reference books were available here on the open shelves, his more specialised material needed to be ordered from its storage areas.

He concentrated his research on the seventeen year period from Caesar's death to Octavian's amazing rise to power as the first emperor of Rome. Miller studied a whole series of works by Roman historians and biographers, noting in chronological order any scrap of information, no matter how trivial. Even so, none of these ancient writers made any reference to the slave. It was as though Damon never existed… and yet, Miller knew the stone at *Maia* proved otherwise.

One evening, frustrated by the day's fruitless search, he was pleased when the bedside telephone disturbed his thoughts. It was Lucy, eager to know of his progress.

"I've got everything I need except for the most important of all. There's nothing on the slave," said Miller. "Unlike the Roman legions, it seems their historians never recognised him."

Lucy sighed. "But didn't your friend, Andreas, say that Damon must have been a famous figure?"

Before Miller could answer he heard Sarah's voice, then Lucy again: "Ben…Sarah's just come in. She wants to say goodnight."

Miller's heart pounded at the sound of his daughter's voice.

"Hi, Ben, how are you? Will you be home in time for my birthday?"

Miller smiled at the excitement in her voice. "Yes, of course. No matter what happens, Sarah, I'll be there."

"Oh, Mum just said you're having a problem with the Roman historians."

"Yeah… I'm afraid old Livy and Suetonius are heavy going."

"I know what you mean," she laughed. "Greek historians are the same. We were given an essay to do at school a few months ago on Alexander the Great…"

In an instant Miller realised he was on the wrong track. Damon was not a Roman, and if anything, Greek history would hold the key.

"Ben? Hello… Are you still there?"

"Sarah, you're an angel! I'll explain when I see you, but you've probably saved me a lot of work…"

Three days later Miller had solved the mystery surrounding the Greek slave. With a sigh of relief he stretched his aching shoulders. So, that old rascal Andreas was right after all, he smiled. Damon had died in 30 BC, three years before Octavian became the emperor Augustus.

Miller placed the bulging folder of research notes inside his briefcase, and for the last time made his way out of the British Library. It was raining, and thunder rumbled around the great building as he descended the steps. He scowled at the ominous skies.

Ben Miller hated the rain; too often it reminded him of his brother's death. Robert was ten, two years younger, but always the one full of mischief and daring… no more than on that fateful day.

It had been a hard winter, but with a slight thaw that afternoon it was raining as they walked home from school. Already yards in front of Ben, his brother suddenly decided on a short cut across the frozen lake. Before Ben realised the danger, Robert was over a fence and calling out for Ben to join him. Ben yelled for him to stop, but Robert was on the lake now making slides across the ice. Ben vaulted the fence but fell awkwardly. He heard the bone crack in his ankle; his brother's laughter echoing through the trees… and then the silence.

In spite of the pain, Ben crawled his way over the glassy surface in a desperate attempt to save his brother. He was too late, and almost perished himself as he also plunged through the ice. All he remembered was someone pulling his hair, dragging him from the murky waters. A stranger out walking his dog heard the boys shouting, but found only Ben in the water.

This was only the beginning of Ben's agony. His father beat him senseless; every blow he suffered deepening the blame and torment he still endured. And even now, almost thirty years later, Ben still couldn't swim. He had never overcome his fear of deep water.

The memories lingered like still photographs he wanted to destroy, but never could. Miller quickened his step down Euston Road, trying to console himself with the knowledge that at least he'd discovered the truth now about Damon.

Back at the guest house Mrs Cooper stopped him in reception. The kindly, buxom lady with an infectious smile handed him two letters.

"A very nice gent brought them in at lunch-time. Bit of alright, 'e was," she winked. Her large bosom heaved with laughter as she nudged Miller with her elbow. "His name's Harry… said you used to work together." She turned back to the reception desk. "Here, 'e left his card."

Miller thanked her, went to his room and changed out of his wet clothes before opening the letters. One looked official with a solicitors' address in London stamped on the envelope. But his eyes were drawn to the second letter. He recognised the writing… it was from his father. He opened it and began to read:

'Dear Ben,
By the time you read this I will be dead and buried.
Knowing I only had a few months left ,I made all the necessary
arrangements for what was needed. I never realised there was so
much to do because when your mother died it was you who dealt
with everything. You were always so organised, just like she was.

'When I look back on my life it is with deep regret. I know the day our Robert died I lost both of my sons. His death broke my heart and I blamed you instead of thanking the Lord for sparing your life. I drove you away, Ben, and for that I'm truly sorry.

I realise this may not mean very much to you now, but I have always followed your career with great pride and admiration for what you achieved. A florist's life would never have suited you, Ben, which is why I've sold the business. Our old house is still in good order, and by leaving you my entire estate I'm sure you will find some use for it.

Perhaps you will settle down with a family of your own soon, and one day even find it in your heart to forgive me.

Goodbye, Ben… and God bless you.'

A tear fell onto the paper as Miller brushed his cheek. All those wasted years, the unanswered letters… and now his father dying alone without him. It hit Ben hard.

He picked up the other letter which informed him that he was a benefactor in his father's estate. Could he please contact them as a matter of urgency? It was dated four days earlier. Miller checked his watch: 16:25. He dialled the number and made an appointment for 09:45 the next morning.

The sorrow in his voice was apparent to Mrs Cooper when she answered his next call to reception. She was concerned when he cancelled his evening meal.

"Is there something wrong dear?" I hope it's not bad news."

"What?"

"The letters I gave you, dear."

"Yes… I'm afraid my father's passed away."

"Oh, I'm so sorry. Can I do anything to help?"

Miller raised a hand to his brow. "Will you have my bill ready for first thing in the morning,, only I'll be leaving before breakfast?"

"Yes, of course. Just leave it to me," she said.

Miller sighed, sat down on the bed and opened his briefcase. He found the picture Lucy had given him and gently touched her smiling face. But his hand was shaking as he was overcome with emotion. Ben Miller unashamedly wept for the loss of a father he hardly knew.

He awoke with a start. The telephone was ringing. "Hello, yes?" he answered, drowsily.

"Ben, it's me, Lucy."

"I'm sorry. I meant to call you… must have dropped off to sleep. Are you okay?"

"Yes, but we've had some awful weather. It's been raining for several days now and rivers are very high; there are flood warnings all over Cumbria."

"What about you and Sarah at Bowness. Is it safe there?"

"We're fine, Ben. Don't worry. In any case, it's been really nice today. Now, before I forget, did Harry find you?"

"I didn't see him, but he left my letters here with Mrs Cooper."

"He's been trying to trace you, and managed to contact your editor. He gave Harry my number and I told him where you were staying in London. Is that alright?"

"Yes…" Miller paused. "My father's died."

"Oh, I'm really sorry, Ben. I know you said you were never close but…"

"He wrote me a letter. Can you believe it, Lucy? After all this time he said he was sorry… and I wasn't even there to bury him."

"Don't reproach yourself, Ben. Your father didn't want to know you after Robert died, did he?"

Miller shook his head. "It doesn't make it any easier."

"I know, Ben. Do you want me to come down to London?"

"There's nothing I'd like more, Lucy, but my father's dealt with everything, even his own funeral. Besides, it's Sarah's birthday on Saturday and you'll have enough to do."

"Are you sure, Ben?"

"Well the other letter was from father's solicitor, and I'm going there tomorrow to sort out the paperwork. My father's left everything to me, Lucy, including the house. I'll stay there tomorrow night and then see you on Saturday."

Lucy smiled at the thought. "Have you any luck with your project?"

"Yes, thanks to Sarah I've found our mysterious slave. I'm done here now, so I'll ring Sarah before I leave father's house on Saturday morning. Will she be at home?"

"Well, it's her friend Alice's birthday too, and I'll be at the Walker's house with her mum, Helen, preparing things for the party. We take turns, and this time it's over there. But the girls will be at my place until late afternoon."

"Good. Then while I'm in the city I'll get Sarah's present: some earrings, perhaps. What do you think?"

"Oh, she'll just be happy to see you, Ben… and so will I. I've really missed you."

His eyes settled on Lucy's photograph again. He'd never denied his feelings for her. "I've always loved you, Lucy," he whispered.

There was a brief pause... "I love you too, Ben. Please hurry home."

Ben Miller smiled as he replaced the receiver. In a sense his time here had seemed like an incredible journey into ancient times. His search for an extraordinary Greek slave who carried the name of 'Caesar' was over. He had uncovered one of Rome's greatest secrets. And this is what he found...

Peter Lathe

ITALY

44 BC

Chapter III

The slaying of Julius Caesar not only caused turmoil and civil unrest in Rome, it also determined a young man's destiny. Caesar's power was absolute. Undefeated at war and devoted to his victorious armies, he followed his great nephew's military career with interest and enthusiasm. Indeed, for Octavian to serve on his kinsman's staff would be a normal procedure, and Caesar was already proud of the young man's achievements.

The previous year while still convalescing from a serious illness, Octavian showed great promise in the Spanish triumph. Caesar announced that the boy would be a worthy successor and, more importantly, made provisions in his will to adopt him.

But in the mayhem following Caesar's murder, Marc Antony knew as surviving consul that he must quickly regain control. This was accomplished by stirring the sympathy of the Roman people as they mourned their greatest leader. Antony seized the opportunity to consolidate his position by announcing that Caesar would have a State funeral. Moreover, he delivered a frenzied speech to the people condemning Caesar's killers, led by Brutus and Cassius.

At the same time, Antony was aware from his private reading of Caesar's will that Octavian was named as heir. He made sure the fact was never publicised. Instead, he authorised the confiscation of Caesar's wealth in the name of the State Treasury. Antony assumed that without this money Octavian would be unable to finance the legions. And without them, there was no power or influence in Rome.

Caesar's adoption of Octavian was also an unexpected blow to Cleopatra. She was living in Rome as Caesar's guest when he died, claiming her child, Caesarion, was Caesar's son and his rightful heir. But Caesar made no provision for any offspring borne to him of the Egyptian queen.

Cleopatra stayed on in Rome for a while following Caesar's death, possibly in the hope of gaining some recognition for the child before Octavian's return to Italy.

Meanwhile, Caesar's heir-apparent was advancing his education in Illyricum. But his time in the town of Apollonia again proved detrimental to his health. Octavian was often plagued by illness, yet despite his frailty his undoubted gift in oratory, together with his military training, singled him out as a promising leader.

He was eighteen years old when he helped to prepare and assemble an army capable of impressing the great man himself. It was Caesar's intention to take Octavian with him on his planned war against the Dacians and Parthians… but this was not to be.

When Octavian received news of Caesar's death he realised his own life could be in jeopardy. His choice was to either stay under the protection of his legions in

Apollonia, or return to Rome and claim his inheritance. Octavian decided to cross the Adriatic and face the dangers that might well befall him in Italy.

In the first hour of that April morning, the ship carrying Octavian and his most trusted friends arrived safely at Brundisium. A messenger on horseback watched them step out on deck. He recognised the portly figure of Maecenas, friend and mentor of Octavian, then the golden hair of the boy himself. The man smiled as he turned his horse and rode towards the hills.

Down in the harbour's marketplace the air was heavy with the smell of raw meat and fish. There was bedlam everywhere as traders shouted at the slaves jostling after the finest food for their masters' tables. Arguments and scuffles spilled over to the quayside, clashing with other slaves ferrying cargo from the ships. But these unruly scenes ended abruptly with the appearance of a Roman centurion and his force of legionaries.

Quintus Glaber brought his men to a halt at the quayside and dismounted. He ordered four foot-soldiers to accompany him and prepared to board a ship. The crowd surged forward to catch a glimpse of the two young Romans who appeared to confront him.

"I have news for Octavian," Glaber called out, his eyes fixing on the tall, broad shouldered youth whose right hand closed on the hilt of his sword.

Marcus Agrippa blocked his path. "That's near enough, centurion. State your business."

Glaber smiled at the young man's courage, but before he could speak a pale youth standing in Agrippa's shadow came forward.

"I am *Caesar* Octavianus!" he snapped.

"Quintus Glaber, my lord!" The centurion's arm crossed his chest in a smart salute. "I am centurion of the

Fourth Cohort of the Tenth Legion. It is an honour for me to escort you to Rome, sire."

"Is the honour you speak of your own noble gesture, or are you to escort me under Marc Antony's orders?"

The young man's gaze was penetrating. Glaber could not analyse the eyes locked onto his. They were the palest of blue, like pools of ice… almost frightening in their emptiness. Momentarily, he was forced to look away.

"Well? What news do you bring, Glaber?"

The centurion handed over a letter and Octavian, assuming it to be from Antony, was surprised to see that it carried the seal of Cornelius Balbus, one of Caesar's most prosperous allies.

'Greetings, my dear Gaius' it began.

'Quintus Glaber is an outstanding soldier. His father was a close friend of Caesar's, and both have served him with loyalty and courage. To claim what is rightfully yours you will need his protection on your journey to Rome. Near the forum in the town of Brundisium you will find Evagoras, the Greek. In my name, draw the gold you need to start recruiting men. I urge you to claim your inheritance and calm the troubled heart of our beloved Rome.'

Octavian told the centurion to wait before handing the letter to Agrippa. They walked to the prow of the ship where Maecenas stood, wrapped in his winter cloak against a chill wind from the sea. He was fussing over his own appearance.

"Look at him. He sickens me!" spat Agrippa. "Rome is on its knees, and all he thinks about is preening himself…"

Octavian restrained him. "He's harmless, Agrippa. You may question his self-indulgence, but Maecenas is my advisor, and like you he is a true friend."

Agrippa thrust the letter into Maecenas' hand, and to Octavian he said: "If you want my opinion, I don't like the look of Glaber. This could well be a trap."

Maecenas looked at him in amusement. "My dear Agrippa, there must be a hundred legionaries out there. If it was a trap the whole deck of this ship would be awash with blood... our blood! Now please, let me read what Balbus has in mind."

Agrippa was seething, but managed to hold his tongue. Abusive words might be seen to undermine Octavian's command, especially in the presence of a centurion.

"Ah...how gracious of him! Balbus has offered money," smiled Maecenas, "and that's our most persuasive asset. Gold will buy your legions, Octavian... one day it might even buy you the Roman Senate!"

"That may be so, but I think Agrippa is right," replied Octavian. "Glaber might have served with Caesar but we should remember the Tenth Legion is one of Antony's. You always said that we should never underestimate him."

Maecenas smiled, be-jewelled fingers stroking his chin. "What a strange coincidence it is that five years ago Caesar laid siege to Brundisium during the civil war. Pompey was surrounded here, apparently trapped inside the city walls, rather like we are. Caesar could have slaughtered them all, but surprisingly the great man hesitated. He waited until the last moment to launch the attack, only to find his adversary had slipped through the net. Pompey and his ships escaped from this very harbour under the cover of darkness."

Maecenas placed a chubby hand on Octavian's shoulder, pointing to the Adriatic. "They negotiated that narrow strait to the open sea and fled to Dyrrhachium."

"What's your point!" snapped Agrippa.

"That the gods play tricks with all men, even the mighty Caesar," said Maecenas. "Nothing is ever as certain as it appears, dear boy. If it was, we would all be dead by now."

The two younger men moved away from him, and Octavian called to the centurion. "Very well, Glaber. Prepare the troops for my inspection."

The centurion again saluted before shouting an order to his men. He then witnessed a rare confidence in one so young, as Octavian addressed his men. The boy raised his arms and the crowds fell silent. Their eyes were upon him, listening with bated breath to his passionate words.

"Valiant soldiers of Caesar!" he cried. "I am Octavian, and in Caesar's name I am proud to accept your protection on our long journey to Rome. All of you have served him with honour and devotion… so let us now be united as one by Caesar's blood. Together, we will seek out and destroy his murderers!"

There was a moment of uneasy silence, and then a cheer from the ranks was echoed wildly by the townspeople who began chanting his name.

Octavian calmed them before delivering his finale: "Comrades! You have my word that before the sun rises again I shall reward your allegiance to me with gold!"

The legionaries roared their approval: "Hail Octavian! Hail Caesar!"

Octavian strode across the quayside, moving along the lines of troops. They responded to him in a flourish: shoulders back, bodies taught in salute. Their tunics gleamed as the rising sun glinted on the brass and weaponry of veterans scarred by the ravages of war. He felt a surge of pride at the fine presentation, and knew his words had lifted their spirits. In their eyes a new hope was already burning.

At the third hour, Octavian's entourage rode out through the marketplace. Their horses were flanked on both sides by foot-soldiers, with cavalry guarding front and rear. Glaber led the column under orders to set up camp on the way to Tarentum, near the villa of Lucius Vario, a wealthy equestrian. As the rugged centurion edged his horse through the cobbled streets he recalled Octavian's last words to him.

"I shall be resting at Vario's villa for the remainder of the day. You will return to Brundisium for the gold at nightfall."

Glaber smiled at the thought of this sickly youth replacing the likes of Marc Antony. He vowed quietly to himself: "By the gods! Caesar's so-called son will never see Rome again."

A few miles to the west of Brundisium a Greek slave walked with his master in the grounds of an estate. It was a morning detail that surprised Damon, for whenever his master returned from Rome an inspection of the estate would normally take several hours.

They would discuss the workload completed, and that which remained, including the duties set aside for bad weather. There was always grain to be moved; wine vats washed and sealed with pitch; the repair of ropes and farming tools, as well as financial accounts and additional chores within the villa. Being the overseer of Vario's estate, Damon ensured that everything the senator needed was prioritised and attended to. But today seemed like no other. His master looked tired and drawn; it was obvious that he was deeply troubled by Caesar's death.

The two men passed through the orchards in silence. They entered a gate near the paved threshing floor and crossed an open courtyard where doves cooed and fluttered around them. Slaves paused in their duties, bowing to Lucius Vario as he moved into the shaded colonnade of his villa. A smell of freshly baked bread drifted from a kitchen window as Damon stood waiting to be dismissed.

Almost as an afterthought, Vario finally spoke. "I think you should check on the farm animals, Damon. Perhaps it's time we sold off any blemished livestock."

It was a task already in hand, but Damon nodded politely. "Would you like to inspect the bridge, sir?" he asked.

"The bridge… you repaired the old bridge?"

"Yes, sir; it's strong enough to take the oxen now. We can plough the far meadows ready for seed, if you wish?"

Vario smiled but said nothing more, and Damon watched him walk slowly away and disappear into the atrium.

The overseer left the courtyard; his tall muscular frame a subject of flattering conversation to the two female slaves he met near the main entrance. Damon walked on into the sunshine where marble statues glistened with water in the fountains and citrus trees lined a road stretching five hundred yards to the highway.

He turned left at the granary, passing the slaves' cells that ran the length of the north-west wing. A narrow path led him to the new bridge over the river. Beyond this, he climbed a hill and sat in the lush grass at the base of an oak tree.

Below him, the villa revealed its rectangular shape and the colonnaded walkway around an open courtyard. A handful of doves circled the terracotta roof, and its white walls dazzled in the sun. He could hear the whinny of horses and the faint rhythmic thud of their hooves as they cantered in the enclosure. Cattle and sheep grazed in open pastures, and between its high grassy banks the river ran away in silence towards the sea.

Damon leaned back, the bark of the great oak easy against his shoulders. In his hand he held a small flute, carved from an olive branch by his late father. He closed his eyes and hazy pictures drifted into his mind forming the image of a child.

A boy of tender years clung to his mother's robes. He was annoyed at the sun burning his face; angry with the Roman soldiers who marshalled and bullied an endless line of people trudging along the Via Appia. The boy was searching for his father among six thousand slaves.

One by one he looked up at these men, their arms outstretched like giant birds: an endless line of brothers, fathers and sons... each of them nailed to a wooden cross. The heat was intense, but the haunted faces of the crucified men made him shiver. He saw the blood dripping from their arms and feet, and people gathering at every cross to weep for the dead and dying. Unmoved by this wave of grief, groups of Roman soldiers worked on relentlessly.

Where the road fell into a hollow he could see them now, pulling on ropes and ladders to raise another laden cross into its hole in the ground. The boy gripped his mother's hand, hurrying her down the slope. Although he barely remembered him, somehow he knew his father was there.

The sound of a nail driven into a man's flesh is like no other. One only hears the dull metal thud of the striking blow... all else is drowned by the scream of pain as flesh and bone shatters and dark crimson blood trickles from the wound.

This was the pain tearing through every sinew of his father's body as they hoisted him on the heavy beam, but never once did he cry out. It was the boy who shouted, throwing himself at a guard with flailing fists. The burly Roman cuffed him a glancing blow and he sprawled in a heap on the ground... the blue sky spinning into blackness.

When he opened his eyes again he felt the gentle hands of his mother holding him, and saw the metal spike they had driven through his father's feet. The child could only watch him suffering now. Each time his body sagged his father would gasp for breath from the enormous pressure on his ribcage. To breathe freely again he had to ease himself upward by bearing down on the nail in his feet. When this pain became unbearable too, his body slumped again. This torturous process was repeated until, utterly drained of his strength, death came at sunrise on the following day.

The boy was comforting his weeping mother as she knelt beneath the cross. He wanted to be strong... but as he saw the light in his father's eyes flicker and die, his own tears began to fall.

There was a man next to his father: another crucified slave whose legs were broken with wooden staves for shouting obscenities at the Roman general, Marcus Crassus. In later years the boy would learn more about Crassus, and also a slave they called Spartacus...

The oak tree stirred; leaves falling around him as a family of crows chattered and played among the branches. Damon rose to his feet, clutching the flute to his chest. He could never forget these images... or that he was that young boy...

Damon descended the hill, recalling that some twenty-eight years had passed since the Senate's campaign against Spartacus. A disaster that saw Roman armies defeated, their generals humiliated and two consuls forced from office by public outrage. Spartacus and his fellow gladiators accumulated a formidable army of slaves, vagabonds and escaped criminals. They reeked so much havoc that the whole of Italy trembled with fear.

When Marcus Crassus and his legions finally crushed the slave revolt, Spartacus had won nine victories, captured the Roman fasces, five legionary eagles and twenty-six standards. The Romans searched the battlefield for his body, without realising that he was one of the six thousand prisoners they later crucified along the Via Appia.

Damon was fifteen years old when he discovered the truth about his father's part in the slave revolt. It was a secret his mother kept in order to protect them, and he swore that whatever was needed, whichever role he had to play, one day he would gain the freedom his father had died for.

He was approaching the bridge when he saw the detachment of soldiers. They were high on a ridge heading due south from the Via Appia; yet close enough for him to distinguish their helmets and the muffled clatter of armour. He watched their formation divide. While the main body of cavalry and foot- soldiers veered away down to the river, a small troop on horseback continued towards the villa.

A farm slave had already alerted his master, and by the time Damon reached the courtyard Vario was descending the villa steps dressed in a white tunic with its purple senatorial stripe. The two men were waiting at the fountains when Octavian's party arrived. Several slaves stood ready to tend the horses as they dismounted.

Vario stepped forward. "Octavian! What a pleasure to see you in such troubled times."

"My dear Vario; it's been more than a year," Octavian said, embracing the senator. His eyes settled on Damon and saw the man's lithe and muscular frame towering over his master. "You certainly know how to choose a bodyguard, Vario, but shouldn't he be armed?"

"Damon is my foreman and secretary," laughed Vario. "A dagger is all he needs here, Octavian. Besides, Damon was one of the best gladiators I ever saw in the arena."

While Vario greeted his other guests, leading them towards the courtyard, Quintus Glaber insisted that Damon show him around the villa grounds. The centurion left two of his men at the entrance and stationed two guards at every perimeter door.

It was on their return that Glaber demanded to see the guests' quarters. "Octavian needs peace and quiet… no disturbances," he said. "Show me his room."

Damon felt uneasy. He dislike the way Glaber carefully inspected Octavian's room, but by the time he discovered the truth it was too late.

With Octavian insisting Agrippa and the centurion return to Brundisium at sundown, Vario - always the genial host - had dinner prepared earlier than usual. The day clouded over before the tenth hour, and his slaves lit braziers against the chilled air in a room on the upper floor.

Its walls were decorated with an array of portraits and country scenes. They were illuminated by hanging lamps, while in the shadows between two marble pillars was a statue of Aesculapius, the god of medicine. At the room's centre stood a rectangular table with two couches set L-shaped around it. This enabled slaves to serve extra food at the two open sides without disturbing the guests.

Octavian noted their efficiency over city slaves. In almost military precision they served an appetiser of tuna fish, garnished with eggs and rue leaves, then bowls of black and white olives and cups of wine. After which, they stood harmlessly in the shadows; but even so, Octavian insisted that Vario dismiss them from the room when talk of Rome began. He would only allow them to return between courses. And rather than clear away dishes and uneaten food after the main meal, the slaves simply removed the table. This was quickly replaced with another, laden with bowls of fruit, nuts, honey cakes and fresh wine.

Octavian sat on the senator's left as guest of honour, and beside him was Agrippa. To Vario's right, were the smiling Maecenas and a rather subdued Quintus Glaber.

"Only chaos rules in Rome," Vario was saying. "Caesar's murder is far worse than you can imagine. His death has caused more panic than when his legions crossed the Rubicon and he marched on the city. People leave in droves, and with those in the country returning to safeguard their business interests, the streets are like a hornet's nest."

Octavian was picking at his food with little appetite. "And what of Antony?" he asked.

"Marc Antony is torn between restoring order and his concern for the Egyptian queen, Cleopatra." A troubled look came to the senator's face. "She claims her son is Caesar's heir."

"Perhaps Glaber can tell us more? He is much closer to Antony than any of us," said Agrippa, his voice heavy with sarcasm.

"Only that he, like Octavian, wants revenge for Caesar's death," Glaber replied. "Antony has vowed to hunt down Brutus and Cassius, and anyone else involved in the conspiracy. But I know nothing of Caesar's heir."

Vario placed a hand on Octavian's shoulder. "Of course you do. He sits beside me," the senator grinned. "Octavian is Caesar's next-of-kin, not the son of an Egyptian whore!"

Octavian saw the tension in the centurion's face and, smiling to himself, he carefully watered down his wine.

Agrippa held a smug expression as he engaged Vario in conversation, asking his opinion on the Senate and what the general feeling might be to Octavian's arrival in Rome.

It was left to Maecenas to lighten the proceedings through dinner. Vario's excellent taste in the rich Opimium wine was loosening his tongue in a sometimes crude, but nonetheless, subtle way. With the exception of Agrippa, who disliked his vulgar innuendoes, Maecenas became the focus of attention.

"Do tell me, Vario," he said, biting into a stuffed date, "where did you find that beautiful Greek god of yours, Damon?"

"He was a gift from Caesar. Damon came to Italy from the Syrian deserts and I first saw him as a gladiator in Capua. Caesar kindly offered him to me as a bodyguard, but he's much more than that."

Octavian had moved from the couch, and stood warming his hands at a brazier. "I can see the Greek is not one of those ugly, lumbering brutes you normally see in Rome, guarding the likes of Cicero."

"No. On the day I watched him with Caesar, he was the only retiarius to survive."

"Ah! The lithesome creatures that fight with net and trident," beamed Maecenas.

Vario smiled at his interest. "Yes...even the mighty Caesar admired Damon's agility and courage..."

"Let us not forget this man is a Greek slave not a Roman!" Glaber interrupted. "His head would be rolling in the dirt if he was matched against some of my legionaries." The centurion rose to join Octavian near the brazier, whispering to the senator as he passed. "Old age weakens your mind, Vario. No wonder Rome trembles over its Senate.'"

Vario ignored him by proclaiming even more loudly to Maecenas the virtues of not only being the owner of a faithful slave, but also the continued success his overseer was achieving with the farm. He politely refused Maecenas' more than generous offer to buy Damon.

With the hour of sunset approaching Octavian prepared a letter, and then spoke privately with Agrippa and Glaber about the gold. He was aware of his friend's fine administration skills, and acknowledged the hold Glaber had over the troops camped by the river. So despite their differences, Octavian was confident that together they would enlist a respectable army of men before they arrived in Rome. Their brief was to return to Brundisium, leaving half the soldiers at the river as an escort for Octavian the following day.

The three men stood at a small table, with Octavian indicating their route on a map. He began by handing Agrippa the letter. "On collection of the gold you will follow the coastal road," he said, "recruiting men through Gnatia to Barium, then inland from Rubi to Beneventum. We will meet again here at the Clanius River between Atella and Capua."

"To travel with oxen and carts over rough terrain in the mountains will be slow." Agrippa's fingers passed through his short-cropped hair. "We have to recruit… so give me twelve days."

Octavian agreed. "In the meantime, I will do what I can across Campania," he said.

Glaber saluted him, declaring he would now inspect the perimeter guards. "The Greek is seeing to our fresh mounts," he added, before leaving the room.

The sun had set when Damon tethered their two horses beside the fountains. He saw a faint glimmer of light across the western sky, but around him the night was already casting her shadows over the earth. The two Roman guards acknowledged his entrance, but beyond them he paused as a figure crossed the courtyard.

In the twilight he quietly made his way towards the open area of the threshing floor. One of the guards had left his post at the south-east gate, and he could make out his identity by his size: a great hulk of a soldier named Fabius. By his stance and manner, the figure beside him was Glaber. The centurion appeared to be issuing orders, but their hushed voices were lost in the heavy night air. Damon heard nothing he could piece together… only the name 'Octavian'.

It was some time before Glaber returned to the villa. Damon followed him and found the party in a jovial mood when he reached the dining room. Vario saw him and went to the hallway.

"The horses are ready, master," Damon said, quietly.

Vario smiled at him. "Very well, but before you retire, Damon, there is something you should know. Octavian will be using my bedroom."

Seeing them together, Glaber made his way to the door, eyeing Damon with menace. "I hope you chose the horses carefully, Slave," he sneered. "We have a long journey and if they fail us… your severed head will hang from a pole!" His hand touched the short sword that hung from a belt at his waist. "Remember…your toy dagger is no match for the gladius."

Damon stared at him, but his eyes showed no sign of the hatred he felt - a rage that was to flare again moments later when Glaber charged his horse at him as he rode away with Agrippa.

Whether it was this or the centurion's earlier rendezvous with the guard that unsettled him, but Damon sensed danger. He heard a drunk but happy Maecenas being escorted to his quarters, and long after the house slaves put out their lamps, he lay without sleep… listening to the sounds of the night.

Vario and Octavian were alone and about to leave the dining room. "I noticed in Spain that your health was not at its best, Octavian. This night you must take my bedroom," said Vario. "The furnace room is behind and it's considerably warmer."

They descended the stairs and walked through the atrium, Octavian offering no objection. As Caesar's heir such privileges were to be expected now.

The hours passed, and barely a handful of stars pierced the darkness as Damon found himself once more approaching the south-east gate. He could make out only one of the guards: a silhouette lounging rather lazily for a Roman against the wall. Damon was an arm's length away before he realised the man was dead. He would have made no sound, for whatever blade it was that killed him sliced through his windpipe. The guard who spoke with Glaber had gone.

Damon ran across the courtyard, shouting a warning as he raced towards the winter bedrooms. One door was ajar as he burst in, dagger drawn. A lamp was still burning and its pale yellow light touched the figure of a man. The marble floor beneath him was stained with blood. Damon stared in disbelief at the gaping wound in Vario's stomach; the wide blade of a Roman gladius had passed clean through his body.

Damon knelt beside him cradling his master's head, and Lucius Vario shivered as the chill of death touched him. He raised a trembling hand to touch Damon's face… but the words he tried to say died on his lips.

Octavian was pleased with the senator's room. It was both spacious and warm, furnished tastefully and decorated with splendid murals which portrayed leaping beasts and gladiatorial scenes. A heavy oak table was set against the far wall and to the right of it was a sleeping couch. The left wall was full of scrolls. They were pigeon holed from floor to ceiling, each encased in leather or cloth and individually labelled with tags. A few remained on the table, and Octavian could see that Vario had earlier been working on his accounts.

Nearby, was a handsome glass chalice. Octavian was surprised by its weight, and admired the way the hanging lamp reflected streams of coloured light from its facets.

He felt tired; his body ached as he lay on the couch, regretting now that he hadn't soaked in the baths before dinner. However, it was more pressing matters that kept him awake: his problem of ensuring credibility in the Senate; how to deal with Marc Antony on his return to Rome; the armies he would need, especially to hunt down Brutus and Cassius. But he had the friendship of Agrippa and the wisdom of Maecenas to guide him, and it was in these comforting thoughts that Octavian began to doze.

The lamplight was dim, and shadows had deepened the corners of the room when he opened his eyes again.

He was already aware that someone lurked in the darkness… and there was a rustle of mail armour as the intruder loomed over him. In the second Octavian rolled off the couch a Roman gladius slashed through it. He was quickly on his feet, but no match for Fabius who sent him reeling across the room with a blow from the back of his hand. The sword was raised to take off his head when someone came crashing through the door.

As the guard spun round to face Damon, Octavian seized his chance to scramble clear. The slave moved quickly between him and the assassin, and Octavian continued to edge towards the door. He knew that even without a helmet or shield Fabius was a formidable opponent. The slave's dagger would be futile against him. With a mail cuirass protecting his body, only the arms and legs were exposed. Repeated dagger thrusts here could weaken him, but the facial area was the real target and the Greek would need to get in very close to deliver a fatal blow.

Octavian could hear voices outside, a woman was crying and lamps were being re-lit in the hallways. Light began streaming in through the open doorway on to a scene that was about to explode into violence and death.

Damon drew first blood: his speed of hand surprised the guard, gashing his left forearm. Fabius snarled. He thrust his sword time and again at the slave, whose skill and agility astounded Octavian. The two men circled each other then once more the dagger found its mark, the point jabbing upwards this time into the Roman's sword arm. Even before the curse reached his lips the slave had kicked him in the chest, driving him backwards into the table.

Fabius lay spread-eagled on its surface, and in an instant the descending blade of a dagger was striking at his throat. The guard turned his head, feeling nothing as the weapon sliced off his earlobe before sticking fast in the table. It left Damon off balance and an easy target.

The guard should have ended it… but hesitated, and in one savage moment Damon lunged at him. The chalice in his hand smashed into the guard's face with tremendous force.

Fabius staggered backwards, slivers of glass embedded in his face… hands clutching at his neck where blood was gushing from a severed jugular. He crashed to the floor at Octavian's feet, his body in convulsions as he died.

Suddenly the doorway was jammed with inquisitive slaves, and perimeter guards came rushing in with Maecenas. All of them shocked by what they saw; it was much later before Octavian could relate his ordeal. When braziers had warmed the dining room again, he sat with Maecenas talking in sombre tones of his narrow escape.

"The worth of our Greek slave is more than any of us imagined," Maecenas enthused. "He saved your life, Octavian… and that makes him priceless! So, what becomes of him now?"

Octavian was dunking morsels of bread in cold water to moisten his throat. "We will know soon enough. I would like you to find Vario's will."

A few minutes later Maecenas returned. He looked stern, and made no effort to hand over the scroll as he pointed back to the hallway. "Damon seeks an audience with you, Octavian. He says it's most urgent… for your ears only."

"That's for me to decide, Maecenas. Send him in. The three of us will discuss the matter together."

Damon entered the room and stood in silence waiting to be addressed.

Maecenas smiled at him. "He has such charming manners, too. Don't you think, Octavian?"

The young Roman nodded, but merely in a gesture for Damon to speak.

"There is something you must know, sir. What happened to the master was a mistake… it was you they wanted to kill."

Octavian put down the pitcher of water. "What are you saying, Damon?"

"It was a plot. The guard and… I believe the centurion, Quintus Glaber, betrayed you. I thought it unusual when I saw the guard away from his post at the gate, especially at dusk. Glaber spoke to him for a long time before he returned to the dining room."

The two Romans stared at him, clearly unsettled by his statement. Maecenas was the first to speak: "My dear boy, that hardly involves Glaber in these awful deeds," he said, helping himself to more wine.

"And you say that darkness was upon you," Octavian added. "So how can you even be sure it was Glaber out there? Did you see his face?"

"No, sir… but I was close enough to see he was a centurion. Only an officer fastens his belt with the gladius on his left side."

The slave met the young man's stare, but for the first time he saw a glimmer of warmth in the Roman's eyes. "I will not forget your courage, Damon, but you should realise that Glaber came to me as one of Caesar's trusted men. You must convince me otherwise."

Damon nodded. "I understand, sir… but was not Fabius also a trusted soldier of Caesar?"

Maecenas winced, thinking Octavian would chastise such a remark from a slave, but Damon was allowed to continue.

"When Glaber said he wanted to inspect the grounds he was not thorough for a man of his standing. He seemed much more concerned about your bedroom, insisting that a clear path be made from the door to your sleeping couch. I remember he laughed, saying you always drank too much wine. This also seemed odd because the master had mentioned that you much preferred water.

"Secondly, I was the only other person who knew that you would be changing bedrooms. The master had explained this to me out in the hallway before Glaber left with your friend, Agrippa. When I found the dead guard and Fabius missing I realised he was after you... but I was too late to save the master."

Octavian had left the couch, pacing the floor in anger. "Yes, of course. The head they wanted was mine! There was no reason to kill Vario; he was just in the wrong place. Fabius went there first only because Glaber told him that was my bedroom." He turned on Maecenas, eyes blazing with fury. "Agrippa was right, and so is Damon. The centurion is Antony's man... only he could have plotted this!"

Maecenas thought it best not to disagree.

At sunrise Octavian sent word to the remaining soldiers by the river that his departure to Rome would be delayed. A messenger rode into the camp leading two horses; they carried the bodies of Fabius and the guard he had murdered. Octavian ordered that one of their comrades should be buried with dignity. The second man, Fabius, was to be stripped of his armour and dumped at the edge of a nearby wood. To the troops who left his corpse as food for the crows and wild beasts... it served as a chilling reminder.

A few hours later the body of Lucius Vario was placed in the atrium. When Octavian entered the small garden he saw Damon standing at the funeral bier, head bowed. The deceased lay before him on an elegant bed: a wooden structure exquisitely carved and inlaid with ivory. Vario was dressed in a white toga and covered with purple blankets, edged with gold embroidery.

His hair was grey, but he looked remarkably handsome for his years; only the faintest of lines marked his face, and his high cheekbones revealed a strong Roman nose and chin. The lips were closed, concealing a gold coin placed on his tongue: this was, as tradition suggested, a reward for Charon the boatman to ferry him across the River Styx to the peaceful lands beyond.

The only sound in the atrium came from a fountain, where water trickled from a bronze figure of Fauna, the country-goddess. As sunlight touched the darkest corners, Octavian paused to moisten his fingers in a basin and touch them to his forehead. He could smell the incense burning over a low brazier and, as he drew nearer, the herbs and perfumes that anointed the senator's body.

"Vario was a good man, Damon. A man of great courage in the face of an enemy," he said. There was a fondness in his voice as he touched the bier. "Caesar thought very highly of him; they fought many victorious battles together. But now, it matters not whether a man is a crucified slave or a Roman general, in death we are all equal."

Damon stared at him with uncertainty. He had confessed to Vario of his father's loyalty to Spartacus, but had the senator kept his secret?

"We must look to the future," Octavian said, disturbing his thoughts. "Come, we have things to discuss about the senator's will. I have sent for Vario's nephew from Tarentum, and after the funeral tomorrow I will be leaving for Rome."

Damon followed the young Roman into a library near the atrium that contained mostly books on poetry and philosophy; a place where Vario often invited him after dinner to read and improve his Latin. Damon always treasured their time together… but now the room felt cold and empty without his master's presence.

He was invited to sit on a folding chair while the two Romans studied Vario's will. Maecenas finally walked over to him, placing a sympathetic hand on his shoulder.

"It's ironic how the gods give… then take away, wouldn't you agree, Damon? Vario bequeaths you two precious gifts, yet with one of them you not only avenge his death, but also save Octavian's life. That broken chalice was rare Alexandrian glass and extremely valuable, my friend… as well as lethal."

Octavian stood at the open doorway staring back into the atrium; his eyes fixed on the bronze statue, curious at how the tiny jets of water almost brought it to life. "The second gift is even more precious," he said, turning to face Damon. "Vario has granted your freedom. He regarded you as a man of intelligence, strength and virtue, so I trust you will understand the reason why he states one condition. Vario requests you to serve in some way to bring justice upon Brutus and Cassius in order to avenge Caesar's death."

There was an awkward silence then Damon stood, addressing both men. "I have grown to respect the master as I do the memory of my own father… and this is something the gods will never take away."

"Do you have any family?" Octavian asked.

"Yes… a wife and daughter, sir. Our home is in Cyprus… but that was a long time ago," he added, quietly.

"What about your parents?"

"We came from the Greek island of Leucas. They were taken into slavery by the Roman army. Both my parents died here in Italy. My father was sent to a gladiator school before…" Damon paused, there was still a danger in talking of the past…

"Yes, of course, but what of your own victories?" asked

Maecenas with a timely interruption. "The senator told me how you fought many times in the arena against overwhelming odds. Perhaps at a more appropriate time you will enlighten us. I'm sure it would be extremely entertaining."

Octavian offered him wine, his eyes searching Damon's face. Again there was a knowing tone to his voice. "Whoever your father was you seem to inherit his courage. But tell me, what happened to Damon the boy before he came to Caesar's attention?"

"I was fifteen years old when my mother died and I was taken into the household of Gaius Salenus. He was a man who found great pleasure in beating his slaves to death. I ran away."

"To where?" asked Maecenas.

"I managed to board a cargo ship bound for Epirus, and eventually made my way to the island of Cyprus. It was there that I learned to farm the land. I married a Cypriot girl. Her name is Hestia."

"Hestia. How delightful," beamed Maecenas. "To us Roman's she's Vesta: a spirit of the household."

Damon lowered his eyes, his mind racing back to the Arabs who seized him. They were faceless now; he remembered only silhouettes... the jingle of tiny bells from their bracelets. "A band of slave traders took me to the Syrian deserts," he said. "I was sold as a gladiator..."

Octavian prompted him. "So, what happened with Caesar?"

"He saw me fight in Capua. Several of our best gladiators died that afternoon, and for some reason the gods spared me. Caesar assigned me to Lucius Vario, and the master always treated me well. He gave me back my life."

Octavian smiled. "How strange that Caesar himself should play a part in bringing us together. What do you think, Maecenas?"

"Oh, it's splendid. Splendid! You certainly need a man like Damon. A man of loyalty and courage; a companion you can trust with your life."

"I agree. Damon is to accompany me to Rome as my personal guard and secretary. He will be rewarded handsomely." The words were spoken as an order not a request.

"But I seek no reward, sire... only to see my family again."

The ice-cold stare returned to Octavian's eyes. "Our priorities are the deaths of Brutus and Cassius, along with that scum, Glaber. The gods demand it and so do I! Nothing is more important than the retribution I have in mind for the death of Caesar. Is it not so, Maecenas?"

Maecenas nodded, and then smiled as Octavian's voice softened again. "But you have my word, Damon, when vengeance is mine you will be given your freedom."

Chapter IV

As a retreat from the crowded city, Marc Antony used a villa that once belonged to Marcus Pompey. It was situated outside the city walls and commanded stunning views from the Pincian Hill. The villa's furnishings were modest, but this was of no consequence to Antony; being Rome's consul at a time like this occupied his every thought.

The heat of the day shimmered over the city as he returned from the Senate House with his closest aide, Canidius. A troop of legionaries escorted them across the Forum, their shields forming a protective wall around the two men as they passed through the Fontinalis Gate and out on to the Via Flaminia.

Antony's body ached, but worst of all his mind was fraught with the recurring image of Caesar's blood-soaked corpse, and the anguish as flames devoured Rome's greatest leader. He was thankful when Canidius dismissed the guards. They climbed the winding steps, through terraced gardens where ivy-covered statues stood neglected among the dense trees and evergreen shrubs.

Antony acknowledged a bodyguard's salute at the villa's entrance, pausing for a moment to catch his breath and look back over the Field of Mars. It surprised him how much the equestrian courses and old marching grounds had diminished. Ugly tenement buildings and warehouses now edged their way along the river. But towering above it all was Pompey's own creation: the city's first permanent theatre. The building was set in a complex of adjoining galleries, marble colonnades and extensive gardens.

In the distance, his eyes followed a veil of mist that charted the Tiber: a long curved arm of the river embracing the Field of Mars.

"What do you see out there, Canidius?" he asked.

"I see only ghosts... of young boys pretending to be soldiers. We trained them, you and I, led them into battle to die in some foreign land far from their beloved Rome." Canidius lowered his eyes. "We have lost so many comrades... and now Caesar."

"Yes," Antony said, quietly. He clasped the man's shoulder. "Come with me, Canidius. We shall drink to old times and fallen heroes."

It was pleasantly warm out on the balcony. The sun had lowered to the tall trees beyond the river, casting red and orange streaks across an indigo sky. To the south loomed the Temple of Jupiter, and beyond the Glaberline Hill lay the great expanse of a city still jostling with people.

"Rome's greatest need is for someone to restore order on land and sea. And by the gods I will do it!" said Antony, defiantly. "I will finish what Caesar was preparing for: war with the Parthians."

Canidius was more objective. "Such glories are won with money as well as legions, Antony. Our men must be paid, the veterans settled on the land promised by Caesar, and ships provided to rid the Adriatic of piracy."

The mellow wine brought a smile of satisfaction to Antony's lips. "There is something you should know, Canidius. Caesar's fortune is safe. I have secured it for this very cause. Our friend Octavian will not claim his inheritance after all."

"But what of Caesar's will? You said Octavian was named as heir."

"That may be so, but whom would you follow, Canidius... a sickly boy with little experience of war and none of command, or a man of destiny?"

Canidius stiffened to attention. "You will always have my loyalty, sir. But before I left Campania the news was that Octavian is making his way to Rome. Does it not concern you?"

"Not any more," said Antony, seemingly amused. "I have changed his plans."

Canidius drained his cup. "Now what have you been up to?" he smiled.

Marc Antony looked to the doorway where an old slave stood, hands clasped in front of him mumbling his apologies. He bowed to both men, before informing his master that the baths were ready.

"Thank you, Siro... and the wine?"

"Yes, master. Your best Falernian is waiting."

Antony nodded, and the slave returned inside the house, his sandal-covered feet shuffling silently across the stone floor.

"Will you join me, Canidius? We can discuss my plans for Rome... and Octavian in private."

They shed their tunics and under garments and entered the baths. The walls and floors throughout were decorated with elaborate frescoes and mosaics, portraying scenes of gladiators and wild beasts in the throes of death. Each of the three rooms contained a sunken pool with water heated and piped from a furnace housed between the kitchen and changing area.

For a short time, Antony and Canidius soaked in warm water before passing through an arched doorway to a second circular pool. A mass of steam obscured its surface, swirling upwards to the domed ceiling as they immersed their bodies in the water.

Antony breathed deeply at the luxury of its soothing heat. "Is it hot enough for you, Canidius?"

"Just as I like it… in fact, the house is a perfect retreat. Pompey chose an impressive site. Close to the city, yet private enough for…"

"Orgies, you mean?" prompted Antony. "I insist you come to the next one!"

Their raunchy laughter echoed around the room as Antony filled two cups from a pitcher conveniently placed at the edge of the pool by the old slave.

"Try this Falernian wine," Antony offered, "it tastes much better than that vinegar Pompey used to drink!"

They drank with relish before a serious tone returned to the consul's voice: "I will begin with Octavian… and his unfortunate end. I can only imagine he must have suffered a similar death to Caesar."

Canidius blinked the steam from his eyes. "By the powers of Jupiter!" he cried. "What are you saying? Has it been confirmed?"

"Not yet, but Quintus Glaber is like you, he never fails me. He bears a letter from Caesar's friend, Balbus. It's a genuine enough reason for our gallant centurion to escort Octavian to Rome. And on their journey, well…" He shrugged, and as he stepped from the pool the scars of battle gleamed white against his weather-beaten skin.

On any other occasion slaves were at hand to cleanse his torso. He would then lie on a cloth-covered bench while the huge hands of his masseur rubbed scented oils into his skin, relieving the tensions of the day. But in need of privacy, Antony had dispensed with their services.

Antony's physique was a marked difference between the two men. Canidius was taller but slight, and whilst he had inherited the good looks of his father, Antony's face was heavy, rather brutish in profile. His dark, piercing eyes were almost as black as his curly hair. Yet there was warmth, even gentleness about him in which his men saw trust... and most women found seductive.

The light from burning lamps turned to a pale orange glow in the steaming heat when Canidius left the water. Antony watched the vapours of steam trailing from his naked body. "Here, cover that thing up... you make me envious," he laughed.

Canidius caught the towel and wrapped it around his waist, smiling to himself as he poured them more wine. He raised his cup to Antony in admiration. "I agree with your treacherous plan. With Octavian disposed of, his share of Caesar's estate will help to strengthen our legions."

Antony smiled. "There's more, my friend. To build our ships and sustain our armies we will also need the great wealth of Cleopatra!"

Canidius wiped the sweat from his face. "Of course, the Egyptian queen is still here in Rome, I believe?"

"Not for long, she sails for Alexandria tonight. I will speak with her before she leaves."

"I hear she's grown into a beautiful and desirable woman."

Antony shook his head in amusement. "It wasn't beauty that lured Caesar into her bed, but there's nothing more desirable than a woman with wealth and power. Anyway, now that Octavian's been taken care of I'm sure Cleopatra will be generous to our cause if she wants her son to be heir."

"You're a genius, Antony. How will Cleopatra be able to resist you?"

Antony smiled his approval. "Let us finish our bathing, and then I must visit her."

Marc Antony emerged from the shadows. Below him, a stairway led down to the river where a small barge awaited its royal passengers. On board he could see the oars already manned by Egyptian slaves, their half-naked bodies shining like black marble in the moonlight.

He called out to the three women crossing the pier, and quickly descended the steps. The woman caressing the brow of an infant wrapped in a blanket looked up. His voice softened. "I must speak with you."

The Queen of Egypt gestured to her handmaidens that they should take her son to the boat.

Antony stood beside her, aware of the sensual way her eyes were upon him. "I would have been here sooner but there is much to do," he said.

"Yes, and you do things so well, Antony, but all of them for Rome… not for me and my son, Caesarion."

"Caesar's death has left Rome in chaos," he said. "You must realise as consul I have to restore order. Brutus, Cassius and the others have to be hunted down. The people demand it."

"These citizens of Rome are the same murderous mob who wanted Caesar dead. Now they shed tears for him and scream for revenge. How convenient it is to have you as their saviour!"

Antony understood her sudden anger; he felt both respect and concern for the young queen. "I am here because I want you to stay. I give you my word, you have nothing to fear."

"You forget Octavian. When he approaches the Senate you cannot deny him the contents of Caesar's will any longer. You told me he is the one named as Caesar's heir, not my son. There is no reason for me to stay now. Caesar and the dream that was to unite Rome and Egypt died with him."

Antony walked with her to the barge. "I only know if Caesar had lived you would have both ruled the world," he said. "But even in death Caesar deserves his power and titles. I will see to it personally that he is deified." He took hold of Cleopatra's arm, helping her aboard.

She turned to him, her voice filled with emotion. "A dead ruler and you want to make him a god, even though Rome burns its heroes on a pyre like rubbish? So, what becomes of me, Antony? All I have left of Caesar is my son."

Marc Antony chose his words carefully so as not to mention Octavian's untimely death. "Give me time and I will come to Alexandria. I know Caesarion is Caesar's true heir, and I shall do everything in my power to unite our countries."

"Yes," Cleopatra whispered, "I believe you will."

The morning after Cleopatra sailed for Egypt a band of men replenished supplies at Nola, a city to the north of Mount Vesuvius. They re-joined their comrades whose number was now close to a legion. Most of the five thousand were Caesar's veterans, found wandering aimlessly around the inns and brothels of harbour towns like Tarentum. The small army headed for the sea on a road that circled the mountain, following a young man who promised them just reward for their loyalty.

The column was brought to a halt, and while the foot-soldiers rested a group of cavalry led their horses to a nearby stream. It was a tranquil place, the valley brimming with wild flowers as far as the eye could see.

Damon lay down in the long grass, his view of the rolling pastures reminiscent of Vario's estate. He thought of the senator's nephew, hoping the frail young man would be strong enough to come to terms with everyday rigours of life on the estate.

Aelius had been devastated by his uncle's sudden death, weeping as Vario's body was borne in the open carriage to the funeral pyre. The senator's hands lay at his sides, his strong features clean and shining with perfumed oil. When the carriage halted, the sound of three legionary horns echoed across the meadow. Romans and slaves mourned together, their heads bowed as Vario was laid on the pyre.

Aelius almost crumpled in grief. He was shaking as he took the flaming torch. Damon stepped forward steadying the boy's hand as together they lit the base of the pyre. Flames roared, and soon only memories remained.

Damon turned his eyes to Mount Vesuvius. The mountain, with its flattened summit lost in the clouds, dominated the skyline around the bay like a majestic pyramid. It was here, somewhere on the high-forested slopes, that his father had taken refuge with Spartacus and his men in the days of the slave revolt. In a spontaneous gesture Damon raised the shepherd's flute to his lips and quietly, so as not to attract attention, he tried to play a few notes.

"By the gods!" cried Maecenas, appearing from nowhere. "For a moment I thought it was someone in violent pain."

Damon spluttered to a halt. "Very funny, Maecenas," he smiled, waving the flute. "I've had this for years and never really tried to play. One day I'll master it, you'll see."

"I'm sure you will. Meanwhile, you should eat."

Damon propped himself up, gratefully accepting a share of bread. He liked Maecenas; admired his oratory skills and exuberant manner. He was sure the man could win a battle with words, while others needed the sword.

"Have you been to the Cup before?" asked Maecenas, sitting beside him.

"No… not if you mean the Bay of Neapolis?"

Maecenas laughed. "Spoken like an ancient Greek. Yes, it was they who named it Neapolis, but Romans call it the Cup… or the Bay of Luxury."

"It gives no pleasure to Octavian. Our journey to Rome troubles him. He looks pale and drawn."

Maecenas agreed. "I'm afraid his health is a constant problem, Damon. But as you're more privileged now to his company, perhaps you will be discreet enough to keep me informed?"

"Yes, I will… but look at him now," he pointed, shaking his head.

To contradict their comments, Octavian could be seen sharing a lecherous joke with a group of legionaries down by the stream.

"Don't be fooled," said Maecenas. "I can hear him wheezing from here. At this time of the year he suffers a tightness of the diaphragm, and catarrh when the Sirocco blows in from Africa. But I'm afraid any extreme weather conditions cause him distress."

This frailty was more apparent to the Greek a few hours later when Octavian seemed overcome by the midday sun. They sheltered for a while on the outskirts of Pompeii before their rejuvenated leader took the city by storm. Damon could only admire his resolve as people flocked to the forum to hear him speak. Slaves, freedmen and soldiers alike, welcomed him as Caesar's son.

As their numbers multiplied, Damon realised that in Octavian he was witnessing the same magnetism Spartacus must have possessed. Men followed them with equal optimism and valour. While his father and Spartacus fought for the freedom of slaves, Octavian would fight for the leadership of Rome... each of them wanting justice.

The following day was much cooler. A light mist hovered over the sea, and through it glided a flotilla of fishing boats and phantom-like trading ships; the larger vessels ferrying cargo and passengers around the coast from Surrentum to Puteoli on the northern rim of the Cup.

It was normally a day's march from Pompeii, but it was mid-afternoon of the second day before they reached the port of Puteoli. The journey had not been easy. Damon was alert to the hostility in some of the fishing villages and farms around Oplontis and Herculaneum. Here, the people feared for their land, accusing Octavian of being a warmonger and thief. Even so, further recruits joined them, including a large detachment of legionaries at Neapolis. The Greek noticed it was their defection that pleased Octavian the most, for he learned their absent commander was a man named Canidius.

In the hills above Puteoli the crisp, pine-scented air was a welcome relief from its port and fishery. Along the wooded ridge either side of a stone-paved road, Damon began to glimpse the great houses in which Roman wealth unashamedly flaunted itself. Their long gardens swept upwards in cultivated tiers, adorned with ostentatious fountains and statues.

At the marble-pillared entrance of one such residence, they dismounted. Now responsible for Octavian's safety, Damon left men guarding the road and, accompanied by Maecenas, he brought up the rear. They followed Octavian into the atrium where a small, corpulent man with a ruddy complexion and flaccid cheeks met them; it was Octavian's stepfather, Marcius Philippus.

He embraced Octavian, who visibly flinched at the greeting. "Where is my mother?" he asked, impatiently.

"Atia is still in Rome comforting Caesar's widow, Calpurnia. But I don't know why," he sighed, "it's been over a month since his death." He turned to Maecenas offering him hospitality. "And who might this be?" he added, with a disparaging glance at Damon.

"My personal guard," Octavian said, curtly. "And before you disapprove… he stays!"

Philippus gestured to the couches. "Well, then perhaps we should all relax together."

They all sat except Octavian, who continually paced the floor as Philippus listened, and then disapproved of his ideals. "The risks are too great, Octavian. You are out of touch with reality… you're merely a boy. Forgive me, but an inexperienced one at that. What can you possibly hope to achieve by going up against the likes of Antony, Marcus Brutus and Gaius Cassius?"

"Lepidus is also a threat. As Caesar's Master of Horse he has a large following. And let us not forget the ominous Sextus Pompey. His fleet dominates Sicilia and the south."

"I have Caesar's name… a talisman that has already given me an army of men," Octavian replied, angry at such a negative response.

Philippus shook his head in despair. "How many men do you have? Is there five, or even ten thousand? You will need more than that against such mighty opposition. Antony is consul, and this alone gives him command of at least five legions," he said.

Philippus took a long drink of yellow wine, and turned his plea to Maecenas. "As his friend, please make him see reason."

Maecenas shrugged. "My dear man… these are worrying times and I appreciate your concern, but Octavian charts his own destiny; we are merely swept along by the tide of his brilliance. How can any of us deny a young man his inheritance?"

Philippus was crestfallen, even glancing to Damon for support, but knew from his sombre expression that he agreed with Maecenas. He tried again with Octavian, this time appealing on Atia's behalf. "Your mother will be desperately upset over this, Octavian," he cried in a wavering voice. "For her sake, will you not at least compromise?"

Octavian sat beside him, and for a moment Damon saw a glimmer of compassion in his eyes as his stepfather made a final appeal.

"Caesar has left you two-thirds of his estate. By all means take it, Octavian, it's yours to live in luxury as a private citizen. But accept his name and you enter a political arena where treachery and murder is part of Caesar's legacy."

Octavian put his hand on his shoulder. "How can I choose my own destiny?" he said, quietly. "If the gods have planned a dangerous eminence, then so be it. I cannot live my life in safety and obscurity."

Philippus bowed his head as the tears welled up inside him.

They stayed overnight at the house and by morning the skies over Campania threatened rain. With Maecenas leaving early to assemble troops down at the port, Octavian and Damon rode on a short distance following the ridge. Between the houses the land was wild and forested, but looking west through the trees Octavian pointed out the red roofs of Baiae and the blue waters of the sea dotted with coloured sails.

The road turned sharply and dipped into a hollow, where it revealed the surprisingly modest facade of a villa. They dismounted in the courtyard and, as if expected, a slave waited to lead their horses away to the stables. Octavian knocked on the heavy oak doors, and to the old servant who opened them he announced his arrival.

"Tell your master, Octavian is here! I wish to speak with him."

The slave led them through a dark hallway which opened into an atrium. Damon waited as Octavian was ushered into an enormous study. The man he had come to see was looking out at the rain. He was silhouetted against the high windows, hands clasped behind him; not turning, but when he spoke his voice was unmistakable. Trained and matured over the years it rang out, crisp and clear.

"So, you bring the rain, Octavian. What other miracles lie in store for us?"

It had been almost three years since Octavian's coming of age; it was his joyous toga day when he last saw the man who Romans loved and hated with equal intensity... Marcus Tullius Cicero.

"Sir... I seek your advice, not to perform miracles," Octavian said.

Cicero, resplendent as ever in a white toga, turned to face him. "Then let me surmise what it could be?" he mused, stroking his chin. "Is it about Caesar and your inheritance? Or even Marc Antony's position in Rome? And perhaps you would like to know what support you might have in the Senate. Tell me; is it one... or all three?"

Octavian smiled. "All three... and to foresee such things could also be deemed a miracle!"

Cicero laughed, gesturing to a nearby couch. "Then we should sit for a while. Would you like some wine... fruit, perhaps?"

Octavian politely declined, his eyes focussing on the man beside him. Cicero seemed to have aged considerably. His face was fleshy, the sharp nose and pointed chin had softened over the years and although his eyes had lost none of their sparkle, the deep furrows across his brow gave him a more sinister appearance. The once dynamic orator was now a portly old man but, as Octavian perceived, still a powerful ally.

"Caesar created armies loyal to himself not the Republic," Cicero began, "that's why I opposed him. We had our differences but one could not fail to admire his abilities. The man had charm, lucidity and fine literary skills. He always led his legions with courage and dignity. Yes, a truly illustrious career..."

Cicero paused for a moment as rain hammered against the shutters and flashes of lightning lit up the room. "I realise now why Caesar chose to end it all."

The words stunned Octavian. "There was no choice," he protested. "My father was murdered by a treacherous mob!"

"I understand your outrage, Octavian, because murder is the scourge of our society. There are many innocent victims who die without reason, butchered by the thugs and robbers who infest the streets of Rome. And whilst others perish at the hands of a jealous husband or lover... sometimes death is a mystery. I believe this of Caesar."

"He died from multiple stab wounds. We know his killers. There's nothing mysterious about that." Octavian said, firmly.

"But I have studied Caesar's actions prior to that fateful meeting on the Ides of March in great detail and, shocking as it may seem, concluded that he initiated his own death."

Octavian felt uneasy, but listened respectfully as Cicero rose from the couch and began to pace the floor speaking in a measured and persuasive tone.

"The savagery of war had taken its toll on Caesar. He was fifty-six years old and the falling sickness he suffered weakened him by the day. He was a proud man. His appearance, the image he portrayed to his legions and the people of Rome made him seem invincible. Caesar had no intention of dying through illness, so when it threatened to destroy him I believe he devised a glorious end."

Octavian disagreed. "I'm sorry, your idea is irrational," he said. "It's true that his illness bothered him at times, but would the greatest of all Romans want to end his life because of it? I think not!"

"Then let us put aside for a moment the fact that Caesar was a supreme soldier and political genius. He desired, as all patricians do when they die, that death is swift, their bloodline continuous, and the reputation they leave us with is honourable and enduring."

He placed his hand on Octavian's shoulder. "You are his bloodline, dear boy. And there was no need for him to suffer a lingering death when he could provoke others to end it swiftly. By doing so, the reputation he leaves us is immortalised by those who conspired to kill him."

"There's no proof that my father would do any of this; it's completely out of character."

"Indeed, this is exactly what Caesar wanted us to believe. His plan was ingenious!"

Octavian poured himself some water from a pitcher, trying to look more interested than angry, but his hand trembled as he drank. If this theory became public it would tarnish Caesar's name and probably destroy his own career.

"There is no evidence of any death wish," Cicero said, sensing the boy's anxiety. "No, Caesar was much too clever for that. What I have is purely circumstantial… and for your ears only."

"I may not agree with your opinion, sir, but I am intrigued. Please continue." Octavian said, selecting a grape and relaxing now into the couch.

Cicero nodded his approval. "My relationship with Caesar was always a battle of intellect. Even now I strive to outmanoeuvre him; his death holds too many unanswered questions," he said, raising a hand to his brow. "Why, for example, after offering deliberate provocation to his enemies did he sack the bodyguards and walk unprotected to meet his killers? The night before, Calpurnia had a vision of his impending death; she pleaded with Caesar to stay at his villa but he ignored her.

"Even on his way to the Senate meeting someone in the crowd gave him a note warning him of the plot to kill him. Did you know it was found after his death...unopened?"

Octavian shook his head. "No. I... "

"Then let me elaborate," Cicero intervened. "Here was a man of high intelligence who never left anything to chance, either on a battlefield or in the political arena. Caesar knew his enemy's every move, and yet, when it comes to his death he's completely defenceless. Now this is what I see as irrational!"

Octavian said nothing. He could see Cicero's point of view but dismissed it as the ramblings of an old man clinging to the last thread of his tattered Republic.

Cicero addressed him again. "Think of the outcome, Octavian. While Caesar achieved everything he desired his killers were left with nothing because in defending the Republic they only ensured its demise."

With this, he returned to the couch, raising a cup of wine to his dry lips. "I respected Caesar as a man, but not his dictatorship."

"Then by taking his name will you oppose me?" Octavian asked.

Cicero's rhetorical manner was suddenly transformed... his voice subdued. "Strange as it may seem, your question was answered many years ago." he smiled. "I was consul at the time; it was New Year's Day and I had escorted Caesar to the Senate House, relating to him and other senators what I had dreamt the night before. It was of a boy with noble features, let down from the heavens by a golden chain. He stood at the temple door, and Jupiter himself bowed down before him."

Cicero caught his breath. "The moment I had related this dream, that very boy took hold of Caesar's hand. I had never seen him before that day. The boy was you, Octavian."

"I, too, have a dream… to serve under you as your junior consul," Octavian lied. "Then we could restore the Republic together." He rose from the couch. "Can I count on your support in the Senate, sir?"

Cicero beamed. "Yes, of course, dear boy. You have my word."

They walked to the door, Cicero's hands clasping the toga at his chest in a typical senatorial pose. "Rome is supposed to be a city of free men, where no-one legally bears arms, but not for long," he said, grimly. "Marc Antony already has a force of henchmen, and their numbers increase daily. So waste no time, Octavian. Claim your inheritance and Caesar's name, and be assured, I will praise your cause in the Senate House."

The two men shook hands and as Octavian thanked him Cicero smiled weakly, knowing the boy was fighting a lost cause. "Remember one thing," he said. "Never turn your back on Antony; you must do whatever it takes to stop him taking control of Rome."

Their horses were waiting in the courtyard, freshly groomed. The rain had stopped, and the earthy smell from the woods mingled with a salty sea as they rode towards Baiae.

Octavian was in a jubilant mood. He looked at the man beside him, who only days before had saved his life. "Damon!" he cried, stirring his horse into a gallop. "Race me to the seashore!"

Chapter V

"You may not agree with it, Maecenas, but your reasoning in this matter lies with your Etruscan ancestors. It is not the military way. Wait here if you wish," Octavian said, walking towards a group of his men.

Agrippa smiled as he went to follow him. "Don't you have the stomach for it, my dear?"

Maecenas shook his head, knowing his protest was futile.

The soldiers continued their savagery until Octavian called a halt. "Enough, I say! He's mine. I will finish it!" His words echoed around the grassy hollow where the prisoner lay... but they came too late as another hail of stones thudded into his body.

It was a familiar voice, yet one the prisoner could not remember. This annoyed him... just like the pain and tiredness in his limbs. He wanted to stand... but also sleep. He watched red streams of blood dripping from his body to the earth. Then he turned his face to the skies, darkened by a hundred figures looking down on him.

It seemed cooler here by the river; a breeze reminding him of his nakedness. He shivered, wanting to cover himself from the cold. His hands reached out blindly, finding the rough bark of pine tree. He tried to stand… to see these faceless men, but the pain in his broken fingers sent shock waves through the rest of his shattered body.

A weak smile passed over his lips as he brushed away the warm, red mist from his eyes. The shadowy figures parted, and through the shaft of light a solitary man approached him down the slope.

"Who are you?" he croaked.

That same voice came to him again in a sinister whisper, and he knew his executioner. But no… surely Octavian was dead! The prisoner cowered as Octavian held something out to him… and he saw a flash as it fell.

The head of Quintus Glaber rolled on the ground, its bloody mess gathering pine needles as Octavian kicked it away.

The days following Cleopatra's departure pleased Marc Antony. He and Canidius had consolidated support among a large number of veterans awaiting settlement under Caesar's plans. But their presence had created a volatile and undesirable situation in the city and Antony wanted them removed. Anxious to increase his prestige with the Senate, he assigned Canidius to lead the veterans away from Rome to take farms and land in the country. The money and papers already secured from Caesar's widow were extremely important to such a cause.

Calpurnia entrusted them to his safekeeping, and Caesar's secretary Faberius was also obedient to him. The

Senate decreed that all Caesar's deeds and intentions should be ratified and, with Faberius' help, Antony made several additions. By subtle manipulation of the Senate, he was able to make generous gifts to those he favoured. Then he made plans to move Brutus and Cassius from Cisalpine Gaul and Syria.

He deemed they would become a spent force without support from their armies, the Senate or the Roman people. It was time to relax and celebrate his good fortune… a night to share with a few friends. Antony knew just the place.

Under the cover of darkness and shabbily dressed, Antony and four of his elite officers made their way to a seedy tenement area near the River Tiber. They passed through narrow streets and alleys which reeked of trash heaps and urine, until Antony saw the tavern. He knocked at the door and a scrawny man greeted them with a toothless smile.

"Welcome, citizens!" he cried, with a courteous bow, his eyes squinting at them each in turn. "Welcome to the best of wines… and all the pleasures you desire."

Antony nodded; there was no sign of recognition. "We want a private room and your finest wine," he said.

"Yes, yes… of course. Just follow me." The little man wrung his hands with glee, ushering them to the stairs at the far side of the room.

The tavern was exactly how Antony remembered it: dark as a dungeon, the air heavy with lamp oil and the smell of spilt wine rotting the floorboards. In his younger days it was a sanctuary for struggling poets, actors and philosophers, where wine and women were equally as cheap; a place where virile youths lost their virginity.

He followed the innkeeper up the creaking stairway, smiling at the memory. A need for a woman began to surge through his veins.

Lurid sighs mingled with drunken laughter across the landing as the innkeeper led them into a large room. Antony surveyed the sparse contents of four couches. They were sturdy and finely crafted… but hardly used for sleeping on. The drapes also seemed much too refined for a brothel.

He walked over to a shuttered window that overlooked the warehouses beside the river. "Now bring us wine, and the best girls you can find… not the old dogs you normally trade!" he growled, removing his hooded cape.

The smile froze on the innkeeper's face when he noticed the dagger now in Antony's hand. He quickly placed the lamp he carried on a low table and scurried from the room… their laughter ringing in his ears.

Antony wanted the youngest and most beautiful of the women, but upon entering the room it was she who moved to him. Now she stood very near, her sensuous eyes smiling as he caressed her long scented hair. Antony led her to a couch, and soon the loud drunken antics of his comrades were a distant murmur as she satisfied his every need.

He was aware at times of other females caressing him; of his oldest officer Dellius leering at him, but he would push them away; his own drunkenness sobered by the intense sexual pleasure the young woman's body offered his…

The tenth hour of night was approaching when Antony returned to the Pincian Hill. He and Dellius shared a joke as they climbed the winding path to the villa. The sky was sprinkled with stars, and a full moon shone through the trees lighting the way. Their laughter alerted a guard who suddenly stepped out from the gardens wielding a sword.

Antony stopped in his tracks. "It is I… Marc Antony and friend," he said, removing his hood.

The guard apologised. "Someone was in the grounds earlier, sir. It's the centurion, Quintus Glaber. I'm afraid… "

"Hail Jupiter!" Antony cried. "I've been waiting for days. Hurry up, my man. Where is he?"

The young man nervously pointed to the cypress trees. "But he's …"

Antony and Dellius brushed passed him, crossing the bridge over a small stream. In a clearing beyond the trees a pool of yellow moonlight touched the face of Glaber. Antony gasped, turning to Dellius in disbelief.

There was a spear embedded in the ground, and displayed on top of it was the centurion's severed head… a surprised expression frozen on his face.

In the shadows nearby, a crippled boy smiled to himself… Octavian would be pleased with his work.

At the centre of the camp red and gold pennants fluttered on the corners of a large tent. In front of it stood two standards mounted with silver eagles. The Romans called them Aquila: the eagle being a symbol of the legion's power. Damon knew that men would lay down their lives rather than lose it to the enemy, for a captured eagle brought disgrace and the legion was often disbanded.

He stood admiring how real they looked in the flickering light of a nearby campfire. Beside them were other standards, gilded and wreathed, bearing the letters 'SPQR' which represented the ancient motto: 'Senatus

Populusque Romanus'. This reminded the legionaries that they fought for the Senate and the Roman people.

Damon was distracted by raised voices coming from within the tent. The flap opened and Marcus Agrippa stormed outside. He breathed deeply, raising his head to the skies as if thankful to be out in the night air.

Damon said: "I suspect all is not well at the meeting?"

"I had to get out! It's that fool Maecenas and his feminine ways." Agrippa spat on the ground as though he had tasted some foul wine. "He even thinks like a woman! Granted he may be wiser in political concerns, but I've warned Octavian to keep him out of military matters... they are for real men!"

Damon was sympathetic. The lasting impression he had of Agrippa was seeing him, sword in hand, leading more than three thousand troops to meet them at the Clanius River. He was full of physical aggression, and opposite to Octavian's calm assurance, they made a perfect foil. Yet Maecenas was very different, and certainly a thorn in Agrippa's side.

"Why do you object to his advice, Agrippa?"

"I object to Maecenas at all times!" he said, angrily.

Damon grinned. "It shows."

Agrippa shook his head. "I worry about what others may think of their relationship... if you know what I mean? It's not just our own men but the opposition. Just imagine what Marc Antony would make of..." His voice trailed away. "Ah... what's the use?"

"Is the master aware of this?"

Agrippa shrugged his shoulders. "Octavian knows exactly how I feel... Anyway, join me for a walk through the camp, I could do with some company," he said, more cheerfully.

The army of men was encamped outside Sinuessa, a town beyond Capua on the western coast. Despite shelter from the tall trees along this stretch of the Via Appia, the two men fastened their cloaks against a chillwind blowing in from the sea. They wandered around the village of tents which held the strangest of armies. Agrippa was in charge of training young men and old farmers, whose weapons ranged from carving knives and farming tools, to anything sharp enough to resemble a spear.

"Just look at them. Octavian has given me this ragged outfit to shape into a fighting force. Is there any hope, Damon?"

"Whatever your indifference is towards Maecenas, the master still regards you as his right hand. You have the strength and ability to achieve many things, Agrippa."

As they walked on, the Roman pointed out that thankfully the main body of men were Caesar's veterans and the deserters from Canidius' legions. Damon observed them to be the disciplined legionaries: well armed and notably armoured, most of them highly experienced in warfare. It was one of these groups who exchanged greetings with the two men. They were invited to share a skin of Posca: a cheap, sour wine the soldiers disposed of in large quantities.

"So, is it true we're off to war again, Agrippa?" asked a bulky, red haired veteran.

"You drink too much, Rufus. Don't you old soldiers think of anything else but your next battle?"

"Yes... my next woman!" said another, poking the fire suggestively with the tip of his sword. A swirl of sparks danced into the air and they all roared with laughter, except Rufus.

"With respect, I was a soldier before you and Octavian were born," he said, passing on the wineskin. "I've been decorated six times and now I'm a Decurion. A rank, I might add, earned through blood and sweat not by patronage. Believe me... there's nothing worse than killing another Roman."

Damon watched the cavalry officer wipe the dribbles of wine from his beard, noticing the deep jagged scar that ran the length of his forearm. "Then why are you here?" he asked.

"Money! That's what I fight for, and war is all I've ever known. Our good leader has promised us land. Perhaps the time is right for me to become a farmer." He stared at Damon. "And what's your reason for living, Greek man?"

"I just want to see my wife and child again."

"Well, I hear that you're the one who saved the general's life. You must have some fine privileges to look forward to?"

"There are no privileges in war, my friend... only death. I'm sure you know that more than any of us."

"Then bring us some cheer, Greek man. Let's have a tune from that flute of yours."

It took Damon by surprise. "I can't play very well, but..."

"We know that... we've heard you before!" roared a drunken voice.

"Quiet!" said Rufus, trying hard to stem the laughter. "Give the Greek a chance."

Damon began to play and Rufus listened for a while before joining in... howling like a wolf. The noise and laughter brought other legionaries over, and dancing and merriment began around the fire. But with the wine came a tiredness that turned men of steel into sleeping babies.

It was time to leave. Damon placed a hand on Rufus' shoulder, thanking him for the wine before he and Agrippa moved away.

At the north-west corner of the camp they sat for a while at the roadside. It was warmer here with the Via Appia banked above them. Beyond this, came the sound of waves battering the seashore.

"I was sorry to hear about Vario... I respected him," Agrippa said, quietly. "He was a fine man."

"Yes. I... I loved him as my father." Damon was surprised by his own words. He'd never spoken of Vario like this before, but the guilt had never left him. "I should have been there to protect him," he said. "That's all he really asked of me."

"You were not to blame for his death, my friend. - It was the will of the gods. It meant Octavian survived because his destiny was already written in the stars."

The words held no reasoning for Damon.

"We have been friends since our days at school," Agrippa continued, "and I bear witness that he is the chosen one. By saving his life you are now a part of his dream for a new Roman world."

Damon looked sharply at the Roman. "What have you seen, Agrippa? Why do the gods choose to let one man live and another die?"

"Before we left Apollonia, Octavian and I visited Theogenes, the astrologer, to consult him about our future careers. I was prophesied such good fortune that Octavian at first declined to offer his own information. But when he did, Theogenes fell to his knees treating Octavian as though he was a god."

Agrippa smiled at the thought. "Do you know that in Rome we have a group of prophets who read the sky for omens?"

"Do you mean the augurs?"

"Yes… they study birds, clouds, lightning and other movements. Well, one day Octavian and I met a prophet on our return to Rome from Velitrae. He offered us bread and wine, and as we sat beside the road a huge shadow came over us."

Agrippa spread his hands in an arc over his head. "Before we could move an eagle swooped down, its talons taking the bread from Octavian's hand. The bird carried it aloft, and to our great surprise it hovered over him, before gliding down again… gently replacing the bread at his feet."

"What happened then?"

"The prophet, just like Theogenes, fell to his knees proclaiming Octavian as the great saviour of Rome."

"He will need all the gods to smile on him if one so young is to replace the mighty Caesar," said Damon.

Agrippa smiled. "I believe they already have… thanks to you."

Damon was intrigued by Agrippa's story because its prophecy was akin to what Octavian had previously told him about Cicero's dream. And unlike Caesar, who had apparently disregarded several warnings of his imminent death, Octavian's belief in these premonitory signs never wavered. It amused Damon when Octavian insisted his footwear should be placed by his bed in such a way that he could never thrust his right foot into the left sandal or boot… as this was a bad omen.

In their short time together he had begun to enjoy the individual trust of the three Romans. Each one confided in him in their different ways… but all in unison to

Octavian's cause. This greatly improved his own education and understanding of friendship. Whether they succeeded or died in the attempt, he realised his own destiny was now in their hands.

A sudden chill made him shiver as he rose to his feet. "We should go back," he said to Agrippa, "there's a storm in the air."

Rain began to fall as they walked through the camp, turning into a relentless downpour by the following day. It was a storm that raged across the Bay of Cajeta slowing the army's progress and forcing them to remain in Formiae.

On the second day they marched to Fundi, where the road carved its way through a mountain pass near Lake Fundanus, before reaching the Pontine Marshes: a swamp district separated from the Tyrrhenian Sea by high sand dunes. The marshes were rife with flies, mosquitoes and disease. By the time they entered a village near Tarracina, several men, including Octavian, had gone down with a fever. A physician was summoned from the town.

"Hey, Greek man. Over here!"

Damon turned to see Rufus grinning at him from the doorway of a small farmhouse. He carried Octavian inside.

The house was dry and warm, with signs that its occupants had fled in sight of the advancing army. A fire still burned, and over it the smell of chicken lingered on a roasting spit; its carcass lay on the table among scraps of bread and vegetables.

Next to the fireplace, hot charcoals smouldered on a stove where fruit juice bubbled in an earthenware pot. Several large amphorae were propped up in a corner, and above them a shelf supported an assortment of jugs and cooking pots. Behind a drawn curtain was a sleeping couch which Rufus dragged out near to the fire.

"Lay the general here. I will bring fresh blankets," he said, closing the door behind him.

Damon could hear him outside shouting orders: "You there! Check the outbuildings for wood, and make sure there's enough to last until morning." There was a pause, and then… "And you two! What are you waiting for? Ride out and find that doctor. He should be here by now!"

When the physician arrived, Octavian lay shivering in front of a blazing fire. Damon had stripped him of his wet clothes and wrapped him in warm blankets, but his breathing was laboured and a painful cough racked his body. The physician went to work.

He was Sicilian: brusque and darkly intense, his eyes flickered over Octavian without sympathy. He turned to Damon. "Has he coughed blood?"

"A little… but his fever worsens by the hour."

The physician checked Octavian's mouth, and noticing the open sores and his struggle to breathe he ordered his assistant to prepare a poultice for the patient's chest. He then mixed a potion of medicinal herbs with a little wine.

Damon put his arm around Octavian's shoulder, easing him up from the couch to sip the honeyed liquid. Meanwhile, the assistant was spreading a black, sticky mess onto a square of fabric. The poultice reeked with a mixture of pine resin, oil and vinegar.

"This will draw out the noxious elements," said the physician, as he smoothed the poultice onto Octavian's bared chest. He took Damon to one side. "Keep him warm and quiet. Use the potion regularly, and you must soak a cloth in this bowl of vinegar, so…" he said, squeezing out the excess. He folded the cloth, placing it on Octavian's brow. "Repeat it throughout the night; it will help reduce his fever."

The Sicilian looked at his patient once more in apathy, and with a swirl of his cloak he was gone; his assistant scurrying after him.

During the night, Octavian's condition deteriorated, yet there was no weakness in his spirit. He had the qualities his troops most desired in a commander: stature, charm… and often brutality, but to Damon he was just a boy in need of someone to watch over him.

Octavian beckoned Damon to sit beside him, his voice hoarse and weak. "Talk to me, Damon… for should I sleep I fear I will never waken." He held out a shaking hand, "Tell me about your home in Cyprus."

Damon took his master's hand, and as he spoke the memories softened his voice to a whisper. "The island is green and fertile… rich in copper, timber and wheat. It has a fine harbour city they call Nea Paphos.

"My home is in the foothills beyond the city walls. It's a simple house approached through vineyards and a meadow of wild flowers. There's a herb garden through the gate and a terrace shaded by an old grapevine. Behind the house, orchards of fruit trees stretch down into a valley filled with olive groves."

He paused to look at Octavian. The young Roman's eyes were closed, but a smile touched the corners of his mouth. He seemed to be picturing it all…

"When the morning sun rises over the Troodos Mountains, I can rest from my work in the vineyards and watch the eagles soar over a valley where wild beasts emerge from the great forests to drink at the river. Then at night, while our baby slept, I would sit with Hestia in the garden and watch the sky fill with stars…"

His voice faltered and he turned away to prepare a fresh cloth for Octavian's brow, relieved that the tears in his eyes were never seen.

Damon nursed the Roman for three more nights without leaving his side.

When Octavian's messenger returned from Rome, a guard escorted him to the farmhouse. He was granted an immediate audience. Octavian had recovered sufficiently to be sitting up on the couch, but his deathly appearance shocked Tibo.

The general's voice was strained and hoarse. "I trust you left Marc Antony my little gift, Tibo?"

"Yes, sir! I was hidden, but close enough to see how much it shocked him."

Octavian turned to Maecenas. "I wonder what surprised Antony the most, the head of Glaber, or the way he underestimated me?" The young messenger appeared nervous. "What concerns you, boy? Is there news from Rome?"

"It… it's not good, general." said Tibo. He looked sheepishly at the occupants of the room, and then to the flagstone floor. Damon handed him a cup of wine, which he gulped down.

"Marc Antony has left Rome. He's joined Canidius in the north to settle more of Caesar's veterans. The people are angry about it, saying his absence is an insult to your good self."

"Well, at least the plebeians are supportive," remarked Maecenas, cheerfully. "What say the patricians, Tibo?"

The messenger's voice trembled. "Sire, the Senate has agreed that Caesar's killers should not stand trial for his murder. And although the consuls have deprived Brutus and Cassius of Macedonia and Syria… they have been compensated. It is said they will govern Cyrene and Creta."

Octavian was livid. "Is there anything else?"

"Only that Cleopatra has sailed back to Alexandria, and Caesar's widow has returned to his villa again on the Janiculan Hill."

Octavian told Damon to summon a guard. "Take him outside. Give him food and wine, I may need him later."

Octavian allowed himself a wry smile as he watched the boy limp away. "The great Marc Antony… fooled by a crippled boy not even old enough to be a soldier." He turned to Damon. "Now find me Agrippa. At first light tomorrow we set out for Rome."

A mixture of fear and excitement gripped Rome with the expected arrival of Octavian at the Capena Gate. But Caesar's heir had already changed his plans. His troops were stationed a few hours journey from the city in the foothills of Mount Alba between Aricia and Bovillae.

Two nights before, oil lamps burned late in the farmhouse at Tarracina as Octavian's council debated the move. An argument Octavian lost.

"I understand your sense of urgency, "Agrippa had said to him, "but this is not the time. Even without Marc Antony's presence Rome is still well protected. Our two legions would be crushed underfoot like acorns."

Both senior officers agreed; as legates with Caesar's army they had experienced too often the hardships of being outnumbered in battle.

Octavian then looked to Maecenas for support, only to hear his mentor praise Agrippa's words.

"What a pleasant surprise, Agrippa. For once I admire your restraint," he said, chewing on a piece of roast chicken.

It was times like this when he annoyed Octavian. Even when Maecenas was eating he gesticulated with every word... his perpetual motions wafting perfume in the air.

"I also agree," Maecenas continued, "it will be far wiser to leave the troops at Aricia than risk inevitable defeat." He waved another chicken leg at Octavian. "I advise patience rather than boldness, my boy. Build up your strength and enter Rome as a citizen. Visit your mother, Octavian. Seek out your inheritance for now, not your enemies."

With mounting impatience, Octavian also conceded to Damon's suggestion that he should be carried in a litter until his health improved.

From Aricia they could see the mist still clinging to the treetops on Mount Alba. The mountain soared into a cloudless sky, and as Octavian watched all but a century of his army head towards its hill towns, sunlight came streaming down across the plains. He had returned to horseback and his pensive mood lightened on the way to Bovillae, pointing out to Damon the estate of Publius Clodius and a villa retreat of Caesar's old rival, Marcus Pompey.

"Like Caesar, both men were murdered," Octavian said. "Pompey's throat was cut as he stepped ashore in Egypt asking for hospitality. A few years earlier Clodius was slaughtered on this very road. It was built by his ancestor, Appius Claudius Caecus."

Octavian referred to the Via Appia, and this first stretch was more than 270 years old. Its construction was unique: a deep trench with a base of tightly wedged large stones. Then a thick layer of smaller stones bound in cement and topped with a compressed compound of gravel and flint. The surface consisted of polygonal stone slabs, so perfectly cut that each retained the other between the outer edging blocks. Its width was cambered to take the rainwater away into draining ditches.

The Via Appia widened as they emerged from the wooded slopes, and Octavian remarked how the road had been built from Rome as a military route for the legions. It ran like an arrow past the eleventh milestone to Bovillae: a drab and dusty place that held a post station and a few houses. Opposite these, lying back from the road - was a large inn with stables at the rear.

They rested long enough here to feed and water the horses before moving out again into the mid-day sun. With the Alban Hills behind them the land took on a placid face; the stillness broken only by the staccato of hooves on the stone highway. An occasional farmhouse and scattered trees marked the countryside as a patchwork of flat open pastures coloured both sides of the road. This natural beauty was soon lost in the sight and pungent smell of trash.

"Welcome to Rome!" Maecenas laughed, turning to Damon. "To reach the living you must first see its dead. It is Roman law that we bury them outside the city walls."

As the great piles of rubbish and debris reduced so the tombs and sepulchres multiplied. Cenotaphs, crumbled and green with age, stood alongside the shiny marble tombs of grand patrician families whose names meant little to a Greek slave. Damon's eyes were fixed on the great city wall and the aqueduct above which carried Rome's water supply.

Lucius Vario had told him so much about the city: its maize of streets and alleyways with regions of shops, artisan yards, workshops and granaries which sprawled around its shrines and temples. And on the hills and ridges above resided Rome's nobility, wealth and the socially aspiring. It was a place he longed to see.

The noise began at the fish markets outside the Capena Gate: a loud cheering and chanting of Octavian's name by Roman citizens, slaves and freedmen, who circled the troops and frequently brought them to a halt. Octavian and Agrippa waved while Maecenas dabbed the tears from his cheeks. Damon was speechless, completely overwhelmed by the crowds and the enormity of what lay inside the city walls.

They were jostled by a mass of people in the Vallis Murcia, along the Circus Maximus to the Forum Boarium, where the meat markets swarmed with well wishers. Their enthusiasm reached a crescendo when Octavian arrived at the Sublicius Bridge. He turned on his horse to acknowledge them before crossing the wooden bridge over the River Tiber. Then the entourage turned their backs to the grimy wharves and warehouses, heading towards the villas and estates that rambled down wooded slopes to the river.

Here, wealthy Romans lazed away their summer days in cultivated gardens, where shady trees cast dappled sunlight over statues and glistening fountains. The noise of the city was lost; there was only the sound of their horses' hooves in the soft earth and cicadas chirping in the high grass.

Octavian sighed. He knew his mother and sister would be waiting for him, but felt it was his duty to first pay his respects to Caesar's widow. A weariness swept over him; it suddenly seemed as though he'd been away for a lifetime.

In the following days it was agreed that Octavian's initial approach to Marc Antony should be one of diplomacy. By the time Antony returned to Rome, Octavian had already claimed his posthumous adoption in Caesar's will through the court officials. He wasted no time in seeking an audience with the consul.

The twenty-first day of May began with a bright, sunny morning. Octavian arrived at the Pincian Hill with the best of intentions, so he was not prepared for the ensuing events.

Meanwhile, the gladiators guarding the villa's entrance were surprised to see their master so early. Marc Antony appeared relaxed considering his tiresome journey, but his mood changed abruptly at the sight of two men ascending the steps.

He gave Damon a cursory glance. "You travel light, Octavian. I should warn you, Rome has changed... even in such peaceful gardens as these one might lose their head."

"I feel no threat from the dead... especially centurions." Octavian replied, icily.

Each stared at the other, until Antony smiled. "It seems we have much to discuss, but privately. The slave stays here."

They passed through the atrium and a flight of stairs led to a room flooded with light. Its centrepiece was a large oak desk, littered with scrolls where Antony had been writing. As they crossed the room a warm breeze drifted through the open doors and shutters, bearing a trace of herbs and flowers from below.

Neither man spoke while Spiro served them wine out on the balcony, but on his departure Antony took the offensive. He was frank, and eager to impose his stature on the young upstart. "So, you waste no time in making trouble," he began. "Your army - if one can call it that - is mine. Those men you recruited in the south are from my legions!"

"They're not yours, but Caesar's. Now they pledge their allegiance to me." Octavian countered.

Antony grinned. "Let me remind you, boy, you are no more than a citizen, and as such you act illegally. I fear you have been misled into thinking anything else. Granted you have accumulated a misguided following. What is it... one legion or two? Yet even you should know that a private citizen can never command an army.... unless you aspire to be another Spartacus, but we all know what happened to him!"

The icy stare from Octavian never wavered as Antony sneered: "You have no official rank, and with no experience of commanding an army... you're out of your depth. I warn you, Octavian, I want those men returned to Canidius!"

Octavian stood, leaning against the balcony with the sun warming his shoulders. "There's one thing you conveniently forget. I am now Caesar's adopted son. I have claimed his inheritance and whatever his name brings me."

Antony slammed his empty wine cup down on the table. "And I am a loyal consul of Rome!" he roared. "Caesar may have left you his name, but Rome will never accept you as his successor. I will see to that!"

"A loyal consul, are you? Then where is your loyalty to the Roman people? Tell me, just what have you done to avenge my father's death? You pose as Caesar's friend and most trusted officer... the one whose oratory stirred such glorious remembrance at his funeral.

"Yes, the same noble Marc Antony who fooled our people into believing that he would bring Caesar's killers to justice. Oh, you quickly opposed the perpetrators then, but now they are free men… and still govern in Greece. I wonder, did you also bribe the Senate with Caesar's gold?"

Antony was taken aback by the young man's boldness. He chose his next words carefully. "I can only see your lack of respect as ignorance, Octavian. It has not even occurred to you that whatever I said and did was to provide for Caesar's immortality. He displeased the Senate; seized authority and only my actions prevented him from being declared a tyrant. The concessions I made to Brutus and Cassius were only to satisfy the Senate. Without me, Caesar would have been dishonoured.'"

"So, with equal generosity you must have protected his estate and my inheritance?"

Antony poured himself more wine and drank it, playing with time. "This wine will ripen the blood in your veins, Octavian. Look at you… you should eat more. You need some flesh on those bones!"

"All I need is the gold coinage you took from Calpurnia for safekeeping; it's the legacy my father left for the people of Rome. If more is required then I will ask to borrow from the Treasury. In exchange, I can offer my own properties for sale."

"My dear Octavian, your informant is not to be trusted. The simple truth is that Caesar left our treasury empty and now his assets are under investigation, including the money I once held for his widow."

Antony smiled broadly, leaning forward in his chair. "It also seems that by way of your inheritance you are now liable to a number of people in dispute with Caesar over certain properties."

Octavian turned deathly white; his eyes blazing as he moved towards Antony, raising his cup. "Then what shall we drink to, loyalty to Caesar or the truth… your sympathy towards Brutus and Cassius for murdering him?"

Marc Antony opened his mouth to speak just as the untouched wine from Octavian's cup drenched his face. The shock took his breath away. He staggered to his feet trying to clear his stinging eyes, but the anger he felt suddenly turned to fits of laughter. When he looked again Octavian had gone.

Chapter VI

The following months were a series of highs and lows for Octavian, as he was both praised and ridiculed in the Senate House. Marc Antony seized every opportunity to slander his name. It became serious enough for Octavian to hold council at his mother's house on the Aventine Hill.

In the dining room two women were organising an evening meal when a young slave announced their visitor. As Damon entered, the older woman greeted him. "So, we meet at last," she smiled. "I am Octavian's mother, Atia. This is my daughter, Octavia."

Damon bowed. "I am honoured, my lady," he said politely.

"Please join us, Damon." Atia gestured for him to sit on a back-less chair, and as they reclined on two adjacent couches Damon was overawed by the room's grandeur.

Its walls were deep red and the windows draped in orange and gold. A marble floor inlaid with rectangular patterns of coloured mosaic, each one portraying a different class of society. They looked so realistic that slaves, legionaries, senators and even the gods seemed alive in the flickering lamplight.

It was a brief encounter for Damon, in which Octavia thanked him for saving her brother's life and Atia said he would always be welcome in her home. But he was soon aware of their fears for Octavian. He listened with a certain distraction as the beauty of both women and their admiring glances made him feel uneasy.

Atia looked beautiful dressed in a white stola; it was edged with gold at the waist and hem, and tied loosely under her bosom. She was without makeup, and the only jewellery she wore was an ivory pin that secured her golden hair in a bun. Her slim body, high cheekbones and cream, marble-like skin gave her the serenity Octavia was yet to achieve.

But in her lovely young daughter Damon could see the striking resemblance to Octavian. Even when she spoke he was aware of that same self-confident manner. Octavia's was another kind of beauty: a vibrant mixture of youth and intelligence that shone with the same intensity as the blue of her eyes. Her undressed hair cascaded down in long tresses and with every movement it shimmered like black silk. She was seventeen, and her delicate frame belied the fact that she was the mother of Gaius Marcellus' son.

When Damon left the dining room he could hear voices in the library. Agrippa and Marcellus had returned from the Senate House to join Octavian, Maecenas and Atia's husband, Philippus. Their meeting had begun.

Lamps were lit in all the darkened rooms and hallways now, reflecting a host of colours from the frescoed walls and mosaic floors. At the end of a hallway opposite the library, Damon stood at a window looking out on the city. To the west, white plumes of smoke curled away from fires near the Tiber and lights glimmered in houses on the Palatine Hill. Beyond it, the Forum and Senate House lay silent as a cluster of stars gathered over the temples and basilicas.

He lowered his eyes to the Circus Maximus: a vast arena that occupied the hollow between the Aventine and Palatine hills. Only weeks before, Octavian had honoured Julius Caesar there with a magnificent series of games. In the fading light he could see the outline of its high walls, the monumental arches and darkened arcade, through which poured thousands of people to witness Rome's *ludi circences*. Between its towers was a processional entrance with the *carceres* for horses and chariots.

Damon recalled the great chariot races, and in the stillness he could almost hear the horses' thundering hooves and the roar of frenzied crowds as charioteers jostled for the bends close to the *spina*... the most dangerous part of the race.

In that instant a shadow crossed the hallway. Damon saw only a glimpse of the figure... but it was enough. In seconds his arm was locked around the man's throat, and with a dagger pressing into his ribcage the man was forced into the library. His hooded cape was torn from his back as he fell in a heap on the floor.

"Balbus! What an unexpected pleasure. How nice of you to drop in," Octavian laughed.

The banker was almost as round as he was tall, his girth making him struggle to find his feet. Philippus lent him a hand, apologising profusely for such barbaric treatment. Balbus eventually made it to a couch, holding his throat and gasping for breath. His eyes shot arrows at the grinning faces around the room.

Apart from his insatiable appetite, he was a remarkable man. His black hair and swarthy looks were unmistakably Spanish. A shrewd citizen of Gades, he had amassed a fortune from silver mines and banking. He befriended Julius Caesar on his first Spanish campaign and now wanted to offer more of his wealth to Octavian's cause. It took him a while to regain his composure.

"I must apologise… I should have known better than to enter unannounced," he said, looking to Octavian. "Words cannot express how sickened I was by the traitor, Quintus Glaber. I trusted him with your safe return. I thank the gods you were spared."

"Trust is something we do not give away lightly," Octavian snapped. "I thought a man of your principles would have known better?"

"I will make amends… I pledged my allegiance to you with gold at Brundisium," cried Balbus, "but there's more. Just tell me what you need!"

Octavian gave the banker a reassuring nod. "Very well. I think you should stay and join our deliberation." He turned away, smiling. "Thank you, Damon… you may stand at the door."

The meeting resumed with Agrippa addressing Octavian. He was distinctly agitated. "When Antony speaks to the Senate it seems that you have no allies," he said with his usual bluntness. "Antony even alleges that you had an unnatural relationship with Caesar in order for you to become his heir. Slander, of course!" he quickly added.

Octavian was taken aback. "That's enough, Agrippa! We know Antony's a liar; it's what he does best."

"Exactly! Our problem is that most of the senators believe him."

"What of the troops? Do they disparage me?"

"Not that I'm aware of, but they prefer a general with vices anyway… whatever they may be."

Maecenas sniggered. "Yes. And if nothing else, the men make up dirty songs… I heard the one about Caesar and King Nicomedes on our journey to Rome."

Octavian gave him a withering glance.

"What the men don't like is confusion," stressed Agrippa. "They joined us not to spend days training for combat and their nights in brothels. They are restless to avenge Caesar… not to talk about it."

"I can sympathise with them, my friend. This is why we are here." Octavian turned to his brother-in-law. "Tell me about Cicero's involvement, Marcellus."

Unlike Agrippa, the man who stood beside him was quietly spoken. Marcellus had a lean sensitive face; his bright blue eyes and ready smile charmed everyone he met. He delivered his words in clear, measured tones.

"Most favourable," he began. "Despite Antony's gibes, the old man dominates every discussion. He continually reminds the Senate of Antony's own moral shortcomings, and praises your purpose. The way you are selling off the properties you've inherited and, more importantly, your intention to use your own estate to pay Caesar's legacy to the people." '

Marcellus began to mimic Cicero's flamboyant style, which lightened the serious faces around him. "This young man is a true servant of Rome," he said, gesturing to Octavian. "Why… even upon his entry to the city a nimbus circles the sun. If the gods acclaim him this divinity, then who are we to deny his loyalty?"

Octavian smiled. Agrippa looked away shaking his head. "I, for one, am not fooled by Cicero's words," he said. "His mind changes like the wind. How can we think about trusting him?"

"I trust no-one outside this room except my mother and Octavia. Cicero only praises me because he hates Antony. Even now he probably sits in his house on the Palatine preparing yet another derogatory speech. He knows I can keep his dream alive to restore the Republic, while on the other side lurks Antony... a would-be dictator!"

Marcellus was pouring two cups of red wine at the table and, handing one to Balbus, he said: "I witnessed them exchanging words on the steps of the Senate House only two days ago. Cicero had complained loudly to a group of senators of the strong smell of wine. Antony was raging. He told Cicero his tongue was too sharp. 'Be careful how you wag it,' he snapped, 'or one day it will cut your own throat!'"

"A common problem... too much talking," Agrippa said, downing his wine. "While Antony strengthens his army we stand gossiping. Our agents report that Canidius has already secured the three legions returning from Macedonia."

Philippus clasped his hands, resting them on his protruding belly. "Then why not join forces with Antony?" he said, thinly.

Octavian laughed. "Please... you sound more like my mother every day."

"Is it so surprising that your mother and I worry about your safety?"

"No. It's a comfort... but not a solution, I'm afraid."

"There is only one solution," Maecenas said. "We must vote: either mount a challenge, or wait."

The result was shared. Octavian, Agrippa and Marcellus wanting to challenge Antony, while the three elders voted for a waiting game.

"A fresh voice is what we need," Octavian said. "A neutral opinion from someone who can be trusted." He turned. "Come and join us, Damon."

"Are you mad!" cried Philippus. "Do you seriously want us to rely on the word of a slave?"

Octavian stood, ignoring him. "Well, Damon... what say you, my friend?"

"With respect, sire, I'm sure my opinion would be inappropriate in such presence."

Philippus and Balbus echoed their agreement.

"Nonsense!" argued Maecenas. "Your ideas are valued here." He looked sternly at Philippus. "Lest some of us forget, we are deeply indebted to this man's services to Octavian and Rome."

Octavian bid Damon to speak.

"Despite any differences, we all desire a safe passage for the master," he began. "I have trained recruits with Agrippa, and he knows the mood and influence of the veterans. If they should lose faith, Antony will hear of it..."

"But Cicero crucifies him in the House," Philippus cut in, "it's only a matter of time before he's driven out of Rome."

Maecenas agreed. "We should wait. Antony's consulship is virtually over. He badly needs Cisalpine Gaul to safeguard his future. As its governor, his power would be extended, and with his army he would be ideally placed to intimidate Rome."

"But Decimus Brutus will never surrender his province," added Balbus. .

"That may be so," Damon said, "but at the moment Cicero only damages Antony's pride, and in doing so spurs him to greater things. With another three legions he now has a formidable army, enough to march on Cisalpine Gaul."

"So, just what are you suggesting?" Philippus asked, impatiently.

"I think the master should rally his legions in the Alban Hills and recruit more experienced troops. He can then compete with Antony on all fronts. Is not the army the true source of Rome's political power? Whoever has the legions in his grasp has Rome by the throat."

"Bravo!" shouted Agrippa. "We have a Greek slave who speaks more like a Roman. Surely, this is a lesson for the faint-hearted?"

Octavian stood and walked over to Balbus. "I have reached a decision," he said, "a compromise." His hand squeezed the banker's shoulder. "The gold from Balbus will increase our powers of persuasion. A gift of five hundred denarii goes to every soldier we recruit."

"But that's two years pay for a serving legionary!" the banker gasped.

Octavian smiled. "With five more legions we will match Antony man for man. In the meantime, let Cicero's tongue continue to wag. I will observe with interest while our campaign grows."

He turned to Agrippa. "By the second hour tomorrow I want you and Marcellus to escort Balbus back to Arretium and recruit for me only the best men his money can buy. I shall return to the Alban Hills with encouraging words for our troops."

"And Maecenas and I?" asked Philippus.

"I need your ears and eyes in Rome. Your presence here is vital. If Cicero's tongue is sharp enough the Senate will bow to his wisdom. We must be prepared to answer their call. Meanwhile, my promise to the Roman people will be kept. You will continue to organise the funding to honour Caesar's legacy."

While Balbus felt decidedly faint trying to calculate the cost, Octavian crossed to the doorway. "Now, stepfather, I think the time has come to try some of mother's excellent food."

With Cicero's words still ringing in his ears, Antony led his legions from Tibur to Ariminum on the eastern border of Cisalpine Gaul. In doing so, he underlined his intention to march on Decimus Brutus. It was a move which incurred further condemnation from the Senate. Some days later they supported Cicero's motion to make Octavian a pro-praetor, and for him to join forces with the new consuls Hirtius and Pansa. But in this position Octavian held no real authority when serving with the consuls because his own army came under their command. It was a tactical plan by Cicero to control Octavian and dispose of Marc Antony while saving Decimus Brutus from a humiliating defeat.

As one year passed into another the first snows of winter began to fall in the mountains. Antony's army had besieged Mutina and, huddled around campfires from the bitter cold, they waited for orders. An icy wind swept flurries of snow through the valley as Antony and Canidius arrived at their tent.

"Morale is low. I've never seen it like this," said Antony, brushing the snow from his cape.

"I'm not surprised. My balls are frozen as hard as walnuts, imagine how the veterans feel out there day after day," said Canidius, warming his hands at a brazier.

Antony paced up and down, a depression shading his face. "Who would have thought the Martian and the

Fourth would desert us, Canidius? I can't believe two of our best legions would join Octavian."

"The men out there are just as angry. And have no fear, brothers or not, they will fight them to the death for you." He poured them wine. "At least we've trapped Decimus Brutus. He hides behind the city walls and he and his men are already weak from famine; they will soon starve to death. So, my friend... we should rejoice in this."

Canidius was raising his cup in salute when the tent flap opened with a rush. It was Dellius, out of breath and his face drawn.

"It's Octavian and Hirtius, sir... they must have circled the mountains from the west. Their camp is in a valley between here and Placentia."

"Show me," Antony said, walking over to the map spread out on a table. "Bring another lamp, Canidius."

Dellius ran his finger along the Via Aemila. "They're here, in this area below Parma, sir. Our agents estimate five or six legions, including the Fourth. Pansa is also on his way from Bononia."

"How many men travel with Pansa?"

"No more than six thousand, general. It's the Martian Legion and one cohort."

Antony was silent, his eyes scanning the map until a smile lit up his face. "Pansa is the tactician. He comes to plot our downfall, so Hirtius and Octavian won't attack us at the city until he arrives."

Canidius nodded. "I know Hirtius, he'll not move in unless he's certain of victory."

"Yes," smiled Antony. "And to ensure this he has to wait for the rest of Pansa's army to come from Bononia. Meanwhile... we attack!"

Canidius grinned. "Pansa's men have to come through the mountain pass."

"Yes. That defile is so narrow men are reduced to a single line."

Dellius looked slightly bemused until Antony enlightened him. "I want you to take one legion and Canidius another."

Antony touched the map with the point of his dagger between Forum Gallorum and the river. "Below the road on both sides in this area there are high reeds and marshes."

Canidius smiled. "So Dellius and me will set the ambush."

"Yes. Then after Pansa has gone through I will be there facing him. At my signal, Canidius, you block the pass behind him. Pansa will find himself both surrounded and outnumbered by three to one."

"We have little time, my lord," Dellius said. "Pansa will probably reach the pass in a few hours."

"Then rally your legion," urged Canidius, "and meet me at the city's north gate in one hour." He turned to Antony and saluted. "My general, I will see you on the Via Aemilia at dawn."

Marc Antony moved forward and embraced each of them in turn. "May the gods be with you," he said.

At first light the wind had ceased and snow fell silently through the grey mists that shrouded the valley. Ten thousand men waited in the marshes, ankle deep in freezing mud. A message came to Canidius and Dellius that Pansa was leading his troops and they were emerging through the defile.

With visibility down to fifty yards, Antony had already moved his cavalry and troops to blockade the Via Aemilia near the river. As the enemy appeared through the mist he signalled the attack with two flaming arrows. Canidius and Dellius raised up their troops from the high reeds, shouting a challenge to Pansa while a century of men sealed the mountain pass behind him.

Pansa reined in his horse, screaming for his men to divide and attack each side of the road. He dismounted, and the troops followed his brave charge down into the marshes.

The Martian legionaries were experienced veterans of war, and despite the ambush their battle lines were drawn without orders; each man in charge of his own destiny. In the marshland and on the road at Forum Gallorum they began to fight Roman against Roman in three separate battles.

Marc Antony led his soldiers on the road, urging them forward from his horse, sword slashing at the enemy; but in the marshes below there were no battle cries. Sometimes it was as though life itself had been suspended. Intermittently, the soldiers drew back from each other exhausted… taking breath before the next encounter. The dull beat of shields parrying enemy blows was lost in the clash of steel against steel ringing through the air.

There could be no charging in the mud and ditches, as they were locked together in close order. A space less than a yard apart was the killing zone for the gladius. From there one could see the fear in a man's eyes and smell the wine on his breath. They would hear his stifled cry and feel the warm splashes of his blood as the short sword cut deep into flesh and bone.

As the hours dragged on, each man to fall was replaced by another… and the passage of time an eternity for the wounded and dying.

To the north of the road Canidius was gaining ground, while on the other side Dellius' troops were forced back by Pansa's savage onslaught. The consul himself appeared invincible; often forging ahead of his comrades with a skill and leadership that gave them added strength. But no one was invincible in the marshes.

Mud and reeds clung to his legs, wrenching away his energy until a weapon found its mark and he fell clutching his side. Pansa was carried from the battle and his troops lost heart, crumbling to defeat. The cohort that led him through the mountains was also slaughtered to the last man. Antony was victorious.

Hirtius was leaving his tent in deep conversation with two of his officers when a messenger arrived. The Spaniard leapt from his horse near the startled general. "Forgive me, sire!" he gasped, falling to his knees in front of Hirtius. "But there's grave danger on the Via Aemilia. It's Marc Antony... his army engages Pansa's troops beyond the river."

Hirtius was already securing his armoured breastplate. "How many men with Antony?"

"It's impossible to tell, sir. The mist lies heavy over the river and marshes."

The consul turned to his officers. "Take two legions around Mutina and move in along the river from the north. I will blockade the road bridge with cavalry and auxiliary until you arrive." He grabbed the messenger roughly by the shoulder. "And you! Get on your feet and ride to warn Octavian. My orders are for him to hold his ground. Tell him to await my return with Pansa."

Hirtius had no reason to expect Pansa's defeat, or that his enemies were regrouping from the marshes. There was no sound of battle up ahead when the ageing consul decided to cross the river. It proved to be a fatal mistake.

Flanked by cavalry, he had deployed his auxiliaries in lines, five deep and some two hundred yards wide, when out of the swirling mists a solid wall of Roman shields marched silently towards them. It was an intimidating sight: a facade of overwhelming numbers and strength no more than twenty yards away and closing fast. The front line of Hirtius' men froze at the sound of a Roman horn. It was the signal for Antony's infantry to throw their javelins… and a volley of death rained from the sky. Hirtius died instantly as a pilum struck his chest from close range. Driven by the weight concentrated behind its small pyramid-shaped head, the weapon pierced his throat.

With their backs to the river the auxiliary was no match for the Roman elite. Their lines were smashed as Antony's men resumed their savagery… killing everything that moved. Weaponry littered the riverside and bodies turned its waters red with blood. But even the victors were exhausted and in disarray when the two legions attacked them from the north.

It was the last hour of daylight when the final battle ceased. A countless number of men had perished and the haunting cries of a thousand more drifted from the marshes.

On the road at Forum Gallorum a solitary messenger boy remained among the lifeless bodies lying in the snow. Tibo had witnessed the carnage, and at its ending he knew the cavalry would not pursue Antony's men into the swamps. Slumped over his horse with an arrowhead lodged in his shoulder, he waited in the darkness for the troops to retreat.

Tibo held on to the horse's mane. "Take me back, Zeus," he whispered… and his black stallion sped away.

His wound bled freely again as they circled Mutina towards Octavian's camp, and his horse slowed to a canter as he left the Via Aemilia. Below him, Tibo could see the village of tents which occupied a whole valley between the two rivers south of Parma. At its centre, heavily guarded, was the general's quarters.

Inside the tent, braziers cast flickering light on the crimson and gold drapes around the chamber walls. As Tibo entered, its canopy billowed slightly and the heavy beams supporting it creaked like the decks of an old ship. Despite his wound, he was greeted without ceremony.

Octavian stopped his discussion with Agrippa. He turned on Tibo, the look in his eyes as cold as the marble bust of Homer beside him. "I expect *you* to bring me the news of Antony's attack, not some miserable Spanish messenger from Hirtius!" he shouted.

Tibo lowered his head. "I'm sorry, sir. I… I was caught up in the battle."

"You failed me!" yelled Octavian, pointing an accusing finger at the boy. "Had I known of Antony's movements before Hirtius the victory over Antony would have been mine. Now the consuls will be covered in glory."

Tibo was shaken. He had lost all feeling in his arm and felt faint from the loss of blood, but the thought of being disgraced gave him the courage to speak. "There was no victory, sire," he said. "Hirtius is dead."

"What?" Octavian looked aghast.

"I saw his body… he lies near the road bridge. Pansa was also badly wounded, general. When they carried him from the marshes he was close to death."

"Go on, Tibo… what else?" urged Agrippa, moving forward.

"The consul was surrounded at dawn. Antony let them through the defile then closed in around them. Pansa must have lost half of the Martian Legion before they broke back through the pass and retreated. Then Hirtius and his men crossed the river, only to be slaughtered."

"And what of Antony?" asked Octavian.

"Another force of cavalry attacked him from the north. He must have suffered heavy losses before being driven into the swamps. I was trapped on the Via Aemilia, sir. I…"

Damon sensed the boy was about to collapse and rushed to his aid, while Octavian was stunned by the enormity of his good fortune. With the death of both consuls, he would be in control of the largest army south of the Alps.

The thought reassured him to the point of forgiveness. "Take him to the surgeon, Damon, and be sure he's cared for properly."

Tibo raised his head. "Thank you, my lord…"

"It is I who should be grateful," Octavian replied, offering a weak smile. "That will be all for now."

Only then did Tibo collapse into Damon's arms and the slave carried him out.

"So, the consuls fall and Antony escapes… but where to?" Agrippa said, his eyes scouring the map.

"Here, to the north beyond the marshland, probably in these woods," Octavian pointed out.

His friend agreed. "Yes, he can re-group there on the high ground and return to Mutina under the cover of darkness."

A surge of excitement ran through Octavian's veins. "Then we must be there to welcome him," he said.

On a wooded hillside north of Forum Gallorum, winter sunlight shone in slanted beams through the snow-covered trees. It gave no warmth to the groups of men huddled together on the frozen ground. After surviving hours of battle they had worked through the night carrying their wounded comrades from the marshes. Now, drenched in foul water and fatigued by their efforts, some of them waited to die in the freezing light of a new day.

Marc Antony walked among them trying to raise their hopes, but the gaunt faces that looked back at him reflected utter defeat. He paused near a sheltered hollow to greet one of his centurions. The normal radiant smile and smart salute was gone. The young soldier sat with his back against a pine tree… helmet in his hand, eyes closed. The morning frost clung to his eyelashes and beard. A sprinkling of snow from the branches above whitened his hair. Antony crouched beside him, but even before he placed a hand on the centurion's shoulder he knew he was dead. Charon had already taken the boy's spirit.

Back at his makeshift quarters he found Canidius waiting. "The men have no will to live," Antony told him. "The place reeks of death. We have to move back to Mutina. Is there any news from Dellius?"

"I'm afraid not. Maybe in another hour," Canidius replied. He wanted to say more… to tell Antony they should retreat from the city, giving their troops time to recover, but he held his tongue. He knew that for every man Antony lost he wanted instant revenge. Although later, when Dellius returned and told of Octavian's imminent advance on Mutina, he spoke out.

"With Hirtius dead his legions have now joined Octavian," reported Dellius. "We are greatly outnumbered, sir."

Antony looked at him sharply. "Did you expect anything else? What do you suggest... that we surrender?"

Dellius smarted at the remark. "No, my lord. Decimus Brutus is still ours for the taking if we can hold Octavian back for a few days..."

"No. I think we should retreat," Canidius said with purpose. "We may have lost a battle but we still have our allies, and with their legions behind us we can rise again and win this campaign."

Antony stepped outside and his two officers followed him, waiting for an answer. Below them the troops were silent, hardly visible now as a bitter wind gathered mist from the marshes swirling it through the trees.

"You're right, Canidius," Antony said, thoughtfully. "We owe these men what is left of their lives." He turned to Dellius. "You and I will hold Mutina for one more day; this will give Canidius time to reach Verona with the wounded. It seems the goddess Fortuna embraces Octavian. And the boy's no fool; he knows his chance is here for the taking."

He managed a smile at the irony of it all. "Come, Dellius, we must get back to the city before it's too late."

Antony's siege of Mutina was broken on the following afternoon. The valiant efforts of his troops held off wave upon wave of Octavian's onslaught, but once more his casualties were heavy. With Dellius wounded, Antony called the retreat. They escaped with less than a two thousand men, passing the night in Histalia before moving on to the city of Verona.

Peter Lathe

In desperate need of comfort for his sick and injured legionaries, Canidius caused great consternation in the city by seizing all the private houses near the west gate. Fearing punishment, most of the owners moved out quietly while protestors were forcibly evicted.

Antony found his friend in a house of luxury. Canidius was lying face down on a couch, naked except for a piece of cloth covering his loins. Two female slaves stood over him massaging scented oils into his aching muscles. When Antony entered the room, Canidius quickly ushered the slave girls away, while trying to conceal his erection.

Antony shook his head, smiling. "Stay where you are, Canidius. There's no need to salute!" He helped himself to wine... his tone serious now. "How are the men?"

"Another fifty died from their wounds in the night. And you Antony?"

"I've less than half a legion left..." Antony paused, his heart heavy with the enormity of his loss. "Octavian is a formidable enemy," he said, earnestly. "He may lack experience, but it's as though Caesar's spirit is guiding him. When the veterans look at him they see Caesar. They fight for Caesar!"

Canidius began to dress. He was fastening his tunic, more aware than most of Antony's mood swings. "There is a way... a compromise." he suggested, cautiously.

Antony paced the room with his hands clasped tightly behind his back, his eyes searching the intricate patterns of the mosaic floor. "You mean a deal with Octavian?"

"Why not? One of your most ingenious letters and..."

"But to bargain we must be equal to his demands. A defeated army can demand nothing... it only pleads for mercy. Look at our troops, Canidius. We cannot compete with Octavian."

"Not now, but given a few months and Pollio, Ventidius, Plancus and even Lepidus will support us. Our joint legions can match Octavian's. You will have the power again to negotiate… or otherwise."

"As ever, Canidius, you have the sexual prowess of a gladiator, but you think like a philosopher," he smiled. "I will write to them all, but first I must bathe and sample Verona's finest food and wine."

Canidius grinned. "I will make arrangements at once, my lord."

The house was silent as Antony entered the study. Braziers burned brightly in each corner of the room and a lamp hung over the writing table. He sat behind it, and drawing the inkstand nearer he spread a piece of parchment before him.

As consul, Antony had scribes to attend to such duties; writing letters was unfamiliar, and speckles of ink appeared on the parchment before the reed began to flow smoothly. He began:

'To my friend, Marcus Aemilius Lepidus, Master of Horse and loyal servant of Rome. Greetings from Marc Antony…'

The words that followed were warm and coated with honey, reminding Lepidus of their long association together, the former glories they had shared with Julius Caesar and the urgency to unite again in order to remain loyal to his cause. His letters to the other three commanders were of similar content. He had no doubts that Pollio and Ventidius would join him with their legions, but persuading Plancus, who was governor of Gallia Comata, appeared more difficult. He had been designated as consul for the following year, and his choice would be between friendship and the Senate.

The fifth letter carried just enough innuendo to plant the seeds of uncertainty in Octavian's mind.

Antony drank the last of his wine. When the ink had dried on Octavian's letter he rolled it up and, as before, slipped the parchment into a cylindrical case. He tied and sealed it and pressed his ring into the soft wax, smiling in satisfaction.

Early the next morning messengers were dispatched to deliver them, and a few hours later Antony gave the order to vacate the city. He and Canidius led what remained of their beleaguered troops towards the safety of the Alps.

Chapter VII

Sleep would not come to Damon. He lay through the long hours of night, his mind drifting between dreams and reality…

There was no place to hide in the open vineyards; even if he ran they would hunt him down long before he reached the forest. The sun was setting beyond the ridge as they rode towards him, their silhouettes black against a burning sky. His heart pounded, for deep down he knew his world was about to crumble.

The horsemen were traders and skilled in the art of abducting slaves. But with Cyprus occupied by the Romans, they avoided the island's copper mines and cities to target the farmers who worked the land for a paltry sum at the harbour markets. These young men had strength and stamina… and reward for them was high in Syria. The desert towns thirsted for blood sports, especially with gladiators.

Damon stood firm. He gripped a staff in readiness to fend off their attack as the riders surrounded him. Four of them held rope-nets, with the remaining six brandishing spears and shields. He could see their eyes now, cold and without expression. Their muscular bodies glistened with sweat, and with every movement came the jingle of tiny bells from the bracelets around their wrists and ankles. He saw only one chance of escape and waited, poised for a net to be thrown as the circle closed in. Then he swung the staff at a white stallion, and as it reared up unseating its rider he caught the reins... desperately holding on as the horses around him began to panic. Damon was almost on the stallion's back when the net came over him and a shield slammed into his shoulder knocking him to the ground. As he tried to regain his footing the point of a spear jabbed into his thigh. Another net was cast before a heavy blow struck him from behind and he sank to his knees.

The earth began to spin, and for one precious moment he saw the image of his wife reaching out to him. He could hear her laughter, and the touch of her hand was as soft as a butterfly's wing. Then there was nothing... only the darkness.

Damon opened his eyes. He was no longer that young man who nurtured his land; the clothes he wore were not those of a Greek farmer, but a Roman. He crossed to the far side of the tent, quietly stoking up the brazier nearest to Octavian's sleeping couch before stepping outside to check on Tibo.

Dawn was breaking with a great stillness over the mountains and a thin mantle of snow covered the valley. He saw a lonely star shining in a wedge of blue sky, and the heat from a thousand campfires cast ripples over the landscape.

He paused outside the hospital enclosure, his eyes scanning a panorama of tents secured in a network of lines inside the square perimeter. Roadways crossed the camp dividing it into four sections, and within these areas the tents were pitched in multiple rows. Every row housed a century of men, and each tent shared by a group of eight soldiers.

He learned from Agrippa that there were six centuries to a cohort, and ten cohorts made up a Roman legion. Each legion had its own cavalry unit of one hundred and twenty men, including scouts and messengers.

Damon entered the hospital tent pleased to find that one such messenger had regained consciousness... but not for long. A surgeon was about to wrench the arrowhead from Tibo's shoulder. Blood spurted from the hole, and even though the boy was hopelessly drunk, his whole body screamed out in protest. The surgeon held a cloth firmly in the gaping wound, doing his best to staunch the flow while his assistant approached with a white-hot iron.

Tibo saw the figures standing over him but their images were blurred and the tent around them wouldn't stop spinning. Strong hands held him down, and all he remembered was the searing pain as the surgeon plunged the iron into his shoulder, cauterizing his wound.

When Tibo awoke there was a table beside him containing a mixture of oils, crushed herbs, an array of surgical instruments and a bloodstained arrowhead. The smell of burning flesh sickened him. He slowly turned his head at the sound of voices to see a doctor washing his hands in a bowl. The man beside him was Damon.

Tibo tried to rise too quickly and the pain set his mind in turmoil. He was aware of his sweat-soaked body, the gaping hole in his shoulder and Damon easing him down again. Then the nightmare scenes and mutilated bodies of the battles at Forum Gallorum consumed him once more.

On his return, Damon could see that most of the legionaries were starting their daily routines. He stopped for a while to admire their highly organised procedures. The sessions of military drill for new recruits had now been increased, and seasoned troops still trained hard and practised with sword and javelin despite the snow. If he was lucky, a man served for twenty years in the army before retiring with a sum of money and a plot of land.

Damon wrapped his cloak around him and tried not to think of his own homestead. He walked across to a tethered horse where Marcellus stood talking to its rider.

"This is Cornelius Gallus," he said, his face ashen. "He brings news from Bononia."

Damon shook the hand of a handsome, slightly built man with a confident air and steady gaze to his brown eyes. He looked in his early twenties, much too young to be holding the crimson-crested helmet of a centurion under his arm. The name was familiar to Damon. He recalled Rufus praising the centurion's heroics at Mutina, where Gallus persuaded hundreds of men from Decimus Brutus' army to join Octavian's cause.

"Is Octavian still sleeping?" asked Marcellus.

Damon nodded. "Yes, sire."

"Then we must wake him. There's been an important development. The second consul has died!"

Damon noticed a strange, almost excited response from Octavian when Gallus reported Pansa's demise. Outwardly, he acted with true Roman virtue and respect, ordering the centurion to arrange an escort for the bodies of Hirtius and Pansa to be taken back to Rome.

"The consuls died as heroes, they must be honoured and treated with dignity," he said. But his eyes were without expression; his mind already surging ahead to a far more important matter: a chance to govern. Rome was now without any consuls.

It was the last hour of daylight when Damon learned of his master's plan. Octavian had invited him to dine along with Agrippa and Marcellus when a messenger arrived. Damon went to receive him and was handed a letter.

He glanced at the seal. "It's from Marc Antony, sire."

Octavian opened the parchment and handed it back. "Read it to me, Damon… slowly, if you please. We must digest every word."

Antony had addressed him as *'Brother'* which brought a smirk to Octavian's face. The letter continued:

'…You have surprised me. I questioned your inexperience and doubted your leadership, but I grant you the victory at Mutina. You deserve just reward from the Senate: a triumph or ovation, perhaps? But I wonder, what are they really whispering in the corridors of Rome? Do they appreciate your endeavour? Allow me to remind you of where you stand, my friend.

'By all means be proud of a battle won, but will you receive any recognition for it from the Senate? Who will they turn to now that Hirtius is dead, and Pansa promises to join him in Hades? Not you, dear boy. No, I expect the supreme command of the armies, including yours, will pass to one of the so-called liberators Decimus Brutus… the very man you released from my grasp.

'Even as I write it puzzles me as to where your loyalty has gone? I remember a young man who once shouted condemnation from the rooftops of Rome and vowed revenge for Caesar's killers, yet here you are handing Decimus Brutus his freedom! I fear you have been trapped in the web of Cicero's words. He flatters your virtues to the Senate, they decorate you as a pro-praetor… and now? Well, that's the easy part. Now they can smile, pat you on the head… and dispose of you!

'I, on the other hand, might have lost a battle but believe me this war is only just beginning. I know my allies, Octavian. Soon the time will come to choose yours.'

It was signed... 'Marc Antony'.

Damon handed back the letter and watched as Octavian strode around in anger, seething at the sarcasm in Antony's words.

Agrippa was the first to speak. "It's typical Antony! Either sour grapes because Cicero tarnished his name and now he's had to run with his tail between his legs, or..." Agrippa paused, rubbing his bearded chin.

"Or what?" shouted Octavian.

"Or else he knows what I've suspected all along. Cicero has changed horses! I always said he couldn't be trusted. It's obvious that he and the Senate have used us for their own ends. With Hirtius and Pansa dead and a disruptive Antony out of the way, they can now select their own consuls... and on their own terms."

Octavian appeared deep in thought. "We can wait," he said, calmly, "Wait for their answer. I will write to them... to Cicero for a decision on my request. It's a simple alternative, but if they refuse to make me consul then I will cross the Rubicon as Caesar did before me. Our legions will march on Rome.

"Tibo will deliver the letter when he's on his feet again. Then he can stay in Rome with Philippus and Maecenas to find out if there's any truth to Antony's ramblings."

In spite of Agrippa's disapproval, it came as no surprise to Damon when the letter Octavian dictated to him was addressed to Cicero. He was, after all, a principal figure in the Senate and no-one could be more astute in approaching the House on Octavian's behalf.

As always, the letter was meticulous in detail, with Octavian insisting it was not only dated but that it also displayed the hour of its composition. It read as a heartfelt plea to Cicero; in reality it was the lie that he'd already proposed to Cicero at his villa. In requesting a consulship until the end of the year, Octavian stressed that the command he desired was merely to settle the veterans of his army in an authorised manner, and that he, Cicero, being an esteemed and experienced statesman, should be the one to govern as senior consul.

However, the letter's underlying bid for power was recognised. There was no direct reply from Cicero, only the Senate's word after a long delay that the election of consuls to replace Hirtius and Pansa was postponed for various reasons and legal objections.

It was early summer before Octavian learned what he needed to know about the Senate's betrayal. Decimus Brutus had been granted a belated triumph; Sextus Pompey given command of the Republic's navy; and confirmation of the re-instatement of Marcus Brutus and Gaius Cassius as governors of Macedonia and Syria: the provinces they had illegally seized.

It was now clear to Octavian that his defeat of Antony would not be recognised. There was to be no triumphant march to Rome, no ovation… nothing! And what enraged him even more was the Senate's audacity in ordering him to relinquish his command to Decimus Brutus. This was a man who had watched his own troops starving to death inside the walls of Mutina rather than face Antony. He and his brother, Marcus, and their conspirator-in-arms Cassius were his enemies now… there would be no surrender to them or the Senate.

Octavian retired to his sleeping couch that night with a troubled mind. But reflecting on his achievements soon began to cheer him. Caesar would have been proud of his victory at Mutina; his legions were steadfast in their loyalty and he was pleased with Damon's report on a young centurion.

So, he mused, Gallus was the man foremost in encouraging the mass desertions from Decimus Brutus to his own standard; an exodus which also prompted Pansa's legions to join him. Yes... Cornelius Gallus will certainly be rewarded in due course.

On that same night, somewhere inside the borders of Gallia Narbonensis, Marc Antony also pondered his fate. He lay in a drunken state, eyes staring into space and a fixed smile on his face. He knew not why, but the goddess Fortuna had returned to him. He could feel her warmth as he rested his weary head against her bosom.

It was Fortuna who steered the ship of humanity, but for the many thousands who worshipped her it was an unpredictable journey. Like a flirtatious lover, she would promise much then leave you floundering in a stormy sea. Antony sighed. He thought it best to enjoy her brief caresses, not live by them. He was a man determined to rule his own destiny. Nevertheless, she ensured he prospered again. Ventidius and Pollio had joined forces with him, and Plancus was on his way to the border with another three legions. For a while, only Lepidus remained neutral until he paid him a visit.

Antony realised the dilemma in which Lepidus must have found himself. He would have heard that Brutus and Cassius once again commanded the provinces in the east with some twenty legions, so should his allegiance be with them and the Senate, or support an old friend's cause?

It was a choice he deliberated for a long time. That was the problem with Lepidus as a leader, he was too hesitant. He would rather act as a mediator between warring parties than risk his own neck in battle.

Antony stirred on his sleeping couch, recalling how Lepidus had been in awe of him walking into their camp. He had enjoyed that; he savoured the rousing welcome from the troops all clamouring to greet him. It was they who answered any question Lepidus had on loyalties. When the two embraced a tumultuous cheer erupted from the ranks.

He convinced Lepidus that by joining him and his three allies, their joint armies would outnumber those of Octavian.

"The boy has little choice," Antony reassured him. "If he wants to avenge Caesar he will join us, otherwise his army will be crushed between two forces. In the meantime, the Senate will reject him at their peril. I have a feeling he will march on Rome."

This conversation with Lepidus, the hopes and doubts of his future all swirled inside Antony's head. He reached out to touch the warmth beside him, and contented that the goddess Fortuna was still near, he fell at last into the silent world of Morpheus.

A slave girl hovered around the table waiting to refill her master's wine cup, her every movement caressed by Tibo's eyes. When he realised, she was now smiling back at him he flushed with embarrassment.

"That will be all, Tibo."

The boy had found himself mesmerised by the slave girl while Maecenas was speaking, and his blush deepened. "I'm sorry? I… Oh yes. Thank you, sir."

Maecenas was holding out his empty cup for the slave girl. "Our host will allow you to sleep in the servants' quarters if you wish, Tibo," he said with a suggestive wink. "I'm sure Kyriki will take care of you."

Tibo was aware of Philippus glaring at him. "I... I must see to the horses... but thank you for the offer, sire," he said, backing away.

Philippus dismissed his slave girl and shuddered, holding his nose in disgust after Tibo left the dining room. "What a vile little creature," he moaned.

Maecenas paused from reading the letter to raise an enquiring eyebrow.

"That messenger," Philippus gasped. "Can you not smell horses?"

"What? Oh... the boy's been riding for days," sighed Maecenas.

"Then all the more reason to visit the public baths before he entered my house. I can't stand the smell of horseflesh and all that sweat."

Maecenas looked at him in annoyance. "Have you no sympathy at all, Philippus? Can you not see the boy carries an awful wound?"

"Well... for someone who appreciates scented oils and perfume your tolerance surprises me."

"Tibo is an exception. You can use a strigil on him until his skin bleeds... but he eats, sleeps and lives with his horse. He knows no other life."

Philippus peeled an orange, trying to look interested in Maecenas' explanation, but failing to see the point. The smell still clung to his sensitive nostrils.

"Some years ago, I found Tibo in a ditch at the side of the Via Appia. It was the time when Caesar crossed the Rubicon and thousands were fleeing from Rome. In the panic, their family cart was overturned crushing the boy's leg. His own parents deserted him… he almost died."

Philippus wiped a trickle of orange juice from the corner of his mouth. "You took him into your home?"

"Yes. He worked in my stables… lived night and day with my horses. I gave him the black stallion he rides now. He named it Zeus."

"Zeus? How odd… he's the Greek god for our Jupiter."

"Unusual, yes," agreed Maecenas, "and so is the fact that despite Tibo's handicap there is no finer horseman in Rome. Life for him has become a never-ending quest to be a Roman soldier. A life, incidentally, he has already dedicated to Octavian… including his sweat. Here, see for yourself just how much Octavian trusts him."

Maecenas handed over the parchment and Philippus began to read, his face slowly draining of colour. "May the gods help us!" he cried. "What in Hades does Octavian mean by this? He says we are to protect his mother and sister… to hide them away or they may be taken hostage! Has he gone mad?"

Philippus was trembling now, his eyes staring at the passage which ended:

'… By the time you receive this letter I will have led my armies across the Rubicon. The waiting is over. It is time for action!'

"No, Philippus, not mad… the boy Octavian has become a man," Maecenas said, proudly. "His dream is about to be realised." He raised his cup in a salute to his absent friend, and savoured the deep red wine.

The reaction of Philippus could be likened to a slave waiting to be thrown into the arena and torn to shreds by a starving lion. He was fearful, ringing his hands in despair as he paced the room.

Maecenas ignored the outburst as his attention focussed on the woman who walked towards him. He greeted her warmly. "Atia! I'm so pleased you can join us after all."

She gave him a weak smile as she sat on a nearby couch, the legacy of a recent illness still ominous in her tired eyes. Atia selected a piece of honey cake from the table, nibbling it like a small bird as she read her son's letter.

Philippus recovered some composure in her presence, waiting in silence for her opinion. She ignored him.

"Octavian is concerned for our safety, Maecenas, are you?" she asked, finally.

"My dear Atia, your son is right to be cautious. You and Octavia are his own flesh and blood. True, there will be panic in the streets long before he reaches the city. But do not trouble yourself; I have the perfect place for you to stay."

Atia touched his shoulder with gratitude as she stood. "Then I must inform Octavia, we have much to prepare." Her voice soured as she spoke to Philippus. "Can you not believe in Octavian as we do, husband? Be proud. Think of him in his hour of glory... not yourself!"

Atia turned on her heel and the two men watched her go... one filled with admiration, the other acute embarrassment.

Out in the stables Tibo relaxed on a pile of hay with his hands clasped behind his head. He seriously considered a visit to the public baths as he watched his horse nuzzle up to a mare in the next stall. It was time, he thought, to establish his own manly impression… from his head to the worn out sandals on his feet.

His mop of blonde hair, washed only by the rain, needed the attention of a proper barber not the drunken legionary he sometimes visited at camp. Perhaps my first shave too, he mused, touching the soft hair around his chin.

He was happy with his features: a strong face with a few blemishes made him look older, more rugged than handsome - like his friend, Damon. Being wounded in the battle at Forum Gallorum had made Tibo feel like a true legionary. His shoulder was sore from the scar that still restricted the use of his arm, but it was healing. Unlike his leg, which every stranger stared at, and many, including Philippus, dismissed him as a useless cripple. But not Kyriki, she had gazed directly into his eyes, and her smile was…

The door creaked and Tibo held his breath, slowly drawing his dagger. The piece of straw he was chewing fell from his gaping mouth at the sound of her voice.

"Tibo? It is I, Kyriki. I bring you some food."

"I'm over here, Kyriki," he whispered.

She reached out in the dim light and he took her hand. He felt shy… but excited by the softness of her touch. Then from outside the stable came the sound of voices and a pool of torchlight suddenly lit the open doorway.

"I'm telling you I saw someone. They might be in here."

"Could be that thief the master warned us about,'" said another. "Come on out, whoever you are!"

Tibo froze… if Kyriki was discovered away from her household duties she would be punished, and the mood Philippus was in spelt disaster. There was only one thing to do. He placed his hand to the girl's lips urging her to be silent, indicating that she lie down in the hay. Hopeful his ploy would protect her, he stepped out of the stall pretending to stifle a yawn. "Can't anyone sleep around here?" he said.

The two men, more startled than he was, turned on him. The first raised his flaming torch to see the intruder, while the older man lunged forward. Tibo found the tip of a spear at his throat.

He raised his hands in protest. "Wait! Be calm. I'm only looking after the horses."

The man holding the spear stood firm. "Who are you?" he demanded.

"I'm Tibo, a messenger with Octavian's army. Check with your master if you don't believe me. And you! Get that torch out of here before you burn down the stables."

To his surprise, the men took fright at the consequence of his warning, and left in a hurry.

Tibo gasped with relief, and turned to find Kyriki rushing into his arms.

"Thank you," she sighed. "You're so brave... but it was stupid of me to come."

Tibo held her close. "No... I was hoping... I wanted to see you again." He felt her tremble when his mouth brushed her cheek and a warm glow came over him as her body melted into his. They kissed... and her moist, parted lips set his heart pounding. Long after she'd gone he could smell her fragrance, and see the smile on her lovely face. It promised so much when they said goodbye.

On the following night, low clouds were hiding the moon when Atia and Octavia left the house on the Aventine. The litter-bearers held a steady pace until they neared the processional entrance of the Circus Maximus. They slowed here, trying not to jostle their passengers over the rough stones leading to the Vicus Tuscus. Maecenas accompanied Octavia in the first litter, closely followed by Philippus and Atia.

"You must refresh my memory of the Vestal Virgins, my dear," said Maecenas lightly.

Octavia blushed in the darkness. "Why, Maecenas! How could you forget their feminine virtues?"

"I know there are six of them, and that they must ensure an eternal flame burns in the temple. Oh, and they serve the goddess Vesta."

Octavia had parted the curtain, but could see nothing past the bulk of her two bodyguards trotting alongside the litter. She waited, expecting Maecenas to elaborate further. "Yes… but what of their sacrifice?"

"What sacrifice?"

"Their chastity vows, of course!"

It was Maecenas' turn to blush.

"You've forgotten that they're chosen as young children to take a vow of chastity and serve the goddess for thirty years?"

"Well… well no," Maecenas stuttered. "However, I did hear there was once a big scandal. Was not the chastity of one Virgin questioned some thirty years ago? I believe her alleged lover was the naughty and infamous Catalina.

"It all came to the fore when he and Cicero were in opposition for consul: a campaign where more than the usual accusations of bribery, corruption and sexual innuendo went on. But much to Cicero's embarrassment, the Vestal Virgin involved was his own sister-in-law! I'm sure she and Catalina were tried in different courts."

"Yes, but they were acquitted; nothing was proven. Ask yourself, Maecenas, as a Vestal Virgin would you risk denying your faith knowing the horrible consequences?"

"I believe if the accused man is found guilty, he is publicly scourged to death, but what else, Octavia?"

"Mother told me that the Virgin is whipped, and then, dressed like a corpse she's carried through the Forum in a closed litter. She is taken to an underground chamber where she watches her own burial as the vault is sealed over her head and she is left to die."

Maecenas shivered. "Oh, the poor dear... buried alive! Why must we be so barbaric?"

The Vicus Tuscus was a long narrow street which led to the Forum Romanum. It ran between a series of high buildings containing small shops, produce, merchants and granaries. Like most of the city streets, it was a dark and dangerous place at night. Bodyguards were a necessity because the undesirables who roamed the city were so desperate they would challenge anyone.

Four such men saw rich pickings in the approaching light of the flaming torches carried by Atia's slaves. But with their bellies full of cheap wine and no feasible plan to deal with ten enormous bodyguards, the ruffians stumbled out of a doorway as if in a suicide pact. They were crushed in seconds. The leading guard torched the first man; two more were smashed to the ground senseless by Octavia's men, while the fourth dropped his dagger and fled.

The front litter lurched, pitching Octavia forward slightly just as a man's screams filled the street. Maecenas peered through the curtain, and then jerked back again at the sight of a human fireball writhing on the ground.

"Maecenas! What's happening out there?"

"Oh… it's nothing to worry about, dear," he said, with as much reassurance as he could muster.

Octavia touched his hand. "Then why are you trembling?"

"It's only a minor incident. There's no need for alarm. Your guards have dealt with it."

The bodyguards had barely paused in the encounter, forging onward across the Via Nova before turning right in the Forum near the temple of the twin gods, Castor and Pollux. The litters came to a halt at the shrine and statue of Vesta. Beyond this, loomed the colonnaded facade of the Domus Publicus. The building also housed the chief priest known as the Pontifex Maximus, but in total seclusion from him was the Atrium Vestae: home of the Vestal Virgins.

While Philippus still pleaded with Atia for forgiveness, Maecenas climbed the wide staircase and knocked on the wooden doors. Covered lanterns hung in small recesses either side of the entrance, and from within he could hear the soft chanting of voices. Atia and Octavia had joined him when the door opened; in the shadows behind it stood one of the Virgins.

Maecenas smiled awkwardly. "We are expected by the Virgo Maxima," he said in a hushed voice.

The figure before him stepped forward and in the glimmer of light he saw a woman of great beauty. She was dressed completely in white: a long flowing stola, and around her shoulders the linen mantle of the Vestals. Her black hair was swept back from her face and held by a wide headband. Her eyes avoided Maecenas, but she gestured with her hand to invite the two women inside.

Maecenas realised he was one step away from the most forbidden place in all of Rome. For a man to cross its threshold was sacrilege; his presence would be deemed as evil intent, punishable by death.

He turned to Atia and bowed graciously. "I will send for you when your son returns," he said, kissing her hand in farewell.

Octavian had already taken his own unlawful step earlier that day. The sun was casting its long shadows over the landscape when he stood alone on the small bridge over the Rubicon River. He was conscious of the critical decision confronting him... of the dilemma Caesar had also faced crossing this same frontier between Cisalpine Gaul and Italy. But unlike Caesar's day on the bridge, no vision came to Octavian; no apparition sat on the riverbank playing a reed pipe, urging him to cross.

'Let us accept this as a sign from the gods,' Caesar had said to his troops.

Octavian gazed into the water, as his legates and centurions waited in silence. He'd summoned more than two hundred officers, and they warmed to him when he addressed them as his friends and comrades.

"I stand before many of you here as Caesar did, and I am humbled that you have shown me the same devotion and courage. Together, we have won a great victory at Mutina... I have word that even Antony acknowledges that!"

Octavian waited for their laughter to abate. "But the Roman Senate offers no such praise. There will be no rewards for us... the true victors. Instead, they choose to honour our enemies: Decimus Brutus, his brother Marcus and Gaius Cassius, the murderers of your beloved leader... and my father, Julius Caesar."

This time Octavian's words were greeted with a roar of disapproval. He held up his hands for calm. "I see only one path for us, my friends. Cross this river and help me become a consul of Rome and all of Caesar's promises to you… his gifts, your land and all the rewards you are entitled to will be paid in full. Furthermore, we will bring my father's murderers to justice!"

The officers shifted uneasily; they knew a campaign like this against the Senate would threaten their careers if it failed. There was some reservation when Octavian ordered them to carry his words to the legions. He waited anxiously on the bridge until fifty thousand voices roared his name.

His silent prayer to the gods was answered.

Chapter VIII

A few miles south of the Rubicon the Via Aemilia came to an end at the town of Ariminium. There it joined the Via Flaminia, the road which continued along the Adriatic coast before turning inland towards Rome. Along this deserted stretch of coastline, Octavian divided his army. He sent Agrippa on to Rome with seven legions, as proof of his power and ultimate intentions to the Senate. He and Marcellus followed with the remainder of his troops.

They journeyed at a slower pace, and their arrival at Narnia on the thirteenth day of August coincided with a festival. It was the feast to Diana, when even slaves were granted a holiday. Octavian ordered a day's rest, and strolling in the town Damon found himself swept along in the bustling crowds.

He enjoyed the noise and merriment as young and old danced together in the streets. Women beckoned from their doorways with bread and wine, and at every corner he saw troops being mobbed by men and boys, eager to join them. It seemed that every step he took was through a shower of rose petals, thrown by laughing maidens from the balconies above.

"Damon! Over here, my friend."

He recognised the voice and saw Cornelius Gallus waving to him from outside a crowded tavern. The man beside him looked anything but a soldier. He stood as Damon approached and extended a soft, almost feminine hand to introduce himself.

"Publius Virgilius Maro," he announced.

Gallus smiled broadly. "Call him Virgil. All his friends do."

Damon thought the stranger to be a little older than Gallus. He reminded him of a young Marc Antony: well built, the same black hair and lustrous eyes; but while Antony's gaze was direct Virgil merely glanced at him shyly, as if wary of any kind of affection.

His embarrassment was evident when Gallus clasped an arm around his shoulder, saying: "This, my friend, is one of Rome's finest poets."

"That's nonsense!" replied Virgil. "Your poetry is much better than mine."

"Ignore him, Damon. I love poetry, but not with the same intensity as Virgil… and it shows in his work. My best is woeful by comparison." He removed his arm, much to his friend's relief.

"You must forgive Gallus. He is a fine soldier but a sycophant where poetry and women are concerned."

"There's no need to be modest, Virgil. Tell Damon about your present work and the commission. I have a feeling it will be something very special."

Damon smiled; it was pleasing that both of them should converse with him in Greek. "Yes. Please do, I'm always interested in poetry," he said. "What are you working on, Virgil?"

"Well… I'm trying to adapt the poems of Theocritus into Latin verse. Do you know of him?"

The poems were familiar to Damon. He was suddenly reminded of Vario again, and the long winter evenings his master had spent with him improving his education. "Theocritus of Syracuse, the poet whose shepherds speak and sing of their flocks and loved ones. Theocritus enriched the island of Sicilia with his poetry, did he not?"

Virgil smiled. "I'm very fond of his pastoral scenes… if only I can reach such elegance."

Gallus passed Damon a cup of wine, his eyes twinkling at their common interest.

The Greek tasted his wine; it was warm but pleasant. "And someone's commissioned you?" he asked.

"A friend of Gallus first expressed an interest. His name is Asinius Pollio. But things have changed of late."

Damon looked enquiringly at Gallus.

"Pollio is - or should I say, was - one of Caesar's most promising officers. He went to Spain in command of two legions shortly before Caesar died." Gallus shrugged. "But now… who knows? I wouldn't be surprised if he's not joined up with Lepidus in the north… or Marc Antony. So, with a timely and most generous offer, Maecenas has stepped in."

He frowned, his voice more serious. "Pollio is a good friend, but as I pointed out to Virgil, I'm afraid that we could soon be on opposite sides if there's a war."

Virgil sighed. "Please! No more, Gallus, we have discussed politics for long enough." He turned to Damon, noticing the smooth piece of olivewood that he rolled in his fingers. "Ah, now that's what I call a shepherd's pipe. Do you play?"

"Barely a note," Damon laughed.

"Well... perhaps one day," Virgil smiled. "But for now, you must excuse me. I have business to attend to in the town." He offered his hand to Damon. "It's been a pleasure meeting you."

"Oh, yes... and good luck with the poems," Damon said, taken by surprise at the poet's sudden departure.

"I'm afraid Virgil's unhappy with the idea of introducing any military element into his poetry," said Gallus, watching him go. "It seems Maecenas is pressing him to try something new. Virgil's more than capable, but he's so damned stubborn... always has been.

"He and I shared one of Octavian and Agrippa's teachers, a Greek rhetorician named Epidius. The man was noted for his patience, but even he despaired of Virgil's introversion."

"Political issues in a pastoral setting?" Damon shook his head. "They are hardly a poetic combination. Slaughter, human or otherwise, is a Roman trait, Gallus, it's nothing new. Your friend Virgil appears to be a man of gentle nature, death and brutality are not of his character. He obviously finds it difficult to write about the things he reviles. We should sympathise with his task."

Gallus shook his head. "We all have something we would like to hide from, Damon... it's a weakness, our Achilles heel." He finished his wine with a flourish. "Believe me; the sooner Virgil overcomes it the greater his poetry will be."

Virgil turned and waved to them before disappearing into the crowds. Damon would not see him again for a few months... and by then every landowner in Italy was in fear of his life.

Meanwhile, in that same hour of the day, Agrippa was leading his army through a countryside that was bracing itself for yet another civil war. Even in the blistering heat of summer there would always be travellers on the road, but the Via Flaminia was deserted. For mile after mile houses lay abandoned and farms locked and shuttered. The surrounding fields were empty of livestock, their frightened owners enclosing them in barns with the vain hope of hiding any sign of wealth and provisions from rampaging soldiers.

Agrippa raised his hand and the signal to halt was passed to the legions. A wailing of horns echoed back through the hills bringing an immediate and uniformed response. To stop a moving army was a skilled manoeuvre, as each section needed to act simultaneously or risk collisions and chaos. The young Roman turned and looked back into the distance, smiling at the precision of it all. Century after century of legionaries became still as the rhythmic sound of their marching faded away.

Then he shielded his eyes from the sun, searching a landscape ahead that shimmered as though the whole countryside was ablaze. But below the ridge was the welcome shade of a wooded valley. He sighed with relief, for somewhere in the forest his scouting party would be waiting with news of Rome.

Tibo and Rufus met him with contrasting reports. They sat under the sprawling boughs of an oak tree eating cheese and coarse bread, washed down with wine.

"The city plebeians rejoice at Octavian's homecoming," Tibo said, "only the Senate trembles with fear. They look upon Cicero for a solution, but an old man's words are meaningless against our mighty army."

Agrippa paused as he reached for more bread. "And what news is there of Octavian's mother and sister?"

"My lord will be pleased to know they're safely hidden away. I must ride out to greet him."

"Yes, but later," laughed Agrippa, ruffling the boy's hair. "Finish your food and wine while Rufus reports his good tidings. You must build up your strength."

Rufus was more subdued. "Tibo forgets to mention how the Via Flaminia closed behind him. He was lucky to escape. The Senate have assembled an army to guard the city."

"What army? There's no force south of here stupid enough to confront us. Where are they hiding?" He looked on as Rufus scratched a groove in the dry earth with a stick indicating the highway, and then another crossing it for the River Tiber.

"They hold the bridge here to the east of Falerii, where the Via Flaminia crosses the Tiber."

"How many legions do they have?"

"No more than two, sir. But our problem is the river; it runs too deep and fast along this stretch for men and horses. We can't get behind them."

Agrippa studied the lines and the enemy positions, slowly chewing his last mouthful of bread. "So, we go through them!" he said. Then in the dirt he drew a circle around an area approaching the river. "So what's here, Rufus?"

"A few scattered trees, but generally the land is flat and open. We would have no cover except under darkness."

"That's perfect. Good news after all, my friend."

Rufus frowned… Agrippa explained: "On our approach we disperse the column and march the troops in battle lines across this open area. A show of force is often more effective than any attack. Let them see our numbers, then they can decide whether to live or die."

It was a reasoning acknowledged by the Republican legions, for when Agrippa's army closed to within a hundred yards of the bridge two legates appeared on horseback, each holding aloft their legion's silver eagle. They had chosen to surrender.

The legates rode towards them and Rufus turned to the young man beside him. "I salute your tactics, Agrippa," he said with a wry smile. "They obviously believe in living a few more years; it's less foolish than being noble and dead."

A few hours later, an evening mist floated across the Field of Mars from the great river, bringing cool relief to the thousands of men setting up camp. As with all legionary bases it was a standard design, and with no deviation between camps and fortresses there was little need for orders. The soldiers instinctively detached themselves into organised groups with picks and shovels. Tent lines were marked out for each century, and the whole canvas village was shaped and erected in typical military precision.

At its central headquarters, Agrippa was closing his address to a select group of centurions: twelve men he knew and trusted who would kill their own mother for the sake of glory. He looked at each in turn as he spoke; their grizzly, unshaven faces were set without emotion... hard as stone.

"...And so, comrades, tomorrow it is. At the second hour use whatever force necessary to enter the Senate House, and target Cicero with our demands. There must be no compromise... or he'll beat you to death with words. Remember that you represent Octavian. Do not fail him!"

Agrippa dismissed them, and the centurions saluted in unison. As they left the tent he found himself smiling at the thought of their mission. It would be like taking coins from a blind beggar.

Long after he'd read the dispatch from Rome, Marc Antony stared at the report. Facing him, four commanders waited patiently for his comments. "Well, gentlemen," he said at last. "The boy soldier is ready to meet us. Octavian's elected himself as consul, together with Pedius."

"Uh, a distant relative," grunted Pollio, "that's no surprise."

"No. Neither is the fact that his adoption has been ratified by the people, or that he's passed a law indicting Caesar's murderers," said Antony. "But, more importantly, the decrees by the Senate declaring us as public enemies have been rescinded. Furthermore, and as I predicted, the Senate also approve his suggestion that we complete the annihilation of Decimus Brutus. There can be no doubt, my friends, that for the time being Octavian is now in control of Rome's political arena."

Asinius Pollio moved forward to embrace his colleague. "You were right to advise patience, Antony. You always insisted that Octavian would need us if he was to overcome the armies of Brutus and Cassius."

Antony allowed himself a smile of satisfaction as Ventidius and Plancus joined in the congratulations. He passed the scroll to the fourth man beside him.

Lepidus read it carefully, his face impassive. He was unable to comprehend how someone, barely twenty years of age, could possibly be a consul of Rome. Caesar himself had to wait until the legal age of forty-three. He handed the despatch to Pollio, and deep in thought he walked away from the group shaking his head at Octavian's audacity.

It was painfully obvious to him that without any military backing the Senate was useless. Struck with consternation, it had been humbled by Octavian; its backbone filleted like a dead fish. And Cicero, so long in prominence, was nowhere to be seen, having already fled to his country villa when the centurions marched into the Senate House demanding Octavian's consulship.

So, here he is, a boy almost equal in military power to their combined legions, now dictating terms. Lepidus was angered by the irony of his position. Once second in command to Julius Caesar, he now had to bargain for recognition of his authority with Caesar's adopted and inexperienced son! He needed some air.

His appearance at the open entrance to the tent caught Tibo's attention. He knew at once that it was Lepidus. The hair was noticeably greyer; his upright stature had rounded slightly at the shoulders; but there was no mistaking those sharp, hawk-like features. Tibo had seen him before at a friend's toga celebration. Lepidus was Caesar's Master of Horse at the time, intimidating the young men from patrician families at the party to enlist in his cavalry units. It still grieved Tibo that his friend believed such promises of grandeur; for a year later he lay dying on some Spanish plain. Lepidus was to blame for that...

It was normal for a messenger to wait before being dismissed, but there seemed to be a long deliberation over Octavian's letter, and Lepidus was clearly angry about something. He vented his temper on a bewildered soldier who happened to be passing.

Such personal details were important to Tibo; he desperately wanted Octavian to be pleased with his report. His eyes lit up as another general appeared and began to converse with Lepidus. Their voices were too distant, even for Tibo's acute ears, so he ventured a few steps towards the two men.

"Stop right there, boy!"

Tibo flinched as a huge hand grabbed him by the scruff of the neck.

"Now get back here!" The standard-bearer was also keen to impress his generals, yanking Tibo backward into the dust. "What's your name, boy?"

"Tibo, sir," he gulped, looking up at the man's huge physique and blazing eyes. "I… I've brought the letter from Rome."

"Then wait here until the general says otherwise. One more step away from me and I'll have you flogged."

A signifer was not someone to mess with. He would be an exceptional soldier to be given the responsibility of carrying his legion's standard. He was also the man who organised a society for legionaries to ensure they had a decent funeral if they were killed in action.

Tibo thought it unwise to argue. He nodded, unable to speak as a callused hand tightened around his throat.

"That's enough! Let him go."

The big man froze and Tibo fell at his feet, coughing and gasping for breath. But he recognised the voice and the image of a lion's head on the man's breastplate… it was Marc Antony.

After a cold November night with clear skies, a mantle of frost sparkled over the city at dawn. Damon placed another blanket over his sleeping master and quietly left the bedroom. He made his way back to the library, warmed his hands at a brazier and continued to record the pile of official documents that Octavian had signed for the Senate. The task was a boring, time-consuming exercise, but he'd learned to appreciate Octavian's meticulous ways. Every detail, no matter how trivial, was dealt with promptly and efficiently. An hour later he stretched out on a nearby couch.

He reflected that even though the fear of civil war still gripped its people, in many ways Rome was slowly returning to normality. Since his inauguration Octavian had worked tirelessly as consul, but in the past three months his efforts were overshadowed with the death of Atia. Her passing echoed Maecenas' words at the reading of Vario's will: 'It's ironic how the gods give... then take away...'

The gods had given Octavian the strength to lead his army in triumph over Antony at Mutina and the courage to carry one of his wounded officers from the battle. These same gods opened their arms to welcome Rome's conquering hero... only to betray him now with the death of his mother.

Atia was both loved and respected in Rome, and her loss so soon after his consulship was a crushing blow to Octavian. His lack of appetite and sleep undoubtedly induced the illness he now suffered. It was against the advice of his private physician and to the consternation of his friends that Octavian prepared to journey north again to meet Marc Antony.

Damon felt uneasy about the situation ahead. He mulled over Antony's reason to meet at the Lavinius River. The location was barely a mile downstream from Forum Gallorum where he had lost thousands of men. Damon wondered how it would affect the moral of those who returned to the scene of one of their homeland's bloodiest battles. Was there an ulterior motive to Antony's recent letter, in which he promised to pursue

Decimus Brutus? It puzzled Damon why Octavian should even confer with someone he suspected of previously plotting to murder him. But, as ordered, he woke his master at the second hour and helped him dress.

By then, storm clouds gathered over the city and before they reached the Field of Mars it was pouring with rain. Agrippa was waiting there with a vast army. Four legions were left for the ageing consul Pedius to guard Rome… but under the watchful eyes of Maecenas.

"In the light of Atia's death it's the most sensible alternative," Damon said, joining Agrippa and Marcellus at the front of the column. "Maecenas will be a great comfort to both Octavia and Philippus."

"Just as well,' Agrippa replied with a grin, "this will be men's work!" He wiped the rain from his face. "How's Octavian bearing up?"

"Badly, I'm afraid. Unless the weather breaks he'll be confined to his litter. He wants to see both of you."

"Right, Marcellus. Let's get this lot moving then."

Orders were quickly passed down the lines, and anxious eyes followed the signifers' as they joined their respective colour guard. The seriousness of this moment was appreciated by Damon, for to encounter a problem while transporting a legion's eagle at the start of a military operation was a bad omen. But all went well, and he soon found himself smiling again at the familiar grunts and grumbles of soldiers trudging through the rain.

He watched as cohort followed cohort from the Field of Mars on to the Via Flaminia in strict formation. Enclosed within the lines of soldiers and cavalry, mules were burdened with baggage and oxen trundled the wagons of equipment towards the Milivian Bridge.

At the centre of the first legion rode a bodyguard of horse around Octavian's litter. The young centurion leading the troop acknowledged him.

"I'm indebted to you, Damon," he called out. "I know my place here beside the general is thanks to you. Call on me whenever you need a friend."

Damon waved before Cornelius Gallus disappeared again into the driving rain.

The apprehensive mood of the men remained for several days. They were unaware of their destination, and the further north they travelled the incessant rainfall turned to sleet in the icy wind from the mountains. There was an uneasy silence among them as they set up camp, east of the Lavinius River.

It was noon, and as a premature darkness settled over the valley Damon was alerted by the sound of someone outside Octavian's tent. He relaxed again when the weary figure of Agrippa appeared at the entrance.

Octavian rose from his bed, shaking off the blanket around his shoulders to give Agrippa a brotherly embrace. "You bring me good news, my friend?"

"Yes. Marc Antony arrives tonight," he said, gratefully accepting a cup of heated wine from Damon. "He'll camp on the far side of the Lavinius. And as you suggested, the meeting will be on the island at dawn tomorrow. There's a punt moored on the river. Marcellus is down there organising a tent."

"Good. Now we'll see just where all this is leading. If we can't settle our differences and he wants another war then..."

"I think not. It was obvious to me that Antony still grieves over the men he lost at Mutina. Marcellus and I found him subdued and quite amiable."

Octavian laughed. "Antony's about as friendly as a wounded lion. He's just licking his wounds waiting to pounce."

"Then why did he take the trouble to save Tibo from a beating at the hands of his own standard bearer?"

"Don't you see, Agrippa? It's for the very reason you stand here telling me!" Octavian said with annoyance. "He knew the boy would report it. Antony wants us to believe he's mellowed, and if our legions hear of it then we have a complacent army on our hands."

Octavian paused to sip some water. "As for Tibo, any other time or place and Antony would have cut his heart out for trying to invade his privacy."

"I don't know what to make of that boy lately," Agrippa said with a shake of his head. "Something bothers him. No one knows the country better; his eyes and ears have saved our men so many times... but he's getting careless."

"Perhaps he's still troubled by that wound. I will speak with him," offered Damon.

An opportunity arose when Marcellus joined them later. The rain had stopped, but a freezing fog engulfed the camp as Damon stepped outside. He found Tibo in a despondent mood emerging from Rufus' tent.

"Do you have problems, Tibo?"

"I've been reprimanded. Rufus says I'll never make a soldier. I've become a liability."

"And are you?"

Tibo ignored the question. "I have to go. I'm on my way to latrine duties."

They walked over the muddy ground towards the latrine block, with Damon unable to prise any answers from him. "Your silence is annoying me," he said, purposely gripping the boy's shoulder. There was no painful reaction.

"It's a personal matter… nothing really."

"I wouldn't call it that neither does Agrippa. When he sees you day-dreaming it has to be serious!"

The boy stopped in his tracks. "Oh, not Agrippa as well," he groaned.

"Don't worry. We can put it right if you tell me who's been bullying you. It often happens with young boys among toughened veterans like these."

"I swear, no-one's having a go at me, it's just…"

Damon smiled. If it wasn't this, then there was only one alternative. He should have known by the boy's recent appearance: his neat, close-cropped hairstyle, the new tunic and sturdy boots. "Who is she?" he asked.

The messenger blushed.

"It's quite normal, Tibo. I can see how much you like the Lady Octavia," he jested. "But in case you've forgotten she's married to Marcellus. Now if you want my advice…"

"All right, there's no need to go on. She's a slave girl."

"So why the secrecy; is there a problem?"

"I'm afraid for her safety. She'll be punished if Caleb finds out. He doesn't approve of me."

"You mean Philippus' freedman?"

Tibo shivered at the thought of Caleb demanding sexual favours from Kyriki. Slaves had no rights or privileges, and although the girl was treated kindly by Octavia, Kyriki was still under Caleb's control. "Her name's Kyriki," he said, quietly.

"Not the Greek girl who serves…"

"Hush! Keep your voice down," Tibo said through clenched teeth, as two legionaries suddenly appeared in front of them out of the mist.

"Be sure to hold your breath if you're going in there," said one, jerking his thumb towards the latrines. "There's a blockage. I've never seen so much sewage."

Damon raised a hand to his mouth trying not to laugh. "It sounds like a gruesome task. I don't envy you, Tibo."

"Never mind the latrines," the boy said, catching Damon by the arm. "I need your help to free Kyriki when we return to Rome. Please, Damon, she's one of your own people. You're my only hope."

Damon saw the anguish in Tibo's eyes and remembered his own desperation as a boy wanting to escape from the savage beatings administered by Gaius Salenus. "I'll do what I can," he promised, "but it will have to be my way. If Octavian hears of this we'll both be sent to the arena… as raw meat for the lions."

The smile spreading over Tibo's face quickly disappeared as Damon suddenly grabbed him by the front of his tunic. He had never heard such menace in his friend's voice before.

"Don't ever forget that my only reason for living is to see my family again," the Greek whispered. "If you utter a word to anyone else, even Kyriki, I'll throw you to the lions myself! Do you understand?"

Tibo felt his feet leave the ground; he was struggling to breathe, and it was all he could do to nod his head in acceptance.

Damon released his grip. "Now pull yourself together, boy. Concentrate on your duties and make amends with Rufus. Let me decide how to help Kyriki," he said, before walking away.

When Tibo reached the latrines it was raining again. Despite this and the stench that choked him, a broad smile returned to his face.

Chapter IX

It felt surprisingly pleasant inside the tent. Braziers were lit an hour before dawn, and couches set around a table of fruit and wine. Lanterns hung low over two portable desks where Damon sat opposite the scribe who accompanied Lepidus. As consul, Octavian occupied the centre couch. Antony sat on his right and Lepidus to the left with places set for Agrippa and Canidius. But as Damon would later mention in his text, the two generals were dismissed before nightfall.

Marc Antony had been the last to arrive on the island with Canidius. He appeared overjoyed to see Octavian. "You look well, my boy. Being a consul of Rome has put some meat on your bones."

To everyone else present Octavian looked gaunt, but as only Antony could be in such company, he was full of charm. Each man was greeted in turn, including Damon, who noticed how smoothly Antony's dominating presence took control of the meeting.

He began by praising Octavian's achievements, before calmly announcing his own contribution to their cause for unity… the death of Decimus Brutus. "When they realised we were closing in, his men deserted him," Antony said, holding out a wine cup for Canidius to fill. "His intention was to join his brother Marcus in Macedonia, but it's a mystery why he chose to venture through a country of barbarian tribes."

"He was dressed in Gallic robes when they captured him," Lepidus added in disgust. "How could a Roman governor stoop so low?"

Antony took a long drink from his cup. "It seems he offended the barbarians too," he laughed. "They sent me what was left of his head. It's back in Mutina… buried somewhere in the town's sewage!"

"An appropriate resting place," Octavian smiled. "I think it's time we discussed a similar fate for his brother and Cassius."

So the meeting began as it would end, in the same chilling overtones. But Damon could not write of its underlying hatred and rivalry; it was not his place to assess personal triumphs or disasters, only to record their agreements. Yet it was apparent that above all, Octavian and Antony were the most powerful figures.

While Antony and Lepidus scrutinised the words written by their scribe, Damon was called upon to read out his own text of the alliance. He stood to address them.

"Gentlemen… you have all agreed to four major terms. I list them in the sequence of your discussions. The first is to bring justice upon Marcus Brutus and Gaius Cassius for the slaying of Julius Caesar. To do so, the legions of Caesar Octavianus, Marcus Antonius and Marcus Aemilius Lepidus will unite and form a Triumvirate. In order to pursue this cause, Caesar Octavianus is to resign as consul of Rome. General

Ventidius will resume in his place as consul until the end of the year."

Damon looked up waiting for comments, but there were none. He continued: "A new magistracy shall be created, empowered by law to deal with any disputes and civil unrest. It will be held jointly by the triumvirs: Caesar Octavianus, Marcus Antonius and Marcus Aemilius Lepidus for a period of five years. Each is to hold consular power, and they alone will designate the yearly magistrates of the city.

"Thirdly, the provinces of Rome will be divided as follows: Caesar Octavianus is to govern Africa, Sardinia, Sicilia and the islands in their vicinity. Marcus Antonius will govern the whole of Gaul, except for the regions bordering the Pyrenees Mountains. These areas, together with Spain, are to be ruled by Marcus Aemilius Lepidus...."

"What about Rome itself?" Lepidus interrupted. "I thought..."

"Let the man finish! It's all here," Antony said brusquely, jabbing his finger at the scroll before them.

"Marcus Aemilius Lepidus will be consul of Rome next year," Damon confirmed. "He will remain in the city with three legions and govern his mountain provinces and Spain by proxy. A joint decision shall be made on the provinces beyond the Adriatic following the wars with Marcus Brutus and Gaius Cassius.'"

Marc Antony listened with interest. "Your writing is quite remarkable for a Greek slave." He frowned, studying Damon's face.

"Remind me, have we met before?"

"Yes, sire. It was at your house on the Pincian Hill."

"But of course, the gladiator… the one who saved young Octavian here from certain death. So, now you're a scribe?"

Canidius grinned. "How nice for you," he taunted. "It must be much safer than wielding a gladius."

"Are you here to discuss the future of Rome, Canidius, or play the fool?" Octavian roared. "Let's get on with it!"

He was shaking… whether in rage or fever it was hard to tell, but it worked. Canidius' face turned to stone and Antony smiled awkwardly, urging Damon to continue.

Their final agreement was a means to encourage the legions to war with promises of land and booty. They targeted the most beautiful cities of Italy, where estates and fertile land would be confiscated in order to colonise the vast army of men. But the fate of these landowners was not disclosed in the presence of Agrippa and Canidius.

Marc Antony called them aside. "It is time to address the men, they have waited long enough." He stood between them, his arms around their shoulders. "Go, my brothers, and allay their fears. Tell them of the Triumvirate… that we are united as one. Let them sleep, rejoicing in our promises."

When the two men left, the triumvirs retired to their makeshift beds; it would be another day before they could face the major problem of financing the legions. Meanwhile, as the news of an alliance reached the armies, joyous scenes erupted as jubilant comrades carried Agrippa and Canidius aloft through their respective camps. By nightfall Antony's campsite was dismantled. Amid cheers and bawdy singsong, his legions crossed the river to join their Roman brothers in Octavian's army.

When the triumvirs reconvened at dawn, Octavian summed up their financial position. "...Wars, internal corruption and extortion have depleted our income from the provinces. In addition, I have emptied the treasury myself."

He met the stare from Lepidus. "Are you so stupid as to think I wouldn't pay my own legions?"

Antony saw the anger in Lepidus. He gripped his arm to restrain him. "Let it go! Octavian had every right to use treasury funds. He was consul."

"And remember, I remain so until I've signed these documents," Octavian added, flippantly.

Antony ignored him. "We shall finance the war with Brutus and Cassius through their own friends and supporters. They are our enemies, too. Each and every one will pay for Caesar's murder. Let their deaths be a lesson to anyone who opposes us. Are we agreed?"

Octavian offered his hand in support. "It's the only solution."

"I think we should be more cautious," Lepidus warned. He appeared uneasy with their boldness. "Some of our officers and men have relatives who are still loyal to Brutus and Cassius. How will they react?"

"Then we must lead by example," said Octavian. "Those we proscribe will include some of our own personal casualties. For example, your brother, Paulus."

The colour drained from Lepidus' face. It was well known that Paulus' wealth had been amassed over the years through his close friendship with Marcus Brutus. More in anguish than aggression, Lepidus turned on a grinning Antony. "Then I choose your uncle, Lucius Caesar. It's no secret that he betrayed us. He is a prominent figure in the group who proclaimed that we were public enemies."

Antony agreed to his uncle's execution without a flicker of emotion. His thoughts were focussed on another man. Now it was his turn. He looked straight at Octavian. "Your friend, Cicero, must die!"

There was a long pause. Octavian shook his head "So… now you pass sentence on Rome's most revered ornament? Cicero is a man of culture and wisdom. He would be a great loss to the Senate… but not to me. I have no objection."

Lepidus was stunned by his casual manner, and for once even Antony was speechless.

Octavian addressed them with a sinister smile. "Come now, gentlemen…why the surprise? Cicero not only slandered you, Antony, he also denied me when I needed him most. Your letter confirmed Agrippa's mistrust of him. What was it the old man said of me? Oh, yes… 'The boy must be flattered, decorated and disposed of.'" The young Roman laughed. "By all means cut out his tongue."

At its conclusion the death list contained some three hundred senators among the three thousand names. For some reason of political correctness, Lepidus insisted on a delay for their execution until the triumvirs arrived in Rome. Antony supported this and prepared to end the meeting, but Octavian had other ideas.

"No!" he said, firmly. "The twelve men we personally surrendered must be executed first. If we are to lead Rome then we should do so by example."

Lepidus shifted uneasily. "But…"

"Consider it done," Antony interrupted. "Get your man here to record them separately and I will personally organise their elimination."

Octavian nodded to Damon, smiling to himself over Antony's burning passion for revenge. "On a final note," he said, "we must ensure the land seizures and distributions are organised efficiently. I suggest we each nominate a man of intelligence and trust."

"Asinius Pollio! He will be the senior officer in command." Antony said, forcibly.

"I have no problem with that." Octavian turned. "What say you Lepidus?"

The commander thought for a moment. "Oh, you can have Varus... Alfenus Varus."

"Very well, then my choice is Cornelius Gallus."

The name brought a smirk to Antony's face, but he managed to hold his tongue regarding the beautiful woman that he'd once stolen from the young centurion.

Damon again confirmed the nominees in his writings, inwardly pleased for Gallus who might well renew his friendship with Asinius Pollio.

Across the river celebrations had dwindled to a few groups of soldiers sprawled around their campfires. None of them with the slightest interest in anything that moved... other than the wineskins that passed between them.

In the heavy mist that settled over the valley, one of Antony's officers led a century of legionaries from the camp. To the drunken guards they appeared as phantom-like figures: apparitions that floated by, seemingly dissolved by the morning fog. In reality, their mission was to hunt down and slaughter twelve of Rome's most wealthy and respected citizens.

Within two weeks they, and most of the three thousand proscribed, were executed.

"I've never seen the markets so deserted," Tibo remarked as he and Damon entered the Forum Bourium.

"It makes me wonder if Rome will ever recover from the killings."

Damon looked around, recalling how masses of people jammed the city streets when Octavian returned to claim his inheritance. Now only small groups huddled together in a marketplace empty of its booths, meat stalls and rubbish. But its emptiness allowed him to see the true splendour of its statues and temples. Near the Circus Maximus, he stood admiring the statue of a naked Hercules.

"There are two more centres for the worship of Hercules on your left. And look," Tibo pointed out, "back there is the Temple of Ceres, the headquarters of the Plebian Aediles."

Like all Roman temples it was set high on a podium, its giant pillars rising into an ominous sky.

"Yes, it's most impressive," Damon said, fastening his cape. "But this wind from the river spells rain. We should hurry."

Being indisposed again with illness, it was Octavian's suggestion that Damon should meet with Maecenas at the Senate House where Lepidus was due to address the Senate. It was also an ideal opportunity for Damon to familiarise himself with the city and, eager to please, Tibo offered to be his guide.

They followed one of the narrow streets from the marketplace which threaded through the Velabrum. Damon observed a region of shops, artisan yards and insulae, where tall apartment buildings leaned across the streets and alleyways on either side, almost blanking out the sky. They crossed a series of stepping-stones, avoiding the mud and manure that caked the roadway. Several loaded carts trundled towards them heading for the Via Appia, their terrified owners a reminder that Antony's henchmen were still stalking the city.

At the Vicus Iubarius, Damon listened with interest as Tibo described the temples on the Glaberline Hill above. The enormous Jupiter Optimus Maximus stood at its summit.

"It's the place where a triumphal parade comes to an end. An honour reserved for generals who capture foreign lands, but one that should have been given to Octavian in my opinion for defeating Antony at Mutina."

Damon noted the bitterness in Tibo's voice. "Then why didn't it happen?" he asked.

"Only the Senate can sanction a triumph… and we know how they denied him his finest hour. They should all be sent to The Rock."

"What's The Rock? I don't understand."

"It's up there on the cliffs, but you can't see it from here. They call it the Tarpeian Rock and it overhangs the cliff-face. By tradition, it's a place of execution."

Tibo ran a finger across his throat. "The guilty are forced to jump; those who are afraid to are thrown from it. Roman traitors and murderers mostly… but we should make an exception for senators."

Damon smiled. "You mentioned a triumphal parade?"

"Yes… an incredible spectacle that follows a special route. It begins at the Campus Martius, passes through the Triumphalis Gate in the Servian Wall and into the Velabrum, and the marketplace we crossed earlier. At the gate a slave would raise a gilded laurel wreath over the general's head, holding it there for the entire journey through the city. The procession enters the Circus Maximus, after which it goes down the Via Triumphalis then turns into the Forum's Via Sacra…'

Damon held the boy playfully at the back of his neck. "Slow down a little, Tibo. Who might be involved in the parade?"

"Well, members of the Senate and magistrates lead the way, followed by a host of musicians, dancers and clowns; then wagons brimming over with the general's spoils of war. Behind them, the sacrificial animals, and more colourful dancers and clowns. After this the general himself, showing off prize captives in front of his chariot, with his legions bringing up the rear."

Damon laughed at the boy's antics. Tibo had stopped walking, his arms gesticulating as though he was the victorious general waving to the crowds.

"Can you picture it Damon? The never-ending procession through streets covered in green rushes and the flowers cascading down from those high tenement windows. And then banquets of food," he said, licking his lips. "But not before the general has terminated his parade up there at the foot of Jupiter's steps. Then he and his lectors enter the great temple to offer the god their laurels of victory."

"Don't worry," Damon assured him, "one day Octavian will have his triumph, and perhaps you could be there with his victorious legions."

Tibo sighed at the thought of such glory, but his heart was elsewhere. His thoughts turned to Kyriki as he hobbled along with his friend.

Inside the podium, beneath the Temple of Saturn, lay the State Treasury; a point overlooked by Tibo because of the noise coming from the Forum Romanum. It had started to rain, but nothing it seemed was going to dampen the spirits of those who wanted to see Cicero. This was to be his final appearance in Rome and a dense crowd gathered in front of the Rostra.

Damon and Tibo managed to reach the orator's platform where, true to form, Marcus Tullius Cicero evoked a mixture of emotions. People were on their knees, weeping and wailing, while others laughed and cheered or shouted abuse. But the old man was immune to it all, for among the beaks of ships captured in war that decorated the Forum wall hung another trophy.

Cicero's head and both of his hands had been hacked off and nailed to the Rostra.

"Marcellus once said that Cicero insulted Marc Antony on the Senate steps, and Antony warned him that wagging such a sharp tongue might one day cut his own throat. Is this what they call Roman politics?" asked Damon.

"I guess so," Tibo said, quietly. He tugged at Damon's sleeve. "Come on, we should find Maecenas."

The Senate House was only a short distance away. A broad flight of steps led up to the huge columns that flanked the entrance. Senate guards manned its doors, which were always open so the eyes of the gods could witness the affairs within.

There was no sign of Maecenas, but Damon recognised some of his men among the groups of servants and guards who waited for their respective masters. He made his way towards them and almost tripped over a man sitting on the steps. "Virgil... what brings you here? Not to listen to the war-mongering, I hope?"

"Hello, Damon. No... I'm waiting to see Maecenas."

"Then we should wait together. Let's go up in the porch where we can shelter from the rain."

They climbed the steps and Damon introduced Tibo. "He's Octavian's youngest and, dare I say it... his most efficient messenger."

Tibo gave his customary bow. "I'm honoured to meet you, sire."

"Virgil is one of Rome's finest poets," Damon said. "He's also a friend of Cornelius Gallus, so be on your best behaviour." He turned to Virgil. "Did you know Gallus and Pollio were in charge of the land seizures and re-distribution?"

"No, I did not!" the poet said in annoyance, his hand visibly shaking as it touched his brow.

"What troubles you, Virgil?"

"I'm sickened by it all, Damon. I'm angry and troubled at the mindless slaughter of our own people! And now we have the persecution of innocent, hard-working farmers by someone I call a friend." He slumped dejected to the floor beside Tibo, his back against the stone pillar.

"But Gallus works under the orders of Asinius Pollio; it's a position given to him by Octavian as reward for his deeds in Mutina."

"Then he should know about my father's farm."

"Why…what's happened, Virgil?"

"The triumvirs are not satisfied with plundering Cremona, now their greed turns to the fertile lands of Mantua. The soldiers have taken the house and farmland; it's something my father spent his whole life creating."

"I'm sure Maecenas will help you," Tibo said, knowingly.

The poet gave him a weak smile, but Damon disagreed. "It's not a good time, Virgil. With Octavian being unwell, Agrippa oversees the armies and Maecenas is representing him in matters of the State. He's here today because Marcus Lepidus addresses the Senate and Octavian has to know every word he utters."

But Virgil was adamant. "Then I'll approach Octavian himself," he said, rising to his feet. "I've wasted enough time."

"An even worse idea," Damon said, holding the poet's arm to restrain him. "When Octavian's indisposed he favours no-one. Even those closest to him suffer his moods." Damon contemplated the favour Gallus owed him. "Perhaps I can help?"

"But how can you? Forgive me, Damon, but you're only…"

"A slave… yes, I realise that only too well, Virgil."

"I'm sorry, I meant no offence."

Damon smiled. "None taken, my friend. What I can tell you is that as we speak, Gallus is on his way back to Rome. Believe me; he will honour my request for you to recover the farm."

The poet sighed with relief. "May the goddess Juno bless you with beautiful children, my friend."

It was a sincere remark, but one that caught Damon unawares. He looked away to hide his sadness.

"Come with me," said Virgil, quietly. "You might be interested to hear what goes on inside the Senate House."

He led them across to an adjacent building, which housed several offices of the State. Its entrance was surprisingly unguarded, and no-one approached them as they stepped through the doors. Damon and Tibo followed the poet down a wide hallway with rooms on either side manned by clerks responsible for the Senate's records and administration.

While Virgil made an enquiry, Damon stood near an open doorway, noting the untidiness inside. Scrolls were littered across a long oak table covered in dust, and the room was crammed with unmarked containers. Piles of rubbish left little space for the clerks to work efficiently.

He compared its chaos with the meticulous ways of Octavian, and winced at the thought of him paying them a visit.

He glanced at Virgil, and it was apparent the young man he spoke with was in awe of the poet. Nothing, it seemed, was too much trouble for the poet. Urging his visitors to be silent, the clerk led them up a flight of steps to the first floor. This was a replica of the twelve rooms below, except that beyond the second office on their right now was a narrow passageway. Near the end of this they heard a roar of jeering and laughter. Whoever it was speaking from the floor of the Senate House met with strong disapproval.

The clerk indicated a place for them to stand, stressing that they keep away from the arched doorway, and never step out on to the balcony. This was a place occupied by several clerks who were on hand to provide the senators with any documents they might require during the proceedings. Damon estimated their position would overlook a point midway along the chamber's floor.

From the stories Vario had told him, he could visualise the Senate House and the scene unfolding there. The senators passed through a vestibule before entering the main rectangular chamber. They would take up their positions at the far end on three tiers of wooden seats. These were constructed in a U- shape with its open end facing them as they walked across a huge mosaic floor. The majestic pillars and the walls around them shone with coloured marble.

On a bleak day such as this, the chamber was illuminated by a series of lamps which hung from its coffered ceiling. This was the light filtering into the passage where they now stood, and with it echoed the voices from below.

Damon realised the Romans had learned a great deal from Greek architecture, and the acoustic properties of their buildings was evident in the Senate House. Every word exchanged by the senators projected to the most distant ears.

"Lepidus has spoken in riddles!" accused one.

"We want the truth!" shouted another. "Why should we, the Senate, choose to sanction a war with Brutus and Cassius?"

There was silence; then came the familiar mocking tones of Marc Antony. "Because we, the Triumvirate, govern Rome!" he cried. "Lepidus thought it was his duty to report to the Senate. But like it or not, there will be no debate. Our plans to destroy Brutus and Cassius will soon be finalised with Octavian." He lowered his voice. "That's if he manages to recover in time."

Antony glared around the benches. "So, you want the truth!" he growled. "Well, Lepidus has already spoken of Brutus, but as you well know Cassius has also defeated Dolabella in Syria. And now, with the exception of Egypt, his armies command the East. Let me remind the Senate that these provinces once provided us with fifty million denarii every year. But none of this money has reached our Treasury since Caesar's death because it feeds and recruits an army led by Cassius. Are you all blind to the fact that this is the man who seeks to destroy you and all of Rome?"

There was a murmuring among the senators, but whatever misgivings Lepidus provoked, no-one offered to challenge Antony. The meeting was at an end.

By the time Damon and Tibo reached the steps of the Senate House again with Virgil, a group of senators appeared in the doorway. Among their sullen faces was a beaming Maecenas.

"My dearest, Virgil, whatever brings you to the Senate?" he said, warmly embracing the poet. "And we have Damon here with young Tibo. By the gods, this must be serious," he laughed.

"I need to speak with you, sire," Virgil said. He glanced uneasily at Damon. "There's a problem… with the poetry."

Maecenas gave Virgil a sympathetic smile. "Oh dear, I sense a troubled mind. If these wretched killings affect us mere mortals… it must play havoc with a poetic genius."

Virgil visibly blushed as Maecenas took his arm, walking him down the Senate steps towards his waiting litter. "Fear not, Virgil, we can discuss the matter on our way to see Octavian."

The poet politely objected. "But I need to read a lot of passages to you, sire. Can we meet on your return?"

"As you wish," Maecenas sighed. "Go to my house and we'll dine together later."

He ordered two of his bodyguards to accompany Virgil, and Damon gave the poet a reassuring nod as they shook hands to say farewell.

"A strange one is Virgil," said Tibo, as they followed Maecenas' entourage from the Forum.

"He's a poet, and all poets want to live in a world of beauty and fantasy," Damon said. "I think Virgil is afraid of reality, it's too brutal for him to understand."

"But why does he question the friendship and loyalty of Gallus, who supposedly confiscated the farm, while he accepts an 'acquired' property without question as a gift from Maecenas?"

This surprised Damon. "Are you sure, Tibo?"

"I heard that a poet now owns this place near Maecenas' house on the Esquiline Hill. It must be Virgil."

"Well, that's typical of Maecenas; his generosity towards Octavian knows no bounds."

Tibo scratched his head. "No... the house is Virgil's."

"Yes, it may be. But if I'm not mistaken this is all about Virgil's poetry... and Octavian's interest in a military theme." Damon smiled at the bewildered expression on Tibo's face. "Remind me to tell you about it when I see you in Cyprus," he whispered.

Tibo stopped in his tracks, eyes widening in surprise. "You have a plan?"

"It's an idea, Tibo, nothing more. Yet the problem with Brutus and Cassius will give us a chance when the armies go to war." Damon placed a hand on the boy's shoulder. "But before we can put anything into action I need some information on the port at Ostia."

"I've been there several times lately for Rufus," Tibo said, excitedly. "He wants to know everything coming in about Sextus Pompey. Our general expects a regular report on what he's up to at sea. There are fears that his naval fleet will seize our grain supply from the east."

"Then find out what you can about the ships in Ostia. We need a friendly merchant returning to Egypt via Cyprus," said Damon.

Tibo realised the importance of his task. He stomach churned, knowing this would probably be their only chance of escape.

When a slave began to announce the arrival of Maecenas he was waved away by Octavia. Her brother was supposed to be resting and she was growing impatient with visitors.

"You're impossible!" she cried, as Octavian spat out a foul-tasting mixture of herbs. "How can you expect to recover when you ignore the doctor's advice?"

Octavian grimaced. "I'm sick, not dying, Octavia. Please… I would like some water."

She stood beside him defiantly. "You can have water after you swallow the medicine."

Octavian shuddered as he tried the concoction again.

"You're so stubborn, Octavian. You should be resting. You are just like mother was, and look what happened…"

She was close to tears as Maecenas crossed the room, but the smile he greeted her with soon disappeared from his face when Octavia turned on him.

"My brother is going nowhere until he's well enough," she snapped, brushing past him to where Damon stood at the door. "And you're not supposed to leave him unattended either!"

Octavia realised her mistake; she remembered Damon's absence had been her brother's idea, and felt guilty when Damon apologised. Her eyes softened towards him, but the frustration of it all was too much for words. Without looking back she walked quickly from the room.

"Oh, such fire and elegance," Maecenas sighed, pouring himself a cup of red wine. "Octavia inherits her mother's beauty and the passions of her brother. If only there was another like her in Rome. Well… I might even consider marriage myself!"

Octavian's laughter turned into a fit of coughing. "Sit down Maecenas," he gasped. "Tell me about the Senate meeting."

Although Damon missed the speech from Lepidus, there was no doubt Maecenas would be repeating almost every word and gesture. He listened from the doorway, surprised by how much the Greeks revered the man who instigated the murder of Julius Caesar.

"... And as you already know," Maecenas was saying, "Brutus was hailed as a hero on his arrival in Greece. Now they honour him with statues and his image appears on coins along with the Liberators' dagger."

He paused to sip his wine. "But Lepidus failed to convince the Senate that such things present a threat to Rome."

Octavian raised his eyebrows.

"Well, you know Lepidus. There's no fire in his belly. His oratory skills are more suited to the House of the Vestal Virgins. The words he spoke were meaningless; it was though he was afraid of upsetting the Senate. He lacked confidence and was constantly interrupted. I have to say it took Marc Antony to rescue the situation," Maecenas said, seriously.

"So, what did Antony have to say?" Octavian asked, suspicious as ever.

"He reminded the senators that with Cassius joining Brutus from the east their combined armies pose an imminent threat to Rome. Antony quickly asserted authority by declaring that war in Greece was the triumvirs' decision, it was not open to discussion by the Senate..."

Octavian smiled. "He seems well briefed on the eastern provinces; Cleopatra, no doubt?"

"Well now that her son's been denied, Cleopatra thinks Rome will accept her through Antony."

Damon stifled a yawn; it had been an eventful day, and with a lengthy discussion to follow, he felt relieved when Octavian suddenly dismissed him for the night.

Over the next few days the young triumvir barely recovered from one illness when another beset him. His lungs became severely infected and he could hardly breathe; but Octavian was never detracted from his quest and yet again, much to the annoyance of his sister, Antony and Lepidus came to the villa for a series of more lengthy meetings. Damon was convinced the triumvirs would soon be ready for war.

Tibo confirmed this on his return from Ostia. He reported a massive contingent of troops moving south towards Brundisium, which overshadowed the boy's good news about the port. But thanks to Octavia's care for her younger brother, Damon was given more freedom of movement. He decided the time was right to visit Kyriki.

Damon waited until nightfall before making his way to the kitchen, where the young slave girl served him chicken and bread with honeyed wine. Not wishing to be overheard he conversed with her in Greek, thanking her for the generous portion. "You must be Kyriki."

"Yes. And you serve the master's stepson, Octavian," she said, shyly.

"I'm Damon, a friend of Tibo's. He's back in Rome and wanted to see you, but tells me it's difficult for you to meet."

Kyriki lowered her eyes. "Yes. I would be punished if Caleb saw us together."

Damon touched her hand. "Don't worry. I will take care of you and Tibo. That's why I'm here."

She smiled at him, and Damon could see why her beauty captivated the boy. Kyriki possessed the same gentle manner as Hestia; their eyes, too, soft and warm, expressed every emotion. But the strain of working long hours in such a busy household was clearly taking its toll on Kyriki. She looked pale and fragile, and Damon sensed that the older slaves were bullying her into extra duties. This was a common practice he had banished as overseer on Vario's estate.

"There's something I want to tell you, Kyriki," he whispered. "I have a plan to set you and Tibo free. But if word reaches Octavian then Tibo and I will be put to death. Do you understand?"

The girl nodded, trembling at the thought.

"I need your help concerning the slaves' quarters. Describe to me the exact layout of your own cell from floor to ceiling. Where and how often the guards patrol? What time the doors are locked at night and opened each morning?"

She answered his questions in great detail, and when Damon left his hopes were high. The cells were similar to those on Vario's estate, but his old master saw no need for locked doors and guards.

"When they lock you in on the second night from now, gather what belongings you have and a warm blanket. Be prepared, Kyriki, for we will have to move fast." He took her tiny hand in his. "Don't worry, you will soon be free," he promised.

Damon paused at the doorway. "I almost forgot... I'll bring Tibo with me."

A broad smile lit up Kyriki's face, and for the first time he saw a trace of colour in her cheeks.

Chapter X

Despite the warmth of that June evening Octavian received his fellow triumvirs wrapped in a blanket. He lay on a sleeping couch shivering and frustrated at his immobility. It annoyed him that Marc Antony was in control of the machinations of war, and enjoying his senior status with every passing hour. Antony left them in no doubt that Brutus and Cassius were preparing to invade Rome. Moreover, his plans to stop them could not be faulted.

"We have fifteen legions distributed between the provinces of Spain, Gaul and Italy; enough to deter any invaders in our absence. I've despatched another eight legions across the Adriatic to Apollonia, and they're under orders to march east and find the most impregnable place to blockade the Via Engratia."

Antony replenished his cup of wine. "No matter how strong the armies of Brutus and Cassius might be, our men will stop them reaching the Adriatic until we arrive."

"How many more legions are moving from Italy?" Lepidus asked.

"Twenty," croaked Octavian in dismay. "Don't you know anything that's going on, Lepidus?"

Antony grinned. "What chance have I got to win a war with a sick boy and a mindless old fool? Which one of you shall I take into battle?"

"My illness will pass… I don't know about his state of mind," Octavian replied. "He's best left in charge of cleaning up the stench from the streets in Rome."

While Antony laughed at the remark, Lepidus glared at Octavian, pointing an accusing finger. "You won't be so flippant when you're up against Brutus," he fumed. "He might well have your balls fed to his pet dog! That is, if you have any, pretty boy?"

Antony ignored them, making his own decision. "Those legions have to be shipped to Macedonia," he demanded. "Half of them are already on the Via Appia, and I will join them in Brundisium. Octavian, I suggest you stop playing games with Hades and get Agrippa to organise all the warships he can muster on the western side of Italy. You take the remaining ten legions down the Via Popillia in support.

"Lepidus, there is much work to be done in Rome. You're the most experienced and trustworthy where the veterans and politicians are concerned. You will govern Rome in our absence, with Plancus as your junior consul."

"Why Plancus?" queried Octavian.

"The man's proved himself in battle, he's an excellent candidate," insisted Lepidus. Unlike your choice - that fool Quintus Pedius. He ran around the city like a headless chicken during the proscriptions. I do believe he died of fright!"

"All right," Octavian said, "but what about Sextus Pompey? Can you keep him at bay, Lepidus?"

"No, Octavian… that's your province," said Antony. "Pompey's your problem. You will have the resources to keep him in the Tuscan Sea. I don't want him anywhere near Brundisium when the troops set sail for Greece."

Lepidus looked at Octavian with a sarcastic smile on his face. "Is it agreed?" he asked, holding out his hand.

Octavian clasped it reluctantly, and then turned to Antony. "We must never underestimate our enemy's strength. Brutus has overwhelmed the Greeks on land and Cassius made fools of their admirals; his was a major success outmanoeuvring the Rhodian fleet. Both of them amassed huge revenues between them."

"All the more for us when we defeat them," Antony smiled. "Now it's time to discuss my plans in more detail. Are you up to it, my boy?"

Octavian shifted unsteadily on the couch, wheezing until Lepidus helped him sit more upright. "Whenever you're ready," he gasped.

The moon had disappeared behind a bank of dark clouds when Tibo left the stables. A short time before he'd watched Marc Antony and Lepidus depart from the villa surrounded by numerous bodyguards: great hulking brutes that would crush a man's skull with a single blow if he was foolish enough to venture near their generals. With one of Philippus' best stallions now ready alongside his own faithful horse, he crouched in the darkness waiting for Damon.

In his hand was a heavy metal lever, and on the ground beside him a coil of rope and several pieces of twine. For a while, nothing stirred except for the lowing of cattle in a distant meadow. Then Tibo heard the guard who patrolled the northern side of the villa grounds; his thick leather soles studded with hobnails, crunched across the gravel towards him.

Tibo gripped the lever in both hands ready to strike, but the footsteps suddenly stopped. There was the sound of a brief struggle followed by a gurgling noise, then a whispered voice: "Tibo… where are you?"

The boy stepped out. "Over here…"

Damon appeared with the guard hanging limp over his shoulder.

"Is he… dead?" gulped Tibo.

"No, just sleeping. Bring the twine and we'll tie him up behind the stables."

The guard's head slumped on his chest. He was bound and gagged, propped in a sitting position and secured to an olive tree down in a grassy hollow.

"That will hold him until sunrise," said Damon. "They'll find him when the search for Kyriki begins." He clasped Tibo's arm. "Give me the rope and stay close. Come on, Kyriki will be waiting."

As soon as Kyriki entered her cell the heavy oak door shut behind her; a key turned the lock and bolts were slammed securely into place. She could not bring herself to believe that anyone, even Damon, would be able to break it down. She felt tired and confused, wondering how Damon could be so sure about setting her free. Yet she did as he asked by collecting her few precious belongings then sat on the bed with a blanket around her shoulders, waiting.

There was no lamp in her cell, the only light came from burning wall torches in the passage above the slaves' quarters: a flickering light that shone through a thick metal grille in the ceiling. This passageway led to the upper floor of the grain stores, and its open arches looked down over fields to the River Tiber beyond.

It could not be seen from the main house, and at night became a sinister place for the female slaves.

Kyriki had warned Damon to check the passage, as it was a haunt for the prying eyes of guards, Caleb the freedman, who remained under the patronage of Philippus. She saw them all at one time or another peering at her through the bars of the ceiling grille, hoping to see her undress.

The thought made Kyriki shiver. She pulled the blanket tightly around her, and in despair of waiting she looked upward to the grille... straight into the gruesome features of Caleb.

The freedman leered at her. "What are you hiding under the blanket, Kyriki?" he grinned, showing his yellow teeth.

"Go away!" she screamed.

"Do as I say. Remove the blanket and your robe for me or I'll..."

In that moment Caleb turned his head and the descending blow from Damon's fist grazed his temple. As he rolled away Tibo kicked him, but Caleb sprung to his feet and wrenching the lever from Tibo's hand. He clamped it across the boy's throat, gripping him from behind.

"Move away, Damon, or the boy dies," he snarled.

Damon stepped back. "There's no need for that, Caleb. A prowler was seen in the grounds and I was sent to investigate. I'm only doing my job."

Caleb's eyes narrowed. "Then you won't mention this to the master?"

"No... not a word."

Tibo felt the pressure ease on his windpipe, then snapped his head back as hard as he could into Caleb's face. The freedman staggered, blood spurting from his broken nose as Tibo wriggled free. But in a wild rage Caleb came after him swinging the metal bar.

With a sweep of his arm Damon sent Tibo sprawling to safety before facing the attacker. Caleb lunged at him and in one smooth action Damon stepped aside, his dagger hissed from its sheath and he buried the blade deep into Caleb's ribcage.

The freedman died on his feet, and Damon withdrew his dagger as the body slumped to the floor.

Tibo scrambled to his feet. "What now?" he gasped, holding a hand to his bruising throat.

"Give me the lever."

Droplets of sweat trickled from Damon's brow, his muscles aching as he struggled to prise away the grille's iron bars. He tried from each side of the until a corner moved, and Tibo watched in awe as the concrete began to crumble, and Damon's incredible strength tore away the grille.

"Pass me the rope," Damon said, breathing heavily. "I'll lower you down to help Kyriki."

The girl was in tears; frightened by the sounds from above she sat huddled in a dark corner of the cell. Then suddenly Tibo was calling her name, reassuring her. She caught her breath at the gaping hole in the ceiling and Damon tying the rope to his waist.

They led the horses quietly across the meadow before Damon took Kyriki in his arms and lifted her on to the stallion's back.

"What about Caleb?" asked Tibo.

Damon placed his hand on the boy's shoulder. "Don't worry, I'll take care of that, just make sure you board that ship. You have the money?"

Tibo nodded, the tears welling up inside as he embraced his friend. "You're like a father to me. How can I ever repay your kindness?"

"Just ride like the wind, Tibo. Find Hestia for me and tell her that one day soon I'll be coming home. "

Damon watched them disappear into the darkness. "May the gods be with you," he whispered.

Philippus paced around the floor of the library, hands clasped tightly behind his back. "You saw nothing?" he cried. "One of my best horses stolen, a slave girl disappears in front of your eyes… and you saw nothing?"

"I was attacked from behind, sire," the guard muttered, sheepishly. "I was…"

"Asleep on duty, more like!" thundered Philippus. He gestured to a legionary standing in the doorway. "Get him out of my sight. Lock him away until I decide his fate," he said, eyes blazing.

Elsewhere in the house, it was the first real night's sleep Octavian had experienced for a long time. Octavia thought it best not to disturb him, so it was mid-day before he was told of the incident. By then Caleb was also reported as missing.

"It's obvious to me that Caleb's taken her," Octavia said to her brother. "He was always creeping around the female slaves, especially Kyriki. I've seen the way he looked at her," she shuddered.

"Try not to burden me with it Octavia. Marc Antony is on his way to Greece and there's a war to think about. I have no time for runaway slaves.'"

Octavia fixed her beautiful blue eyes upon him, pleading. "But I'm really concerned for Kyriki. Like you, dear brother, she suffers ill health. Please help me to find her."

"Oh… very well," he said, impatiently. "I'll have my own men investigate the matter."

Octavia kissed him on the cheek.

"Now be off with you," he smiled. "And send Damon in to help me dress. Agrippa will be here soon."

"More meetings?" she frowned.

"This will be the last before we leave for Macedonia."

Agrippa arrived within the hour, pleased to see that Octavian was eating some bread and honey in the dining room. "Such plain fare for someone with an aristocratic name like Caesar," he smiled, embracing his friend, "but it's a start. At least you seem more like your old self, doesn't he, Damon?"

"Yes sir. Much better, thanks to the Lady Octavia."

"So, what have you been up to Damon?" asked Agrippa. "I hear there's a problem with the guard. Some intruder, I'm told."

"Not in the house," Octavian replied. "No-one would get past Damon, you know that. A freedman and one of the slaves have disappeared. For some reason, Octavia likes the girl, so I promised to help with the search.'"

He turned to Damon. "It's unlikely that Caleb and the girl would hide in the city. They're on horseback, so I think he's heading for the countryside or even Ostia. While I speak with Agrippa, send two good men to pick up their trail, Damon. But warn them I want results not excuses."

Damon left the room breathing a sigh of relief. They all seemed to believe it was Caleb on the run and this would give Tibo and Kyriki a few more hours to make good their escape. With Tibo's experience as a scout and messenger, the boy was sure to spend time covering their tracks near the river. This would be enough to confuse any pursuers until they reached the port of Ostia.

In the villa grounds, Damon briefed two guards on Octavian's theory, and they were about to mount up when a familiar voice called out. "Wait... I know Caleb. Tell the general he's nothing to fear. I'll find them, Greek man."

Damon turned to see the grinning face of Rufus, the veteran's red hair longer and wilder than ever. "Rufus! I thought you were in Ostia?" said Damon, clasping the man's shoulder.

"I was, but it seems I arrived just in time." He addressed one of the guards. "Are these fresh horses?"

"Yes, sir."

"Then I'll take yours. You can carry on your duties here.

You're with me," Rufus said to the younger man as he mounted the horse. "Brief me along the way."

He winked at Damon. "Give me a few days. Oh, and if you see Tibo tell him to join our legion on its way to Caulonia. That boy's forever giving me trouble... but I love him," he said, raising his hand to Damon as he rode away.

Back in the dining room, Octavian looked on with fondness as Agrippa shared his bread and honey. Their friendship had grown stronger over the years, as each admired and respected the other's ability and courage. He felt no need to prolong the talk of war, for Agrippa was more astute than he in planning military tactics on land or sea.

With battle plans already agreed, most of their time was spent in light-hearted chat about their ideas for the future. But inevitably, Marc Antony crept into the conversation.

"One of my reservations about this war is that Brutus and Cassius won't be our only concern," Agrippa began. "After their defeat we will have to be wary of Antony stealing all the victory laurels."

Octavian rubbed his chin thoughtfully. "Yes. He will push his troops beyond the limit to glorify his status in Rome. We have to match him at every stage of the war."

"But your health is…"

Octavian raised his hand to silence him. "I have to lead my legions by example, Agrippa; it hardly inspires confidence if the men see me carried to the battlefield in a litter. But I will need you beside me, which is why I've chosen Salvidienus to command the fleet."

He clasped Agrippa's arm. "We shall win this war, my friend, and one day the whole Roman Empire will be ours!"

Agrippa's smile disguised his deep concern for Octavian, for the threat of losing his closest friend was greater than ever. Brutus and Cassius had murdered Caesar, now they were more than ready to destroy his son.

The town of Ostia spread eastwards from the sea along the south bank of the Tiber. Merchant ships and large vessels docked at the port's main harbour; their cargo being stored in warehouses or loaded on barges for transporting upstream to Rome. There was also a river harbour, and south of the high wall enclosing the town, a small coastal marina for fishing boats and pleasure crafts.

An odd cluster of workshops, temples and warehouses lined the waterfront, and near the Marina Gate was a small inn. Its location outside the walls mainly attracted fishermen, or the odd traveller from Laurentum, so the innkeeper was pleasantly surprised when a young couple from Rome arrived. The boy paid him a generous sum.

As the pastel shades of dawn streaked across the morning sky, Tibo awoke to the cries of hungry sea birds swooping over the rooftops. He opened a shuttered window in the attic room and blinked at the salty mist drifting in from the sea. Even at this hour a number of legionaries patrolled the town, so he was happy to hear the noise already rising from the fish markets. The crowds would provide cover for him and Kyriki when they reached the waterfront.

He checked what remained of the money: half to pay their passage, the rest he would give to Hestia when they reached Cyprus. He tied the two bags securely under his tunic before waking Kyriki, and together they set out to find the ship.

To avoid the town they crossed a stretch of sand dunes until Kyriki stopped outside a block of stables, sheltered from the sea by a row of warehouses. "Let's go inside," she said, tugging on Tibo's hand.

"No. I can't," he said, quietly.

"But you will never see Zeus again," she pleaded

"I sold him last night, remember? He... he's not my horse anymore."

There came a noise from the barn and a rugged looking grey haired man stepped out to greet them. He was tall and muscular, with deep scars etched white on his suntanned limbs. Tibo saw him as a gladiator or a legionary in his younger days.

"Can I help you?' asked the man. "We have some fine horses…" He paused, and a smile of recognition lit up his face. 'Oh, you've had a change of mind about the horses, my lady?"

"No! She just wants to see them one last time," said Tibo, stepping forward.

"I understand." He gestured for Kyriki to go inside. "Be careful now, that black stallion is a strange creature. He's bred to be a military horse if you ask me; not a spot of white on him anywhere." He glanced at Tibo's crippled leg. "I suppose he was too much for you to handle, eh son?"

Tibo smiled, picturing the big man trying to ride Zeus himself and being promptly thrown to the ground. "Yes," he replied. "I shall need two placid mares for when we return to Rome in a few days time."

"Then why not have a look for yourself while I fetch some hay?"

Kyriki had already ventured inside the barn, which was a long wooden building with stalls along both sides and across the far end. The air was warm and heavy with the smell of hay and fresh dung, but she could see the stables were mainly clean and tidy. The light flooding in through its entrance doors never reached the distant stalls, where unopened shutters cast them in darkness.

The girl walked slowly peering into every stall, while in the darkness ahead Zeus stirred, ears pricked forward to the sound of her footsteps. When she found him Zeus lowered his head and she stroked his face, caressing the soft, wide nostrils as she whispered his name. But his eyes were fixed on the figure approaching them through the sunlight.

Tibo felt no shame in hugging Zeus. He was no longer a soldier but a boy again, remembering the day

Maecenas had given him the young colt and how close they'd become. Through the complexities of life and on the battlefields of war they were inseparable.

He kissed the horse, as he always did at the start of every day. "I will never forget you, Zeus," he said, quickly brushing away his tears.

"Please forgive me."

Kyriki held Tibo's hand as they walked away. The boy hesitated at the entrance doors, but as much as he wanted to he never looked back.

Rufus was tired and hungry. His search throughout the night covered every avenue of escape from the villa to the upper reaches of Rome, but it produced nothing. Yet still desperate to please Octavian, his diligence was rewarded on the way to Ostia. A few miles into the journey he called a halt and sent his companion to water their horses at a stream near the river. Up ahead, voices were raised and the guard reported back to Rufus that he'd seen a group of fishermen dragging a body from the Tiber.

The corpse seemed beyond immediate recognition, but kneeling over it Rufus identified something quite unusual: half of the man's right ear was missing. There was only one person he knew with such an injury, as he'd witnessed a legionary bite off someone's earlobe in a brawl. It was Caleb.

Rufus ordered the young legionary back to Rome with the body and rode on to Ostia, alone with his thoughts. Nothing made sense to him. A young girl would never have the strength to kill a brute like Caleb; it was obvious that someone else had… but who and why? Caleb was supposed to have released the girl and they'd ridden away together… so where was she? Puzzled by it all, Rufus urged his horse into a gallop as the walls of the town loomed up ahead. "Perhaps the answer to it all lies here in Ostia?" he mumbled to himself, hopefully.

Rufus entered town through the Roman Gate and followed the main road that ran through the centre. He ignored the street on his right leading to the barracks; it was pointless questioning soldiers, as their minds would be on war not a runaway slave girl. But another, unexpected option came to him near the Temple of Jupiter when his horse stumbled and pulled up lame. Rufus dismounted, and was cursing his luck when an old comrade approached him.

"You look worn out, Rufus. Was it a rough night in the brothel?"

Rufus laughed. "And you look well; retirement suits you, Gaius."

"Why don't you bathe, eat at the tavern over there then we can catch up on old times. You know where my place is, Rufus. Here, I'll take the horse."

Rufus avoided the baths, but his rumbling belly welcomed food and wine at the tavern. A short time later, he found his way to Gaius' stables and went inside.

"The horse will be fine in a few days," Gaius said, greeting him warmly. "It's nothing that rest won't cure. Will you need another?"

Rufus nodded. "I'm looking for someone, but I have to return to Rome when I've found her," he said, eying the horses.

"So that's why you visit the brothels! Searching for a regular woman, eh?"

"I'll take this horse, Gaius. And no, it's a young Greek girl I'm after not a prostitute. I ask you, Rome's on the brink of war and I'm chasing a runaway slave girl for Octavian!" He turned to his friend. "I don't suppose you've seen her? She's a pretty thing with long black hair. Suffers with her breathing, I'm told."

"Greek, you say?" Gaius scratched his head. "No. I can't say I have."

Rufus led the horse out into the sunshine. He knew Gaius was lying but it was understandable. The man had no cause to help Octavian, since the triumvirs had put his brother to death barely six months ago during the proscriptions.

As if to verify this, Gaius looked him in the eye. "We fought side by side with Caesar, you and I, Rufus. But as for Octavian?" He spat on the ground.

The two men shook hands and Rufus mounted the horse to be on his way.

"Another war… when will it ever end?" Gaius said to himself, then: "May the gods spare you," he called out, raising his hand as Rufus set out across the sand dunes.

The Decurion waved back, smiling. He was convinced now that he knew Caleb's killer. He leaned forward on the horse, stroking its shiny black mane. "Take me to your master, Zeus," he whispered.

Soon after his meeting at Caulonia with Sextus Pompey, Octavian briefed Agrippa on the favourable deal he'd made. Pompey was now lifting the blockade on Rome's grain supply. Damon was in attendance, but his mind was elsewhere when a slave announced the arrival of Rufus. The decurion offered a smart salute to Octavian and Agrippa.

"Ah, Rufus, you bring news of the slave girl" said Octavian, eyeing the man's dishevelled appearance.

"It's not good, sir. The body from the river was Caleb; it has been confirmed by your stepfather, Philippus, in Rome."

"And how did he die?"

"A knife wound, sir. Dead before he hit the water, I'd say."

"What else can we expect!" cried Agrippa. "The streets of Rome are rife with thieves who would slit your throat for the pleasure of it. Yet we've just entertained Sextus Pompey, the biggest pirate of all."

Octavian ignored him. "What of the girl?"

"She probably suffered the same fate. Her body could well have reached Ostia and the open sea by now."

Octavian shrugged his shoulders. "Octavia will be grieved by this, but enough time has been wasted. We have a war to win." He dismissed Rufus, telling him to get food from the kitchen then report back to his legion.

The decurion saluted, a smile hovering at the corners of his mouth as he turned to see the confused look on Damon's face.

At the first opportune moment, Damon went after him. He found Rufus sitting among the sand dunes chewing on a crust of thick honey-coated bread. Nearby, grazing on a patch of dewy grass was a black stallion.

"You have Tibo's horse... where's the boy?" asked Damon.

Rufus smiled up at him. "I thought you might tell me, Greek man. I found Zeus in Ostia... and that was really odd."

Damon said nothing as he sat down beside the Roman. He assumed Rufus would continue to speculate, but instead Rufus asked to see his dagger. Without thought, he handed it over.

"It's good steel... and has a nice balance," said Rufus, thrusting the weapon at some imaginary foe. "But nothing compares to the gladius." He gave it back, and Damon returned it to the sheath at his waist.

"I believe you killed Caleb," Rufus said, suddenly. "I think Tibo saw him take the girl and asked you to help. When I discovered he'd sold Zeus in Ostia I realised his desperation. That horse meant everything to Tibo, and the only reason he would ever leave it…"

He slowly shook his head in disbelief. "No wonder he walked around in a dream, the stupid boy was in love! He and the girl, did they board a ship?"

Damon smiled at him. "You have a remarkable imagination, Rufus. You have a theory, nothing else."

Rufus threw away the remnants of bread. "I could have said all this to Octavian but he's enough to worry about; besides, I owe you a favour."

"A favour… why?"

"When you saved the general's life, you saved mine. The life I've dreamed of ever since I joined the army. Octavian is the only one I trust to keep his promise of money and land when I retire. Without him all our dreams will turn to dust."

The decurion rose to his feet, a knowing expression on his face as he climbed on Zeus' back. "I heard that it took more than twenty stab wounds to kill Caesar. They slashed at him wildly; there was no skill in his execution. Caleb was different; he died from one thrust of a dagger wielded by an expert."

He turned the horse ready to ride away. "It's no coincidence that your narrow blade matches the wound in his body." He grinned at Damon. "Farewell, Greek man! I hope we meet again in Greece."

Chapter XI

On board the cargo ship Tibo and a kind member of the crew made Kyriki as comfortable as they could, but even in a sheltered corner on deck her breathing laboured. Tibo fretted over her constant sickness. The morsels of food she ate were wretched up again soon afterwards.

On the sixth night of the voyage a freak storm forced passengers below deck. There was no light in the hold; it was a cold and damp place infested with rats. Grain and scraps of food from around the ship ensured an ideal breeding ground, and although the crew culled their numbers they could never destroy the rats completely. The dead only served to nourish the living, and most of the survivors were large, black rats.

Kyriki hated them… and they sensed it. In the darkness she could hear their squeaks and gnawing, and although her body ached from exhaustion she was afraid to fall asleep. Kyriki snuggled up to Tibo for comfort and warmth, but it was several hours before the storm abated.

When it did, and the ship rocked gently in the calmer seas, she closed her eyes.

Tibo awoke as tiny beams of sunlight threaded through the deck above. He sat up... then shouted in horror as he scooped away the rats crawling over Kyriki. As the vermin scurried away, Tibo knelt beside Kyriki. He shook her gently. "It's all right, you're safe now. We can go on deck, Kyriki. The sun's shining..."

She opened her eyes and smiled at him as he took her hand, pressing it to his lips. "Are we nearly there?" she asked.

"Yes, Kyriki... we're free!"

Tibo helped her up on deck where they stood at the ship's rail. In the distance the island of Creta glistening in the sun, and Kyriki wept tears of joy at the sight of her homeland. Then she smiled as Tibo brushed a lock of hair from her face and kissed her forehead.

"I love you," he whispered, holding her close.

The Romans occupied twelve major cities on the island of Cyprus, with Nea Paphos as its capital. The walled city was in close proximity to the sea and offered a fine harbour and anchorage for trading ships. It contained many splendid villas, marble temples, theatres and public buildings.

Tibo and Kyriki walked the streets hand-in-hand, spellbound by its grandeur. They could hardly believe such a beautiful place would be their new home.

It was late afternoon when they reached the north gate of the city where Tibo bought a horse from the nearby stables. With Kyriki's arms wrapped tightly around his waist, he rode the horse along a track which climbed steadily through the forest. They journeyed across large areas of open ground where the Romans had felled cypress and pine for the building of ships. Now open to the sun, these tracts of land were cultivated with vines and fruit trees by Cypriot farmers and peasants. Tibo saw them as friendly folk, always greeting them with a wave as they passed by.

After three hours he stopped the horse on a high ridge, and to the east was Damon's land. But as they rode down into the valley Tibo saw neglected vines wilting in the sun and orchards standing barren in the long, parched grass. He tethered his horse to an old carob tree and helped Kyriki dismount.

"This has to be Damon's home," he said, caressing her face… and her smile melted his heart as they strolled across the meadow towards a stone-built house.

A woman stood in the open doorway, smiling as they entered the gate. Her perfumed hair fell in long tresses to her waist… black as a raven's wing. When she smiled her beauty defied even Damon's description.

Tibo bowed his head. "You must be Hestia."

She nodded in surprise.

"My name is Tibo and this is Kyriki. We come from Rome… from Damon. I'm his friend," he said, proudly. "Damon will soon be home." He smiled, placing the bag of gold at her feet. "He sends you this."

Hestia thanked him. The boy spoke in a strange mixture of Greek and Latin but she understood, and the sound of Damon's name made her tremble. She felt faint, and for a moment held on to Tibo for support. Then she began to cry.

"Mama! There's a horse down in…" The girl stopped in her stride, shocked to see her mother in the arms of a handsome young man. And the girl beside him looked so pale and weak.

There was a long pause before Hestia wiped her eyes. "Athena, this is Tibo and Kyriki. They bring us joyous news from Rome. Your father lives!"

The young couple laughed as Athena and her mother danced around the floor hugging each other. It was a special day for them all, and soon they were celebrating with a wholesome meal and village wine. In the evening, with Kyriki tucked up safe and warm in bed, Tibo sat outside with Hestia and Athena.

"When the slave traders took Damon, I always dreamed he would come back to us. So many years now… I can't believe that he's alive."

Tibo reassured her by saying that only day's before the voyage Damon had helped him free Kyriki. He answered an endless stream of questions about Damon, and long after Athena retired to her room he sat with Hestia under the stars. He told her of Damon's heroic deeds, and how much the Roman soldiers admired him for saving Octavian's life.

Hestia listened in awe. Tibo's kind and polite, she thought. And he's a messenger for a Roman general, so he must also be very brave. Yet even when he smiles there's concern in his eyes. I wonder why?

"You speak our language in a strange way," she said, not like Kyriki."

"Then you must blame Damon, he taught me."

Hestia laughed. "I'd like you and Kyriki to stay with us, Tibo. This is your home now."

"I can only stay for a little while. Will you look after Kyriki for me when I return to my legion?" Tibo lowered his eyes. "I have to help in the war alongside Damon."

"But you said he was coming home."

"He is, just as soon as Brutus and Cassius are defeated he will be freed by Octavian."

"Who are these men, Tibo? Please explain... is Damon still in danger?"

Tibo sighed. He knew he had to tell Hestia everything now. But the next morning when Kyriki woke him with a kiss, he made a decision that would change his life forever.

Octavian was greeted at Brundisium with the news he wanted to hear: the blockade was lifted.

"Your deal with Pompey seems to be working," Agrippa said as they crested a hill. "If only he knew what you're up to."

From the harbour below a mass exodus of ships was underway. Thousands of men, arms and equipment – together with horses and pack animals – were crammed aboard ships that lay so low in the water it seemed they would never survive the Adriatic. Nevertheless, over the next few days more than four hundred vessels left Brundisium. Half of them were destined for Apollonia, the rest further north on the western coast of Macedonia.

Octavian's army made camp in the hills beyond Apollonia, and at sunset Damon announced a visitor.

"Just as I expected," mocked Antony, breezing into the tent. "You're in no fit state to walk never mind lead an army!"

Octavian lay on a couch, propped up with cushions. "You know how much I detest the sea, Antony. I'm resting."

"Resting! You look ready for Hades to me. But rest easy, my friend, I will take command from here."

Octavian glared at him. "I will lead my legions, and in my absence, Agrippa... not you! You underestimated me before at Mutina and lost. So lest you forget, Antony, while you did nothing before to save Caesar, I will give my life to avenge his death."

Antony was shaken by the response. "As you wish," he shrugged. "But be warned, we cannot prolong this war. Brutus and Cassius will be aware of our limited food supplies and they will avoid a decisive battle for as long as possible."

Octavian agreed. "Yes, I know they'll wait for us to starve."

"Our reports show their armies are moving west on the Via Egnatia. The legions I sent ahead hold the passes beyond Philippi, and if I leave at daybreak I can reinforce their position." Antony shifted uneasily, his tone softened. "Why don't you stay here for a while; gather your strength, then follow me later?"

Knowing that it would be suicide for Antony to spearhead an attack without him, Octavian relented. "Perhaps I should. Give me three days."

The town of Philippi stood on a rocky plateau above the Ganga River plain. Antony arrived there furious that the enemy had scaled narrow mountain tracks to avoid the trap set by his men in the passes. The Liberators now occupied Philippi in two secure camps: Cassius to the south of the Via Egnatia, and Brutus a mile to the north.

Antony chose to build an enormous camp near the salt marshes to accommodate his and Octavian's joint armies, with the idea of taking Cassius first. His foul mood was still in evidence when he saw Damon helping Octavian from his horse.

He stormed through a group of legionaries. "You're pathetic!" he yelled. "I have a decrepit old slave in Rome with more energy!"

"Look at your own failings before you criticise mine, Antony, or tell me it's untrue that the enemy have slipped by your so-called elite troops! Remind me... how many got through?"

"Only nineteen legions!" shouted Agrippa to roars of laughter.

Antony's face reddened. "That's enough!" he cried. "Now... when you can rouse yourself, Octavian, we have urgent matters to discuss." With this he turned on his heel, brushing passed Agrippa before disappearing inside his tent.

There were a few objections to Antony's ideas, mainly from Agrippa, who still thought the older man was out to steal their glory. But as an observer, Damon saw the brilliance in Antony's tactics. The mild winter and long hot summer in Macedonia had dried up the rivers and marshland, so he wanted to cut a channel through the high grass and reeds for a transistor road. Once this was constructed it would allow him to attack Cassius on two fronts.

"We will start work at dawn tomorrow," Octavian told his officers later that night. "I've also agreed for Antony to take command in the first battle. We will hold ground here, then..." he smiled, "I take care of Brutus!"

With the battle being fought a mile distant no one saw the need for a sizeable force to be left in the camp. But it proved to be a fatal mistake for those who remained, as only a handful survived.

When the war began at Philippi a great pall of dust signalled its fury. Surprised by Antony's attack from the marshes, Cassius was defeated and died in the onslaught. But unexpectedly, small pockets of his troops broke through Antony's rearguard and headed for the triumvirs' camp.

Alerted by the sudden cries and clash of steel, Damon bundled Octavian out of the tent. "Stay close to me, sire. This way! Make for the perimeter wall."

A choking dust cloud was now over the camp, and through it the enemy troops surged after them. Within fifty yards Damon had slain three of Cassius' men, Octavian a fourth; but for every one that fell others came at them through the swirling dust.

They fought with their backs to the wall, Octavian gasping for breath as he slashed out with his gladius until he could hold out no longer and collapsed to his knees. With a sword in one hand and his dagger in the other, Damon shielded him… his body splashed with enemy blood as he killed at random. He was almost unscathed until a young recruit who lay dying at his feet lunged upward, sinking his gladius into Damon's body.

Having seen some of the enemy charge through the marshes, Agrippa ordered a century of men to hunt them down. They quickly regained control of the camp while Agrippa and six veterans searched for Octavian. They found him near the perimeter with blood gushing from a head wound.

Damon lay beside him. The pain was leaving his body now, and through the shadows around him he could feel the sun on his face… the strong arms lifted him as someone called his name…

There was a gate, and beyond it he wandered through a garden where the smell of orange blossom lingered in the cool night air. He gazed at a star-filled sky, listening to the warmth of her laughter, and once more he felt the touch of her hand… soft as a butterfly's wing. "Hestia!" he whispered.

From the mists of time came a jingle of tiny bells… and her image faded away.

Tibo paused to wipe the sweat from his brow, smiling as he saw Kyriki approaching him across the meadow. Ever since she persuaded him to stay at the farm she increasingly occupied his thoughts. Seeing her health improve every day reminded him that he was right not to return to the bloodshed and despair of Rome. The work was arduous here, but in two months he'd made a significant progress in the vineyards and orchards. He felt no regrets.

Hestia encouraged him, while Kyriki and Athena constantly praised his efforts, and even though he knew little about farming he enjoyed the challenge.

"Damon will be so pleased when he returns," Kyriki said, greeting him with a kiss.

Tibo blushed. "I must go to Nea Paphos today; there may be news of the war. Would you like to come with me?"

"Of course, otherwise the people will never understand your Greek," she laughed.

"I might approach the Roman garrison. They will tell me if Octavian's victorious."

"Please don't, Tibo. Someone might recognise you."

He took her hand. "It's the only way, Kyriki. The guards will know what's happened. Come…" he smiled, "we can be back before nightfall. I promise to be careful."

They left the farm at noon with Kyriki mounted on the horse behind Tibo. She was content with his silence, snuggling up closer as the winding track descended into the forest. It was cooler here; the air fresh with the smell of pine. Birdsong always drifted through the trees, where startled deer ran down grassy slopes to a stream in the valley below.

Tibo always warmed to its tranquillity... he could understand why Damon longed to return here. When they reached the city walls, Tibo left the horse to be fed and watered at the stables while he and Kyriki made their way through the crowds towards the harbour. Tibo's hopes were raised at the sight of a Roman galley anchored out in the bay. And as they stood on the steps of a temple he could see a group of legionaries along the waterfront.

He squeezed Kyriki's hand. "Stay here and wait for me. Perhaps I won't need to speak to the guards after all." Before she could protest, Tibo was moving towards the Romans.

He knew that Cyprus was part of the eastern provinces under the control of Marc Antony, so they were certain to be his men. He joined other citizens enthralled by the mighty Roman ship with its three banks of oars protruded from either side of her belly.

Tibo ventured nearer to the soldiers, close enough to hear their conversation. They were full of wine; their mood loud and jovial. "He fell on his sword, I was told," said one. "A noble way out, I suppose..."

"The *only* way out with the likes of Antony breathing down his neck," laughed another.

"Never mind Cassius," began a third man, "all Rome is talking about right now is news about the man who saved Octavian's skin at Philippi. I don't know much, only that a rearguard was breached by enemy troops who stormed into Octavian's camp. Whoever it was held the ground and fought them off single-handed. They say he should be awarded the Corona Civica... if he lives. But reports say he's too badly wounded..."

Tibo turned away... his stomach churning. He knew it was Damon. There was no-one close enough to protect

Octavian, other than Agrippa, and these men would know of him.

It was every soldier's dream to be awarded the Corona Civica: a crown of oak leaves given to a man who saved the lives of others and held the ground on which he stood until the battle ceased. The Corona Civica was the second highest honour awarded for valour... but at that moment it meant nothing to Tibo. All he wanted was his friend to be alive.

He decided to wait; perhaps he could find out more about the hero's identity before voicing his fears to Hestia and Athena, but it was with a heavy heart that he walked back to Kyriki.

Cornelius Gallus stood at the prow of the ship, thankful that in a few hours he would be back in Italy. Octavian had singled him out to escort the wounded. On the deck lay more than three hundred men, with military surgeons working non-stop tending their wounds.

Gallus walked among them offering hope and a prayer to the gods, but under his feet the deck reddened with blood. It poured from bodies slashed open by swords and spears, and pierced with arrowheads buried too deep for a surgeon to extract. He was saddened by the sight and sounds of dying comrades. The war-weary veterans and raw recruits: men and boys of great courage who would never see their homeland again.

At the ship's stern Gallus descended a short flight of steps to where a soldier stood in the doorway of a small cabin. "Any change, Marcus?" he asked.

"No sir. I'm afraid he's... "

Gallus pushed by him... the man lying on a makeshift bed was stirring. "By the gods, he's back from the dead!"

"Where am I, Cornelius?"

"You're sailing the Adriatic, my friend. We're in sight of Brundisium."

Damon gripped his arm. "Octavian?"

"Alive, thanks to you, and plotting the destruction of Brutus now Cassius is dead." He grinned at Damon. "His orders are for me to escort you to his villa at Baiae. The climate around the Cup is much milder over the winter months. You can rest there. Musa will look after you."

"No… I must return to my home in Cyprus to die." Damon tried to raise himself up from the bed but the sheer pain of movement caused him to vomit blood.

"Marcus! Get Musa over here quickly," urged Gallus.

A thin man with long white hair arrived with Marcus. His tired, dishevelled look and bloodstained robes belied his status as one of Rome's finest physicians. He checked Damon's wound and settled him down again before speaking to Gallus up on deck.

"There is nothing more I can do," he said, quietly. "Damon had lost so much blood before I cauterized that gaping hole in his stomach." The physician wiped the beads of sweat from his brow. "Look around you, Cornelius. You can see the terrible wounds a gladius inflicts on the human body. I'm afraid Damon will die if a major organ has been damaged."

"When will you know, Musa?"

"His determination is amazing… but only time will tell. If he makes it to Baiae there may be a chance."

It was December before the armies of Brutus conceded defeat. At sunrise on the second day Marc Antony sat in his tent brooding over his future. His men would normally expect to see him out on the battlefield consoling the wounded and celebrating his victory, but not at Philippi. He was drunk... and in mourning.

Antony sat with his head in his hands, exhausted from the lack of sleep and tormented by the series of events that saw his dream of replacing Caesar as leader of the Roman Empire slowly disintegrate. His plans to eliminate Octavian had failed. He reflected with growing anger at the incompetence of Glaber, who should have killed Octavian before he even started to campaign. Then he fretted over his humiliation at the hands of Cicero in the Senate House; the crushing defeat he suffered at Mutina; and how that bloody Greek slave saved Octavian's life not once... but twice! He poured himself more wine, gulped it down and hurled the cup into the ground, shattering it to tiny pieces.

Antony stood ashen-faced, staring at the figure lying on a nearby couch. "Brutus... my brother," he cried. "Forgive me. I had no wish for it to end this way." As he reached out to adjust his own scarlet cloak that covered Brutus' body, Octavian and Agrippa entered his tent. The latter carried a sack which he placed on the table.

"You should be celebrating with our troops, not grieving for a useless corpse," said Octavian in disgust at seeing Antony's drunkenness. "What kind of a Roman general loves his enemy?"

"What do you want? Have you come here to gloat?" snapped Antony.

"You could say that, but there's something else I have in mind," Octavian said, approaching the couch. "You honour him with your cloak, I see... how touching."

"Brutus was a man of great courage, and I... I respect his status as a general and a... a noble man. He will be honoured. Yes... with a military funeral," Antony slurred.

"Honoured? Did you hear that, Agrippa? Antony is to honour Caesar's killer!"

Antony pointed a finger at them. "And I expect your own legions to be there."

Octavian and Agrippa looked at each other and burst into simultaneous laughter. "Well I suggest you go and tell them yourself," said Agrippa. "They'll probably burn you on the same pyre!"

Their mockery riled Antony. "I'm in command here!" he roared, swaying slightly on his feet.

Octavian moved towards him, his eyes glittering like crystals of ice. "You will never command me, Antony," he said in a sinister voice. "Before I'm done that lion you so boldly display as your image will be no more than a bleating lamb!"

For the first time, Marc Antony was seen to take a backward step. "What do you want?" he asked again, quietly.

Without dropping his stare Octavian pointed to Brutus. "A simple compromise: I want his head… you do as you please with the rest."

Before Antony could react Agrippa drew his gladius, and in one lightening blow across the throat severed Brutus' head.

Octavian grabbed a handful of black curly hair and picked it up. "There… quite painless," he smiled, stuffing it inside the sack Agrippa was now holding out.

Antony was sickened. "It will rot before you reach Rome."

"Not if it's pickled," Agrippa said with a grin.

Antony turned away in disgust, pouring himself a fresh cup of wine. When he looked back he found himself alone again with Brutus.

Whatever the war had proven, whoever its heroes, nothing ever compared with the glories of nature to Virgil. It was a poet's dream walking across this meadow in springtime, for the hills around Baiae were coloured by a vibrancy of wild flowers. Virgil was tired but exhilarated when he reached the villa after his long trek.

It was no surprise to find it heavily guarded, for the man he had come to see epitomised true Roman ideals. Virgil was eyed suspiciously until he was seen by one of the house slaves. The old man was eventually allowed to escort Virgil out to the terrace. Set in the splendour of a wooded hillside, the huge manicured gardens rambled down a gentle slope through an avenue of marble statues and fountain pools to a panoramic view around the Bay of Neapolis.

When Virgil reached the last pair of statues, he stood at the top of a flight of steps that led down to a large rectangular colonnade. The floor within was decorated in a stunning mosaic that sparkled as the morning sun cast golden threads of light through its colours. At the far corner, resting against a marble pillar was the lone figure of a man.

Damon sat facing the sea, his fingers caressing the old flute he held to his lips playing a Greek lullaby... the notes close to perfection.

Virgil waited until he'd finished. "Bravo!" he cried, offering polite applause as he descended the marble steps.

Damon stood to greet him. "I've had too much time to practice," he said, smiling as they shook hands. "How are you, Virgil?"

"Ah! The hero of all Rome... and he asks the wellbeing of a mere poet. You never change, Damon. I'm honoured to be your friend. Now, more to the point... how are you?"

"Oh, Musa keeps me alive. His methods are unusual: 'alternative cures,' he calls them, but I am getting stronger."

Neither man realised the significance of Damon's remarks, but in the years ahead Musa was to become Octavian's personal physician, and his unusual methods would cure the general's poor health.

"Will you return to Rome?" asked Virgil.

"No. When Musa is happy for me to travel, I shall go home to Cyprus."

"Of course, Gallus tells me you're a free man."

"You saw Gallus?"

"Yes, he came to Siro's villa on his way to Rome."

"Is he your friend, the philosopher?"

Virgil nodded, his voice softening. "I'm afraid he died recently and left me his villa. It's up in the hills not too far from here… a peaceful place."

"Then you must be in need of refreshment. Come, we will go back and sit out on the terrace."

Damon walked slowly towards the steps, holding on to Virgil's arm for support. "Did Gallus mention your father's land?"

Virgil grinned. "He said you threatened him… in a friendly way, but the decision now rests with Octavian."

"Did someone mention my name?"

The two men looked up to see Octavian standing at the top of the steps, immaculately dressed in his crimson cape and a magnificent cuirass. The breastplate shone with the figures of men and women portrayed in Roman scenes. There were mythical beasts, a horse-drawn chariot, stags and domestic animals, all carved in intricate detail.

Virgil witnessed a rare moment of emotion from the young Roman leader as he came down to help Damon, and embraced him without hesitation. He saw Octavian's eyes fill with tears; not only of gratitude, but joy at the sight of Damon on his feet again. There was no need for words as each embraced the other like long lost brothers.

"And you must be Virgil," said Octavian, finally turning to face the poet.

"Yes, sire."

"Maecenas is in raptures over your work, and so is Cornelius Gallus. He tells me that there's a problem over your father's home."

"It was confiscated in the land seizures," replied Virgil in annoyance.

Octavian looked at Damon, who nodded in agreement. "A lifetime's work; everything was taken," he said. "Will you return it to Virgil?"

"Since you ask, Damon, it's the least I can do." He turned to the poet. "There is one condition, Virgil. In exchange for the deeds you must come to Rome and discuss your poetry with me in more detail. I should like to hear it."

The poet sighed with relief. "Thank you, sire. I will be honoured."

When the three men reached the villa, slaves began to serve fruit and wine out on the terrace. Octavian dismissed them before outlining his plans for Rome's future. There would have to be more land confiscated for the benefit of one hundred and fifty thousand veterans, so they may retire to a peaceful rural life. This, in turn, would recreate the vast farming communities of their forefathers in Italy.

"It won't be easy to find a compromise," Octavian said. "The Roman people still have hardships to face, but eventually I hope to eradicate the suffering of the last hundred years of civil wars."

"What of the Triumvirate?" asked Damon, after a lengthy discussion and talk of Philippi.

"Antony has gone to restore order in the eastern provinces, and as for Lepidus, his competence and leadership is always in question. Who knows what will become of him?" Octavian said with a shrug.

The young Roman stood, placing his hand on Damon's shoulder. "My dear friend, nothing in my life would please me more than to bestow upon you the highest honours in Rome. I can never repay your courage and devotion, Damon. It saddens my heart that you will soon be leaving for Cyprus… "

There was a long pause while Octavian gathered his emotions. "I have brought you gold… it is only what your loyalty and dedication deserve," he added quickly, knowing Damon would object. "But there's enough to help you farm your land again back home. So, when you're strong again, the guards will escort you to Brundisium… and so will Musa. One of my ships will be waiting there."

Damon rose slowly from the couch. "Perhaps one day we will meet again, sire," he said, as they shook hands.

Octavian nodded. "May the gods be with you." He turned, bid farewell to Virgil… and with a swirl of his crimson cape he walked away.

"I must go too," smiled Virgil. "You need to rest."

"We never spoke of Theocritus and your poems to Latin verse. Are they complete?"

Virgil laughed. "Not yet. I work too slowly, often losing faith in my ability. So it's wonderfully refreshing when I see something that rekindles my imagination. Today, for example, the beauty of nature and the joys of friendship are all around me."

Virgil offered his hand. "I am proud to have met you, Damon. You are an extraordinary man. I will never forget what you did for my father."

Damon shook his hand warmly, and then watched him disappear into the woodland. And even though this was to be their last meeting, Virgil remained true to his word; he would remember Damon the way he knew best... in his poetry.

As Damon reclined on the couch again, Musa joined him. "A generous gift awaits you," he said.

"Oh, you mean Octavian's gold?"

"No. One of his men came by earlier and left a horse for you at the stables. He was a strange, wild looking soldier... but a beautiful black stallion. He called it Zeus."

Chapter XII

Spring blossomed into summer, and for the first time in fifteen years Damon returned to Cyprus. On the ridge overlooking his land he thanked the six Roman guards for escorting him.

The old centurion smiled, inwardly in awe of this remarkable man. "It's an honour, sir," he said. "I speak for all our comrades in Octavian's army. We wish you well, sir."

With a smart salute, the men reined in their horses to return to the harbour at Nea Paphos.

Damon watched them go, shaking his head at the irony of a Greek slave being addressed as 'sir' by a Roman centurion. His father would have been proud of his freedom. He reached down to stroke the neck of his horse as it nibbled the dewy grass. "Come on, Zeus… it's time to go home."

It was the most beautiful of days to Damon. The trees across the valley were in full bloom, and the smell of orange blossom drifted to him on the breeze. There was a horse grazing in the meadow, and beyond the forests a panorama of mountains soared into an endless blue sky.

He dismounted at the carob tree, tethering the pack-horse before allowing Zeus to run free. But the long journey from Baiae had taken its toll: the pain from his wound returned with a vengeance. He was forced to rest until it passed.

There was utter silence around him, as though all of nature held its breath waiting for him to walk to the house. He sensed that someone was watching him, and when a figure suddenly emerged from the garden his heart pounded. "Hestia?' he whispered, then as loud as he could, "Hestia! Hestia!"

She came towards him... hesitant at first, and then running across the meadow into his outstretched arms. They had both lived for this moment and neither wanted to let go. Tears mingled with laughter, as they lay in the grass showering each other with kisses.

Hestia traced her fingers across his brow and let them follow the features of his rugged face, smiling as Damon closed his eyes to her touch. Some mornings she used to wake him like this and they would just lie together, safe in each other's arms.

"Damon, let's go to the house," she said, suddenly. "There's someone special waiting for you... a young lady named Athena." As they walked together, she told him about Tibo and Kyriki.

Out on the terrace behind the house, there was no mistaking Tibo. Through the fruit trees Damon recognised his sun-bleached hair and the familiar limp as the boy carried an armful of bracken to a burning fire. Beside him was a laughing and much healthier Kyriki... but the beauty of another young girl took his breath away.

Tibo stopped, open-mouthed, the bracken falling to the ground when he saw his friend. Athena followed his stare and knew at once it was her father. "Papa!" she cried, rushing towards him. "Papa... you're home!"

Damon was overwhelmed... speechless as this strange, beautiful girl threw her arms around his neck. He held her, and when the reality of it all dawned upon him, tears welled up inside as Hestia joined in their warm embrace.

Tibo watched them... smiling, yet saddened by the sight of his ailing friend. The report he overheard at the harbour that day was true, and it was obvious now Damon had saved Octavian again. But the cost to his own life was painful to see. Before him was just a shadow of the man he once knew. His muscular frame, emaciated through loss of weight, was proof enough that Damon carried a terrible wound. As he lay inside the hospital tent following the battle at Mutina, he had seen so many soldiers like this... and few survived.

It was his fault. All Damon had lived for was to see Hestia and his daughter again, but helping him and Kyriki escape had led to this. "I'm so sorry..." he said, his heart full of remorse and grief. "I never thought it would end like..."

Damon smiled at the boy. "There's no time for regrets, Tibo. We are all together now." He held out his hand to Kyriki, who also embraced him.

When the waves of emotion finally ebbed away, Damon took Tibo aside. "You have done remarkable things here, my friend. Hestia tells me how hard you worked to rescue the vines and fruit trees. Thanks to you I'm sure we will have a fine crop this year."

Tibo blushed. "Athena tells me things... and Kyriki helps now she's stronger."

"Well I'm proud of you all," Damon said, putting his arm around the boy's shoulder. "I bring you a gift from Baiae. There's a pack-horse in the meadow with a chest full of gold coinage. Will you bring it up to the house?"

"Of course... anything for you," said Tibo, preparing to go. "But I don't need money, seeing that you're alive is reward enough for me."

Damon smiled. "It's not money, although there's more than we can ever use. No... you will see for yourself at the old carob tree."

After Tibo unloaded the chest and put the horse to graze, he looked around for something else. He searched the grass, even in the branches of the tree, but there was nothing. He shielded his eyes from the sun to gaze across the meadow. No, nothing... except Damon's horse drinking at the stream. He was half way back to the house before he realised there was something familiar. By then Damon, Hestia and the two girls all stood at the gate, laughing and pointing behind him. Tibo lay down the chest and, as he turned there was Zeus galloping towards him.

While Damon settled down to enjoy his new life as a husband and father, Octavian's plan to establish himself as Rome's favourite son suffered serious setbacks. His only comfort was the unyielding friendship and support of Agrippa and Maecenas... and the pleasure he found in writing his own private letters to Damon. The first of which, arrived in Cyprus during the late summer of the year 40 BC. With no desire to reveal his failings, however, Octavian concealed his disastrous attempts to honour the promise he'd made to thousands of war veterans.

The reward of money and land owed to them was slow to materialise and, with their loyalty dishonoured, open anarchy and desertions took place on a scale unheard of in the Roman army. As a result, opposition to Octavian escalated across the whole of Italy.

But with his usual political flair and unfailing belief, he came through… and one evening, as the sun was setting beyond the hills of Rome, he wrote to Damon:

'*My dear and trusted friend,*

I hope your health has now greatly improved. Musa informed me that all should be well providing you continue to follow his diet and exercise advice. I must say I find him rather strange for a physician; nonetheless, his remedies are effective. If this dreadful coughing and wheezing doesn't abate, I might even try his methods myself. Who knows?

'*The situation in Rome is much improved. I never realised what a difficult task awaited me here after Philippi. The thousands of veterans from that war and those left in Italy rightly expected their rewards, but even now our money resources have still not recovered. In addition, we had the farmers' reluctance to share their land, so finding a solution without more bloodshed has been extremely tiring.*

'*To make matters worse, Antony's detestable wife, Fulvia, conspired with his brother, Lucius, against me. Fulvia manipulated Lucius to incite the Roman people by saying that the two of them represented Antony's standing in Rome. I was furious to learn of their treachery, for previously, as a token of gratitude to Antony's major role in the defeat of Brutus and Cassius, I married his stepdaughter, Clodia. But in reproach of Fulvia's actions I promptly divorced the girl and sent her back untouched – still a virgin.*

'*As consul, Lucius had called upon the likes of Pollio, Ventidius and Plancus for military support; it was to no avail, for* our friend Agrippa took my legions and blockaded them in at Perusia. *Under siege, and without a word from Antony himself, the three generals withdrew their troops and Lucius was left to starve like Decimus Brutus at Mutina. Fulvia fled to Greece and I spared Lucius as an act of goodwill to Antony. The fool is now exiled in Spain.*

'*My leniency pleased the people and our armies, yet even as I write I'm sure that such a betrayal of my status and trust reeks of Antony. The only reason he never conducted the uprising himself was – so my agents inform me – the infatuation he has for the Egyptian queen, Cleopatra. I understand she carries his child… perhaps the spell she weaves will become an advantage to me!*

'*Meanwhile, a more immediate threat infests itself. Sextus Pompey has broken the verbal agreement we made at Caulonia and once again blocks our grain supply from the east. Ahenobarbus and his fleet also harass our western sea towns up to Ostia. It is inevitable that they will have to be dealt with. But first, I am to accompany my legions to Brundisium. Marc Antony has been informed of Fulvia and Lucius' exile, and is on his way to visit his wife in Greece. I am aware that the armies on both sides are sick of war, but a show of power is needed to curb any intention Antony might have of taking control.*

'*Agrippa often mentions your name, especially when I'm unwell or in a foul mood. As you know, he dislikes Maecenas, yet speaks of you with the highest regard. Indeed, we both miss your presence immensely. I am blessed with Agrippa's long and faithful friendship, and the life you gave back to me, Damon, in the face of impossible odds.*'

Damon read it aloud, and while Hestia and Athena listened with increasing admiration for his prominence in such a powerful country, Damon was concerned with its content. Only Tibo and Kyriki understood that the day was drawing near when Rome's two strongest political gladiators would enter the arena to fight for the Roman Empire.

"It sounds like another war is coming," Tibo remarked, as he and Damon went out to the vineyards.

"Yes... I fear for Octavian, as not only can Antony rely on the likes of Pollio, Ventidius and Plancus but the fleets of Sextus Pompey and Ahenobarbus could also support him. Octavian will be outnumbered on every front."

Tibo wiped his brow as they walked between the rows of ripening grapes. "He's been victorious before," he said, earnestly, "and not even Marc Antony can outsmart him."

"Well, that's true. He may not be Rome's greatest general but his achievements are remarkable. We tend to forget that Octavian is barely twenty-two years old. He has an inventive and tactical genius in Agrippa, an expert in political persuasion with Maecenas… and all together they make formidable opponents.

"It's a grave situation, Tibo, but their world is no longer ours. We have so much to look forward to here."

Tibo swallowed the grape he was chewing, and nodded his approval to its sweetness. "Yes," he grinned, "the grape harvest, and then the birth of your child… and my wedding to Kyriki in the spring!"

Damon waited until after the birth of his son before he replied to Octavian's letter. Hestia had been through a difficult pregnancy and he wanted to be sure the announcement was a joyous one. "I've told Octavian all about our son," he said, excitedly showing Hestia the scroll.

"But you address him as Caesar."

"Yes, to please him... Octavian is very proud of the name."

"Have you mentioned Tibo?"

Damon nodded. "Octavian has to know the truth. I owe him an explanation." He kissed Hestia and the tiny infant in her arms. "I'll return before sunset," he promised.

She smiled at him, but as always, a chill touched her skin when he left the house.

Damon's confession never reached Octavian, for when he arrived at Nea Paphos the harbour was empty. Marc Antony had recalled all the Roman galleys and an embargo was in force, isolating the island. It was almost two years before trading resumed in the Mediterranean and news from Rome reached Cyprus again. By then, Tibo had married his beautiful Kyriki... and another letter arrived from Octavian. It started well...

'... and the conflict was avoided. The armies refused to fight their own comrades, and after much discussion, Antony and I made a pact at Brundisium. Antony remains in control of the eastern provinces, including Macedonia, and I have Italy, Illyricum, Dalmatia and the west. Both parties will assist each other with troops and ships whenever necessary. We have dispatched Lepidus to Africa out of the way!

'I am sorry to tell you that Marcellus is dead. He was a good man and his passing saddens me. I cannot say this of Fulvia. Antony's wife died in Greece and, although my dear sister, Octavia, was still mourning Marcellus, she agreed to my request and married Antony. As you can imagine, there was much rejoicing among our armies and the people of Rome. I was unable to compliment the occasion with a marriage-tie myself, as in a moment of madness after Perusia, I married Scribonia.

'Maecenas thought it was highly amusing that I should marry someone older than him! On the other hand, Philippus advised the betrothal as a peaceful gesture to Sextus Pompey, who is a relative of Scribonia.

'With the east – west territories agreed upon, it was crucial that Antony and I meet Sextus Pompey so that trading routes might flow again. Pompey now governs Sicilia, Sardinia, Corsica and the Peloponnese, but none of this changes my plans for his elimination. When Agrippa returns from Gaul I will give him complete control of building and commanding a fleet of ships capable of destroying Pompey and the other pirates, so that our seas are free of their scavenging once and for all…"

Damon passed the scroll to Tibo, who read it with deep concern. "I'm so glad you came back, Damon."

"So am I, my son. Believe me, this is where I will end my days."

There was no foreboding in his remark, but Tibo always remembered it because soon another day would dawn when all their lives and even the future of Cyprus rested on Damon's shoulders.

In the eleventh year following Caesar's death, Octavian made a supreme effort to finally win over the Roman people. At his own financial sacrifice he placed Agrippa at the forefront of a programme that would virtually transform Rome into a city of marble. As usual, Agrippa relished the challenge and his remarkable skill, whether in command of an army or designing restoration projects, shone through with equal brilliance.

Even Maecenas shouted his praises in the Senate House to Octavian's growing number of supporters. But in the library of his house on the Esquiline Hill he now entertained a man of more questionable principles.

"Octavian will be here within the hour," he told his guest, and the man smiled with noticeable unease. "Remember to address him as Caesar," added Maecenas. "He will take it as a mark of respect, and then the rest is up to you.'

The man nodded, his eyes shifting around the room. There was not the usual drabness of shuttered windows for Maecenas; his were covered by elegant drapes in colours that blended perfectly with the images of naked water nymphs dancing across the blue mosaic floor.

They exchanged pleasantries until Octavian arrived, and then the mood changed dramatically.

"What's the meaning of this, Maecenas?" he demanded. "You bring me here to meet Plancus! This man changes sides more than Cicero ever did!"

He went to turn on his heel, but Maecenas caught his arm. "Please… just listen to him. His news from Alexandria is astonishing!"

The young Roman relented, and Plancus began a long informative speech which brought an incredulous smile from Octavian. "Well, I trust you can verify all this, general?"

Plancus nodded. "But of course, Caesar. I was the witness to Antony's will."

Octavian clenched his fist in elation. "So, the great Marc Antony has denounced his homeland to be buried like some Egyptian mummy! Even the doubters will submit when I produce such evidence to the Senate. I trust you know the location of his will, Plancus?"

"Indeed I do, Caesar. As we speak it's in the Temple of the Vestal Virgins."

"Oh, goodness me!" cried Maecenas. "How can we possibly…?"

"Come now, Maecenas, it should not be a problem to someone of your esteem and persuasive talents." grinned Octavian.

"What! You mean you want me to…?"

Both men were laughing at him as the flustered Maecenas hurriedly poured himself more wine and drained his cup in one swallow.

The Senate House was stunned into silence; all eyes were on Octavian as he paced the floor. In his right hand he held a scroll bearing Marc Antony's seal. At this point it remained unopened while he waited for a response to the damning speech he had just delivered against Antony. Eventually a senator mumbled his protest.

"Speak out, senator!" Octavian cried. "Stand up. Let us hear so your defence of the enemies of Rome!"

The frail and aging figure of Aulus Sabinus stood, and with a trembling hand he wiped his brow before addressing the Senate. "It is true that Antony's long absence from Rome must be questioned, but what harm has it done?" he said, his voice surprisingly steady now.

"He has carried out everything expected of him in the eastern provinces, and with respect, Octavian, some of us here today are of the opinion that your personal feud with Antony overshadows the fine and generous work you have achieved yourself in Rome and the west."

Senators began to stir, nodding and voicing their agreement amongst themselves. Aulus Sabinus welcomed the support and resumed his attack on Octavian with renewed confidence. "You want us to believe there's a threat from Egypt, but Marc Antony controls Cleopatra's armies and her fleet, so Egypt's untold wealth will surely benefit Rome if the peaceful alliance between us continues?"

Again, a group of senators echoed their approval, and Maecenas sat increasingly agitated chewing on his finger... it was going badly for Octavian. Why didn't he silence them once and for all?

Octavian remained composed. "You speak as if you look out across the ocean, Sabinus. The sea is calm... and while Antony's sun rises in the east, mine sets in the west; but it never occurs to you what lies beneath the surface. Well let me assure you that below this calm water Rome is drowning in apathy. Once more you are all ignorant to the dangers of one of its own generals conspiring to conquer the Roman Empire!"

Octavian raised the scroll in the air, shaking it at the senators. "Marc Antony has denounced Rome... and in doing so declares he is her enemy! I have the proof right here! Allow me... No! I will call upon Aulus Sabinus to read this document to the House."

Octavian strode forward, handing the scroll to Sabinus. He smiled at the old senator. "Please... tell them what you hold."

Sabinus gazed in disbelief. "I have a will... signed and sealed by Marc Antony."

A murmur echoed around the Senate House, men craning forward on the benches as Sabinus began to read it out. Maecenas sighed, smiling with relief amid the fury that erupted from Octavian's supporters. They were in uproar that their man should be seen as the wrongdoer and aggressor in all this.

Octavian called for order as the senator completed his reading. "Now, Aulus, for the record, please read out the principal witness to this will.'

"It is Lucius Plancus."

Octavian stroked his chin; it was time to throw the final dice. "Ah… one of Antony's most trusted generals, is he not, Aulus?"

The senator nodded.

"Then if anyone is qualified to authenticate this document, it is he?"

Sabinus agreed. "Yes, without any doubt."

Octavian turned to Maecenas and nodded, and with a permanent grin on his face Maecenas ambled across to the large, open doorway. When he returned moments later, his announcement was met with an audible gasp. "My dear conscript fathers, I present the handsome and valiant, Lucius Munatius Plancus!"

Soon afterwards, Octavian sat at the head of a council of war. The decision he made elevated, without question, his standing as Rome's political and military leader. Octavian's declaration of war was not against Marc Antony, but the Egyptian queen, Cleopatra. It served the same purpose… the same end, but in the eyes of the Senate it was Rome against Egypt, not Roman against Roman.

The day had been a tiring one, and Octavian was grateful when he could relax that evening with some of his closest aides at his house on the Aventine Hill. For once, he chose to drink some sweet yellow wine, content to observe friends celebrating his success.

There was Marcus Titius, a fearless officer who, like his uncle, Lucius Plancus, led by example on the battlefield. A man highly regarded by Antony. Alongside him was Cornelius Gallus. This young man had always impressed him; his courage, leadership and excellent administration skills deservedly moved him through the ranks. He was now a fine officer.

Octavian smiled to himself at the next unlikely pair: Agrippa and Maecenas. Agrippa was his closest friend and his greatest general and admiral, who also proved himself a genius in architectural design and construction.

A lump came to Octavian's throat as he realised in that moment he felt proud of Agrippa above all others. After years of discord he and Maecenas were actually on friendly terms! He had even accepted Maecenas' decision to marry Terentia; it was a sham, of course, but Terentia was happy with the situation, and Agrippa accepted that.

Octavian's eyes settled on Maecenas and, as always, he felt assured by the man's warmth and friendship. His advice in all matters was crucial to their cause, and his guidance meant they were now one step away from glory. It was a step that Octavian would not take without him.

But his circle of friends was incomplete, and Octavian's thoughts turned to Damon... the man whom he could never forget; the slave who became his saviour and friend. The young Roman leader raised the cup to his lips in a silent toast.

"You seem deep in thought, my lord?"

Octavian turned to his guest of honour. "It's just an absent friend, Plancus. He's a Greek... a hero of Rome."

Agrippa, Maecenas and Gallus heard him, and all three said in unison: "Damon!" as they raised their cups of wine together.

Several nights later, a slave once again announced to Octavian the arrival of Agrippa. "My apologies for the lateness of the hour," he said, removing his cape in a flourish. "I have good news, my friend. Marc Antony is on the move. Our messengers report that Canidius leads sixteen legions towards Ephesus, and Antony and

Cleopatra have left Alexandria with the entire Egyptian fleet."

Octavian smiled. "So, he looks for a battle at sea with Canidius in a supporting role?" He clasped an arm around Agrippa's shoulder. "Come… let us study the maps in the library."'

Agrippa outlined Antony's possible destination before making a surprising suggestion. He traced his finger in a large circle and in the centre pointed to an island. "This is Luecas… and no-one knows the sea currents, its safe harbours and surrounding terrain better than one man…"

Octavian looked at him. "Damon?"

"Yes. We need him, Octavian. Whatever Antony's plans are, wherever he moves, Damon will have all the answers. There's no need for him to fight, but his ideas and knowledge can win this war for us."

"Then I will send for him at once," Octavian said. "I know the very man to persuade him."

As he approached the edge of the forest, Tibo sensed there was something wrong down in the city. He could see the north gate was closed and the walls above manned by soldiers, but even from this distance he could tell they were not Romans. He tethered Zeus to a pine tree, whispering words of comfort to him before joining a group of Cypriot farmers on foot as they headed for the harbour markets.

Nearer the city walls Tibo recognised the guards to be Egyptian.

The group was allowed to enter the city, and Tibo made his way through the sun-baked streets towards the garrison. A notice on its gates confirmed what Damon said would be their worst fears: Cyprus was now under

Egyptian control, and further orders regarding land seizures and Cypriot labour would be issued in the coming months.

Tibo was furious, shouting to a Roman guard who was watching him closely. "Hey! What goes on? Why are you leaving us to the scum of the east?"

"Hold your tongue!" rasped the guard, drawing his gladius. "You should all know by now about the donations from Marc Antony."

"Donations… what donations?" asked Tibo.

"Antony has given sovereignty of lands in the east to Cleopatra and her children. Cyprus is now under their rule. This whole island will be swarming with Egyptian troops by winter."

Seeing that Tibo had calmed down, the guard sheathed his sword, moving closer. "Your Greek has a trace of Latin. Are you Roman?"

"My father was," Tibo said, cautiously. "Where are you from?"

"The north-east of Italy: Ariminium."

"Oh, near the Rubicon?"

"Yes. I can't wait to return. I've done my service; it's time to take my well-earned money and a nice piece of land. All twenty of us here will retire. These Egyptians can manage until the next lot arrives. I…"

The smile of satisfaction suddenly disappeared from the guard's face as a Roman voice yelled at him from the high wall. "You there, assemble the guard! A ship is closing fast… a Roman galley!"

When Tibo reached the harbour a crowd already four deep lined the sea front. Out in the bay, a fully manned trireme was moving at speed; its three banks of oars cutting through the calm waters in perfect unison. Tibo could hardly believe his eyes, for the galley carried the unmistakable colours of Octavian's fleet. He turned and laughed as a roar came from the garrison, where the Egyptian guards ran around in blind panic.

The crowd watched in awe as one hundred and fifty Roman troops poured from the ship on to the quayside. A group formed a solid shield of armour around the officer in command, but just a glimpse of the man was enough for Tibo. He quickly made his way through the crowd and up to the north gate, which was now deserted. When he reached the top of the hill Tibo stood gasping for breath. There was no-one behind him as he climbed on Zeus' back, but it was only a matter of time before Cornelius Gallus reached the farm.

Cornelias Gallus had the finest qualities of a Roman aristocrat. His good looks, charming manner and brilliant military career endeared him to a growing number of wealthy women in Roman society. He was a poet of some repute... but also a ruthless killer. As he approached Damon's house, nothing was further from his mind than the Egyptian guards that lay slaughtered back in the city garrison. The twenty Romans were held in chains.

But one thing truly saddened him... the appearance of Damon.

His friend greeted him with the usual warmth and firm handshake, but Gallus could hardly believe how frail he looked; it was painfully obvious that Damon was dying from the wound he sustained at Philippi.

Gallus was visibly shaken, his sad green eyes turned to the woman at Damon's side. "You must be Hestia? Damon always spoke of your beauty. It's an honour," he said, graciously kissing her hand.

"And I am Athena," announced the young lady holding Damon's hand. I'm the daughter my father never knew for fifteen years because the Arabs seized him." Her eyes fixed on Gallus, unwavering. "I have a little brother now. Do you come to take my father away from him?"

The Roman smiled at her, admiring her spirit. "I have journeyed from Rome with a message from Octavian. He asks for your father's advice... and sends his good wishes to Tibo."

Athena trembled as she gripped Damon's hand. "Papa?"

"Please, don't be alarmed," said Gallus. "Tibo is in no danger and neither is your father."

Damon looked at him sharply. "But how does Octavian...?"

"You know him as well as anyone, Damon... nothing escapes him. He has eyes and ears in every corner of the Roman Empire."

Damon nodded. "Athena, find Tibo and your brother. Tell them we have a special guest for dinner."

A small boy ran to hide behind his father, and then Tibo entered the room.

Gallus rose to greet him. "A farmer's life suits you, Tibo. You've grown into a fine young man."

Tibo smiled uneasily, and relieved that he'd told Kyriki to hide. He shook hands with Gallus. "It's good to see you again, sir."

Gallus felt the tension around him, and did his best to alleviate the anxiety of the two women. His flattery and good humour over their meal almost convinced Athena that all was well... but not Hestia. There was fear in her eyes as Damon kissed her before he went outside to talk with the Roman.

Gallus wasted no time in explaining the purpose of his visit. "Octavian needs your help, Damon. Marc

Antony and Cleopatra are in Greece with the Egyptian fleet, supported on land by a substantial army led by Canidius. Our sources indicate their destination is in the Ionian Sea."

"And what exactly does Octavian want from me?"

"He asks for your presence at his side, but only to advise him… to plan Antony's downfall."

Damon shook his head. "Look at me, Cornelius. I am a dying man. I have been parted from Hestia for a lifetime. I have a beautiful daughter whom I never knew as a child… and now a son who I will never see grow up to be a man. How can I leave them when the next sunrise could be my last?"

Gallus looked at him, suddenly overwhelmed with compassion. He reached out placing his hand on Damon's shoulder. "If there was some other way to protect you and your family I would do it, my friend. But the truth is Cyprus now belongs to Cleopatra, and if Octavian is defeated you will all become slaves to Egypt. This island is an essential part of her plans; its forestry will provide the materials to build Antony a massive fleet for future conquests."

"Tibo has already told me of the notices in the city regarding land seizures…"

"Then you must realise that there is only one way to survive here. Return with me to Greece, and Antony's defeat will ensure this island's freedom."

Damon stood, and for a few moments he watched a lone eagle circling over the great forest. "There are conditions," he said, firmly. "I want ten of your best legionaries guarding my family until this is over. And Tibo stays here."

He looked back at the Roman. "I want your solemn promise, Cornelius, that if the boy has done wrong by the army he will be given a full pardon."

"You have my word, Damon. I respect your wishes and admire your decision. I have business at the garrison now. We will set sail at daybreak."

The two men shook hands and returned to the house: Gallus to say goodbye and Damon to reason with his family.

Chapter XIII

Damon kept himself occupied during the long voyage. Gallus provided the maps he needed and in his small, but comfortable room below the main deck he studied the islands and anchorage in the Ionian Sea. He concluded that the one place where Marc Antony would site his vast fleet and army was in and around the Gulf of Ambracia. He envisaged every move Antony might make on land and sea, and countered it. Being familiar with Antony's military tactics at Philippi was helpful, but Damon was sure a battle at sea was imminent… and this would favour Octavian, especially with Agrippa in command of his fleet.

Gallus had told him all about Agrippa's defeat of Sextus Pompey off the coast of Sicilia. How he created war galleys much heavier in design and capable of ramming Pompey's ships or moving in alongside, and then boarding them in military style attacks with devastating results.

"Agrippa's victory over Sextus Pompey will not be lost on Antony… nor will Pompey's escape," said

Damon, as he and Gallus stood at the prow of the ship. "He will have Cleopatra in mind if he senses defeat."

"But their fleet outnumbers ours, and despite the thousands of troops he lost in Parthia, Antony still has nineteen legions for us to contend with. This is not a situation that warrants a plan of escape," remarked Gallus. "Besides, Pompey's escape was short-lived. After crawling his way back to Antony, he then enlisted another force in Syria. But one of Antony's generals discovered the plot and unlike Lepidus, Pompey was put to death."

Damon shook his head. "So... what's happened to Lepidus?"

"When Pompey's fleet was defeated by Agrippa his legions surrendered to Lepidus, who then thought he could take on Octavian. He failed miserably, and now he's in permanent exile."

Damon smiled. "I can't see Octavian being so lenient with Marc Antony. There's no doubt Agrippa will defeat him at sea, but only the right tactics will trap Antony. He needs a supply route from Egypt, and I believe he'll try to secure the Corinthian Gulf because this passage could also provide an escape route back to Alexandria."

Gallus laughed. "I admire your faith in Agrippa... and I see your point, Damon, but Antony's a military man. He'll fight his war on land, so let's not forget his vast army."

"But surely, the quality of Octavian's troops will balance the odds. I would imagine a large number of Antony's men were recruited from the east; they're not Roman."

Damon pulled his cloak around him from the cool breeze. "If Octavian accepts my ideas there will hardly be any bloodshed on land. Be assured, Cornelius, whoever loses this sea battle will surrender his land forces."

Gallus disagreed, but said nothing. When Damon returned to his quarters he stood for a while, his eyes a searching the night sky. Stars twinkled and the moon cast a silvery light across the ocean. He wondered if Octavian could defeat Antony again and become supreme commander of the Roman Empire. And he thought of a dying man's last wish, hoping the gods would give Damon the strength to survive and return to his beloved family. Gallus smiled at his friend's incredible courage and convictions, and with a final glance at heavens he went below to check on the oarsmen.

Damon gave up any hope of sleep when a drumbeat used for the rowing speed of the oarsmen quickened its pace. He moved a lamp across to his small table and began to write.

Lucius Vario had often encouraged him to record events, his thoughts and wishes, but managing the senator's estate back then there never seemed time. Poetry was only something he admired in others, like Theocritus and Virgil. But slowly, the words began to flow and by dawn a poem of some credibility emerged. Yet he was far from satisfied, and spent endless hours revising it.

Damon completed the poem on their last day at sea and gave it to Gallus as a token of their friendship. "I ask a favour, Cornelius," he said with a smile.

"Then name it!"

"Only break this seal when the war is over. You will understand why when you read the poem."

"Whatever you say, my friend; at least I will have something special to look forward to... if I live that long."

When the two men parted at Octavian's headquarters in Brundisium, it was to be their last farewell. Cornelius Gallus would survive the coming war, and only then did he read Damon's poem… its content amazed him.

Anger was etched on the face of Marc Antony as he paced the deck of his flagship, anchored in the Gulf of Ambracia. He turned his fury on the group of senior officers he had summoned to a meeting. "Why is it when confronted with a simple task, admirals become incompetent fools?" he roared.

It was a question none of the admirals dared to answer. Canidius intervened. "I'm certain the attacks were not Octavian's idea; he hasn't the tactical brains of a goat! We know Agrippa commands their fleet, but even he never resorts to hit and run warfare. It's as though they already knew the location of our ships… our every move. We all expected the assault to come from the north."

"So these four idiots fall asleep in the south!" cried Antony. "Not only did Agrippa take Methone and half the Peloponnesus from them, but he's captured every bloody island in the Ionian Sea and destroyed over a hundred of our vessels! This gave Octavian the freedom to descend on us from Brundisium."

"If the enemy know so much, my lord, then perhaps there's an informer in our midst," said Insteius, nervously.

Antony glared at him. "There's no need for traitors with such incompetent officers like you on the seas," he snarled. "What's happening now in the north?"

The admiral was stunned by the sudden question, and his inability to utter a word enraged Antony even more. But Canidius, calm and assured as ever, took control of the situation.

"Octavian's sixteen legions occupy the Mikhalitzi Hill, some five miles north. Our army outnumbers his and we can handle any military attack he launches. We may have lost the islands, sire, but our main fleet still matches Agrippa's. However, I still believe a land battle will favour us."

Antony felt more at ease. "Thank you, Canidius." He turned to the others. "You had best gather your thoughts; I want a full report from each of you to brief Cleopatra. I should remind you that half of this fleet is Egyptian." He turned away from them with a dismissive gesture, and poured himself and Canidius a large cup of wine.

Octavian's fleet of warships were anchored in the Ionian Sea near the island of Leucas; their eastern flank blockaded the Gulf of Ambracia. The channelled entrance to the Gulf at Actium was narrow; its waters too shallow to allow passage of more than one war galley. On the peninsula either side, Antony had mounted powerful slingshots that ensured enemy ships kept a safe distance from the shore. As it stood, there was no way in for Octavian... no way out for Antony.

Octavian and Agrippa contemplated this on board Octavian's flagship under the sheer north-west cliffs of Leucas. They studied two maps: the first indicated Antony's past and current occupied sites, the latest comprehensive details only reported to Octavian a few hours earlier. A second map, compiled by Damon several days before, was identical.

Agrippa smiled with satisfaction. "What did I tell you? Damon has foreseen Antony's every move! Thanks to him we have Antony and Cleopatra trapped."

Octavian pointed to Actium. "Look at this, he even marked Antony's campsite and how he would fortify the Gulf's entrance," he replied, equally impressed. "His predictions are uncanny; it's as though he was privy to Antony's briefings!" He turned to Agrippa. "By the way, how is Damon?"

"Still resting, I would imagine. He hasn't slept for days."

But Damon was awake... disturbed by the screeching of gulls around the cliffs of Leucas. He felt refreshed despite the constant pain he suffered, and slowly made his way to Octavian's quarters.

Both men greeted him warmly, and over a light meal of fruit and water they decided to take the initiative and force Antony's hand.

"Who commands our army?" Damon asked.

"Titius and Cornelius Gallus," replied Octavian.

"Don't worry, Damon. We have everything in place now, just as you planned," smiled Agrippa.

Damon glanced at the maps. "Your men are well prepared, sire... they can draw water from the nearby river and food from our supply ships in the Gomaros Bay, but Antony will try to draw your legions off the hill. If they hold their positions, his only option is to do battle at sea."

"I agree," said Agrippa, eager to engage the enemy ships again.

"Then I will offer the challenge... to lift the blockade and fight Antony in the open sea."

Both Roman leaders offered war: Octavian at sea and Antony on land, but each refused. But as the stifling heat of late August intensified in the stagnant marshes of Actium, fever and dysentery ravaged through Antony's camp. With no fresh water and dwindling food supplies, his men were dying and deserting in large numbers.

Antony again sent for Canidius and his four admirals: Sosius, Publicola, Insteius and Marcus Octavius... but this time in the presence of Cleopatra.

Canidius was not easily impressed with anything other than Roman ideals, but as he boarded the queen's vessel the splendour of its polished decks, purple sails... and especially her scantily-clad handmaidens, fired his imagination considerably.

Cleopatra smiled at his wandering eyes, as he saluted Antony and politely bowed to her. "Welcome, Canidius. Please join us," she said, gesturing to a couch beside the one she and Antony shared. The four admirals sat grim faced on fold-up chairs.

"Perhaps you will begin, Canidius," said Antony, knowing that his friend would be brutally honest.

"Our army is in serious trouble, my lord. We've lost at least a legion of men from this fever and another from desertions; those who remain grow weaker by the day. Octavian will know this by now because I have news that Quintus Dellius has deserted."

He looked at Cleopatra. "I must now respect the queen's wishes to fight at sea."

Cleopatra smiled at him warmly, and Canidius sensed the sexual aura in her every movement.

Antony addressed his admirals. "We also lost Ahenobarbus. Let's hope his fever spreads to Octavian's camp. This means you, Sosius, are now the senior. I trust you can speak for the other three?" he said, curtly.

"Yes, sire!"

The man who stood to answer was tall and thin; his black hair and beard evoked a sinister look, yet there was a genuine trust in his soft blue eyes. Still offended by

Antony's previous outburst, he was determined to redeem himself. "The fever is of great concern, my lord. We have no alternative but to break out of the Gulf. In doing so, we have a plan on how to engage Agrippa's fleet with a possible escape route if required."

Sosius paused, embarrassed as Cleopatra's eyes met his. "Please go on," she urged.

The admiral cleared his throat. "This disease is rapidly spreading through our rowing crews, and rather than surrender any unmanned ships to Octavian, we suggest they are destroyed."

Antony turned to Cleopatra, who nodded her agreement. "Then burn them!" he said.

Sosius then approached them with a map, and explained his plan of escape. "Before we lost Leucas to Agrippa, I studied how the wind moves around the island. At the eighth hour a good sailing breeze rises up from the north-west, and if we can keep the enemy ships at bay in the open sea it's possible for Queen Cleopatra and a squadron of her ships to sail through."

"Sail through?" Antony laughed.

"Yes, my lord. Unusual in Roman warfare, I know. But if we carry the sails on board ready to hoist... then with sails and powerful oars we can out-run any of their ships."

As the eighth hour approached on the second day in September, a group of bodyguards bearing a litter emerged from the forest on the island of Leucas. The men crossed the grass-covered slopes, and breathing heavily from their arduous climb, they came to a halt near the edge of the north cliffs.

Two of Octavian's henchmen helped Damon from the litter, while another moved closer to the cliff edge. "Over here!" he yelled. "The fleets are already engaged."

Damon walked towards him, thankful for the freshening breeze in his face. Out to sea he could determine the battle formations: Antony's ships had advanced in three squadrons. Agrippa was fighting him in the north, Arruntius in the centre and Lurius, with Octavian on board the nearest squadron to the island.

It was not difficult for Damon to see the outcome, as Antony's ships appeared sluggish and outnumbered. His three squadrons were being hit with a hail of fire-brands and the whole sky seemed ablaze as balls of fire arced through the air with murderous consistency. Damon could hear the clang of grappling irons as Octavian's ships drew alongside the enemy, and then the faint clash of swords as they boarded them. Arrows thudded into flesh, and the cries of death rang out across the water as burning men leapt overboard into a sea darkened with debris and blood.

In the north Agrippa's ships overwhelmed Antony's, and the few that remained surrendered or retreated back to the Gulf. Octavian and Lurius were also victorious, but in an attempt to outflank the enemy on his right Arruntius left a wide margin in the centre.

"By the gods... look there!" pointed one of the guards.

Damon shielded his eyes, and through the billowing smoke and flames he watched in disbelief as the purple sails of Cleopatra's vessel appeared. This was closely followed by a small number of her ships... all of them in full sail.

A light craft brought up the rear, and on board Marc Antony looked back in shame as his ships floundered to defeat. At the north-east corner of Leucas he pulled alongside an Egyptian vessel, casting the boat adrift. Up on the deck, he paused to stem the flow of blood from his gashed forehead. It was then that he noticed a group of men high on the cliff top.

They were Roman except for one, and Antony stared at the man for a long time. The distance was too great to recognise him, but he wore the robes of a Greek. As the Egyptian rowers increased their speed, a cold shiver touched Antony's skin. He knew it was Damon.

Marc Antony went below decks in search of wine. He found a darkened corner and sat on a coil of rope. "It's not over yet," he repeated to himself. "Cleopatra is safe. We have money and treasures in Egypt and Canidius will bring my legions through Macedonia…"

He raised the bottle of wine. "I will rise again!" he cried, without conviction. Then he drank until the images of yet another defeat faded away…

The whole population of Cyprus seemed to have gathered at Nea Paphos for the return of their favourite son. A century of Roman soldiers formed a pathway for Damon along the quayside, each and every one offering a smart salute as he passed them by. At the far end he could see Tibo and Kyriki waiting with his beloved family, and shielding them from the cheering crowds was the ten huge legionaries Gallus had left to guard them.

Even the strength of the cordon around Damon buckled under the force of well-wishers: men, women and children all wanting to touch, or even catch a glimpse of the man who had saved their island from Egyptian rule and slavery. Damon thought he might be swept away by the rush, but a Roman officer was quick to react with an order to double the guard. The man was familiar to

Damon, but without his beard and hair cropped to his skull, he was not easily recognised. He stepped forward offering his hand.

Damon saw the jagged white scar on his arm. "Rufus!" he cried, embracing him, "I knew that drunken old barber would catch up with you one day... or is there a woman?"

Rufus roared with laughter. "It's true! Can you believe I have a most gracious and very rich lady waiting in Ostia for me? But I couldn't retire without saying goodbye to you, my friend... and Tibo, of course!" he grinned.

"Now... stay close to me; the litter-bearers are up ahead with orders to take you and your family home."

Damon followed Rufus until he embraced Hestia and his children, while a deafening cheer greeted their joyful reunion. The celebrations followed them from the harbour to the north gate, through a never-ending shower of flowers and rose-petals thrown from every balcony. It reminded Damon of the day he first met Virgil at Narnia when the Romans were celebrating the goddess, Dianna. He also remembered walking in Rome with Tibo, and the boy's wish to be part of a triumphal march. He glanced behind him, happy to see Tibo and Kyriki waving to the crowds... perhaps his wish came true after all.

A few months later, Octavian reclined on a royal couch in the Palace of the Ptomelies also reflecting on past events. True, the victory at Actium was a hollow one, considering Antony and Cleopatra's escape, but the capture of Alexandria and their subsequent deaths proved his superiority. Canidius had been a thorn in his side, yet he respected the general's courage. The man refused to surrender his legions after the Battle of Actium, and even when they deserted him in vast numbers he journeyed on to Egypt… faithful to Antony until the end.

Octavian should have been elated. Caesar's death was avenged, and now he was the supreme commander of the Roman Empire… and yet, his heart was heavy as he read the letter from Rufus.

"You look troubled, my lord," said Cornelius Gallus, entering his room. "Is there bad news from Rome?"

"No… Rufus tells me that Damon is near to death. Help me, Cornelius, I must go to him."

"A ship will be ready for you at first light. I will see to it personally, sire."

"And the other matter, concerning Antony and Fulvia's son, Antyllus?"

"He's been put to death… and so has Cleopatra's son, Caesarion," said Gallus with a smile. "May I suggest you retire for a few hours while I organise the loading of Cleopatra's treasure; it's already underway."

"Then I must see it for myself."

The two men left the room and entered a long marble and mosaic corridor. Roman guards stood at every doorway and centurions marshalled a continuous line of Egyptian slaves. The men and boys bearing chests encrusted with jewels and weighted with gold, while women carried trays of golden dinnerware and trinkets.

Octavian stared in amazement at this procession of enormous wealth; it would finance his entire army and everything Rome desired for its people. "Wait!" he called to a female slave. "Bring me your tray."

The girl trembled in fear as she placed it at his feet, bowing repeatedly. Octavian removed an object and let the slave girl continue on her way.

Gallus looked on, bewildered. "But sire, you have the entire wealth of the Ptomelies to choose from. May I ask why a simple agate cup?"

"It reminds me of a chalice that once belonged to a very special man. It was the most valuable object Damon ever possessed… yet he smashed it to pieces in order to save my life."

Gallus smiled. "I understand," he said, quietly. "Damon has no need for riches… only the love of his family. May I accompany you to pay my respects, sire?"

"No, I'm afraid there is too much to do here in Egypt. I want you to stay, Gallus. You have served me well over the years, and as reward for your courage and loyalty I am making you governor of all Egypt."

Gallus saluted, thanking his commander for such a great honour. Octavian clasped an arm around his shoulder. "I think you're right, Cornelius, a few hours sleep might do me good."

Gallus watched him go; surprised by the way Octavian had matured. His confidence and charisma was always evident, but there seemed an inner calm and serenity about him. Gallus smiled… this could only be attributed to a good woman, he thought… Octavian's third wife, Livia Drusilla, one of the most beautiful women in Rome…

His demeanour changed abruptly when a slave stumbled behind him and a heavy casket crashed to the floor. Gallus turned to see one of his centurions grab the slave by his hair and haul him to his feet. "Take him out, Publius… but please, no more bloodshed. Just let these creatures see how their new governor rules. The market place will do nicely. Hang him!"

Damon was carried from the house by Octavian's guards and Tibo to his favourite place. He lay where he and Hestia used to sit and watch the night sky fill with stars. A mist began to rise from the valley as the first rays of sunlight caressed the earth, turning the heads of sleepy flowers until a fusion of colour rippled through the high grass. Birdsong filled the air, and Damon watched as wild animals came down the slope to drink at the stream. This was his kind of morning... his last sunrise.

He held out his hands, and in turn Tibo, Kyriki and his family kissed him, each with a lingering embrace. There came the cry of a lone eagle swooping down across the meadow. For a few moments its huge shadow hovered over them... then another cry, and it was gone.

Damon clung on to Hestia and smiled as she traced her fingers over his brow... her touch as soft as a butterfly's wing... her lips taking the last breath of his life.

On the high ridge overlooking Damon's land two men stood beside his tombstone. Octavian placed the agate cup among the flowers and Tibo looked on in silence as the most powerful man in the Roman Empire was reduced to tears.

When Octavian finally turned away from the grave, his pale blue eyes settled on Tibo. "The gods will take care of him now... but his memory must never die. You were a fine and courageous messenger for me, Tibo, so I know you will serve Damon's family with honour."

Tibo stood proud; firmly shaking the hand Octavian offered him. "I will, sire... you have my word as a Roman."

Octavian walked back to the troop of legionaries and mounted his horse, but as they prepared to leave the ridge he held up his hand. "Wait! Did you hear it?" he asked.

The men listened…. only a gentle breeze rustled through the trees. "Sorry, my lord, there's nothing," said Rufus.

Octavian smiled; he was the only one to hear it… the melancholy sound of a shepherd's flute.

Peter Lathe

CUMBRIA

APRIL 4th 1987

Chapter XIV

The coastal road south-west from Bowness-on-Solway leads to the Victorian market town of Silloth. At 3 pm on Sarah's birthday, a young couple sat on a bench there along the promenade. It was a pleasant spot beneath the old bandstand, where the day offered clear views of the Scottish coast and Mount Criffel. As they talked excitedly about their wedding plans, a surprisingly warm breeze drifted in off the Solway.

Joe Adams paused in mid-sentence and suddenly walked to the edge of the promenade. He looked down at the water. In all his twenty-three years he'd never seen this happen before at Silloth. The current had stopped flowing... the sea was perfectly still. Joe stood there amazed as the water level rose dramatically until it was only two feet below him. Then, as if someone had opened a giant sluice-gate, the Solway raced away at incredible speed towards the sea.

"What's wrong, Joe?"

He turned back to his bride-to-be, trying to steady his voice. "Oh… it's nothing, Sue. I think we should go now. What about a trip to Keswick?"

The incident unsettled him, and later he realised his decision to leave Silloth was a blessing… it certainly saved their lives. What Joe Adams witnessed was seen by others along the Solway coastline; but they, unlike him, assumed it to be the turning tide. In fact, this was something far more sinister.

Five minutes after the couple walked away from the sea, a telephone was ringing in the gravedigger's cottage at Bowness-on-Solway. Still fuming over the boy next door breaking a window in his garden shed, George rose from his armchair to answer it. "Yes. What is it?" he snapped.

"Don't yell at me, you old windbag! You shouldn't be snoozing anyway on such a nice day. This is the second time I've called."

"But Elsie, I'm… "

"Never mind, just listen. I saw Reverend Thomas earlier. He needs a lift to Silloth, and I said you'd take him."

"What now? There's some football on TV!"

His wife smiled. "Goodness me, I completely forgot. Anyway, I should think the Reverend's waiting at the lych-gate by now. Oh, and George… "

"Yes, dear?"

"Do drive carefully. You know how nervous he is."

George put down the receiver, and muttered to himself. Missing the game was bad enough, but Elsie was at her sister's again… and this meant cooking his own tea. He took off his overalls, washed his hands and went out to open the garage doors. Inside was his pride and joy: a shiny blue Morris Minor.

George grinned at the throaty roar of its engine as he turned the ignition key. "Now then me little beauty, show me what you can do today," he said.

The vicar was waiting near Lucy's house. Having noticed Sarah and Alice outside, he'd carefully made his way down the steep hill to offer his best wishes for their birthday. George arrived some ten minutes later. He smoothly manoeuvred his Morris Minor in a three-point turn before helping the vicar into the passenger seat. The two girls waved them off, and the shiny blue car purred away back up the hill.

A few hundred yards away from where Sarah and Alice stood, their mothers' discussion on the male ego was interrupted by the return of Tom Walker.

"Well... talk of the devil," laughed Helen, tapping her husband's hand as he reached for a sausage roll.

He smiled, kissing her cheek. "Hi, Lucy," he said, as their eyes met. "What time's your friend due back from London?"

"About five, I guess."

"I hope he's hungry. Just look at this food," he said, rubbing his hands together. "I'm starving!"

"Don't they ever feed you at the golf club?" Helen teased, placing a few morsels on a plate for him. "There you are. Now go watch TV or something while Lucy and I finish the girls' birthday cake."

Tom winked at Lucy, and kissed Helen again before leaving the kitchen. He went upstairs to the spare room, smiling as he thought how much happier Lucy seemed lately. Whoever Ben Miller was, he'd certainly made a big impression.

Walker was handsome in a rugged way. His muscular frame imposed strength and fitness, but he was a gentle and dedicated family man. A skilled carpenter by trade, he was well liked in the small community and could often be seen next door helping two elderly brothers restore their old rowing boat.

The spare room also reflected his passion for sport with an array of trophies. Cups and medals for golf, swimming and tennis filled a large cabinet, while on top of it stood Alice's awards for swimming.

He put down his now empty plate, and picked up the shield his daughter had won at school, three years in a row. He felt particularly proud of this one because he'd taught both Alice and Sarah to swim at an early age.

The carpenter sat down, turning his attention to an Admiralty Chart of the Solway Firth spread out on his desk. Although the archaeologists had left the village, reports were circulating now of plans to construct a tidal barrage across the Solway from Bowness to Annan in Scotland. 'A feasibility study in Renewable Tidal Technology' they called it, but Tom Walker was doing his own calculations on behalf of the village committee. Protection of the environment and its wildlife was a priority in this area.

His measurements from the chart in nautical miles noted the intended dam would be 1.5 miles in length. A parallel line west from Bowness to the Irish Sea was a distance of 42 miles. At this point, a vertical line from St Bees Head across the mouth of the Solway Firth to the Mull of Galloway was almost identical: 42.5 miles.

Tom's calculations proved significant to one critical issue... the fault system located in the Irish Sea. Ironically, Walker had highlighted its proximity on his chart. But he, nor anyone else, could foresee what was already in motion.

Before he arrived home and George's car left Bowness, this fault was activated when Joe Adams saw the Solway waters surge away from him in Silloth. The ocean floor had erupted in the Irish Sea with a huge earthquake, and Cumbria was about to suffer the worst disaster in its history.

Although the earthquake was smaller on the Richter scale than the one in 1607 which struck the Bristol Channel, it produced the same devastating result. Both estuaries are funnel-shaped, and a tidal wave reaching a constricted space proves catastrophic.

Unlike a tsunami out in the deeper oceans which can travel at the speed of a jet aircraft, the wave striking the Solway entrance moved significantly slower in the shallower water. Nevertheless, it increased in both height and speed as it roared through the coastal villages, leaving a trail of death and destruction.

In the aftermath, onlookers had reported a wave some twelve feet high and seemingly endless in length approaching the coast, but the wave hit Maryport before emergency bulletins were broadcast on television and radio. By then it was too late. After such a bad spell of weather, most people were outdoors making the most of a dry, sunny afternoon.

George was in a more cheerful mood driving from the village, as the Reverend Thomas praised his vintage car. "I thought we'd take the coast road to Silloth, only she could do with a run," he said. "The old battery needs charging up a bit."

"That's fine with me, George. I've got plenty of time," the vicar replied.

George nodded his appreciation and said: "The verse you gave our mason for the headstone was most appropriate, Reverend."

"Well thank you. Henry liked it as well, and you know how fussy he is doing inscriptions."

"Oh, by the way," said George, "did that chap, Miller, come back to see you?"

"No. Speaking to young Sarah just now, she mentioned he's in London." The vicar tapped George's arm. "Don't worry, my friend, he'll never find anything."

George chuckled. "No-one ever will now."

After some four miles they passed through Cardunnock, a small village along the estuary. It was here that George felt the steering wheel judder in his hands. He knew at once it was a puncture and quickly stopped the car.

"I'm sorry, Reverend," he groaned, "but the front tyre's gone. Can you get out while I jack up the car?"

As the vicar struggled out on his walking stick, George opened the car boot to retrieve the jack and spare wheel. The road was narrow, so the vicar stood on the grass verge opposite, saying: "I'll give you a shout if I see anything coming, George."

The gravedigger prised off the hubcap. "They say bad luck comes in threes, don't they Reverend? Well this is the second today."

"The second?"

"Oh, that rogue of a boy next door broke my shed window earlier. Makes me wonder what I'm in for with number three!"

George didn't have long to wait. As he loosened the last wheel-nut there was a low rumble like distant thunder. Both men turned to face the oncoming force racing towards them over the Cardunnock Flats. The

Reverend Thomas raised his walking stick in a feeble effort to protect himself. George was frozen to the spot in fear as the thirty foot wave tossed them away like driftwood.

Their remains were later found on Bowness Common some two miles away. In the same area George's shiny blue Morris Minor lay wedged high in the boughs of an oak tree.

Alice's ankle was hurting again, and she was impatient to see what was happening at home. They would be waiting for them now. "Come on, Sarah," she called up the stairs, "it's nearly time for our party." As if by magic the telephone rang; it was her mother asking if they were ready.

Meanwhile, Sarah was checking Ben's room one last time. She wanted it to be really nice for his return. He's so kind to ring me this morning, she thought, considering his father's just died. Sarah smiled with satisfaction at her housework and went towards the door. In passing the window she noticed the darkness. At first glance it seemed like a black storm cloud over the Solway... but there was something strange about it. Her eyes were drawn to the skyline, where the cloud rolled over in cascades of dazzling whiteness. It seemed as though a myriad of stars were falling from the heavens.

Seconds ticked away before Sarah realised the cloud heading towards her was an enormous wall of water. She screamed for Alice as she raced down the stairs. Her friend was just answering the phone when Sarah grabbed her hand. "Run, Alice! For God's sake, run with me!"

In those terrifying moments the girls had no more than three minutes to live.

Ben Miller opened his eyes as the last of the Cumbrian fells flashed by his window seat on the train. It had been a tiring and eventful trip to London, and he was relieved when the train slowed on its approach to Carlisle Station. He looked at his watch and smiled, almost 4:20pm. Lucy and Sarah would be waiting for him now, and he felt overjoyed to be seeing them again. Ben hoped that Sarah would be as happy as he was to know he was her real father.

Miller walked briskly from the station to find an unusual gathering outside. There was confusion everywhere with TV crews, radio and a familiar throng of reporters piling into cars and vans. Distant sirens wailed in the city, as police cars and ambulances raced through the streets.

Miller stopped a female reporter. "Excuse me. What's going on?"

"Haven't you heard?" she said, her voice trembling. "A tidal wave has devastated the Solway Coast. The death toll is high with hundreds more still missing."

Miller caught his breath, trying to absorb the sudden shock to his system.

The young woman saw the colour drain from his face. "Are you alright?"

"I… I have to get to Bowness," he said, struggling for some composure. "My family's there."

The reporter took hold of his arm. "You have children? I'll help you get your car through this lot."

"No, I… I need a taxi."

She walked him across the road. "Here's my car. Jump in, I'm heading that way."

Miller remembered very little of the journey, only the sound of rescue helicopters overhead, and at some point the reporter kindly pulling over at a phone box for him.

His hand was shaking when he dialled Lucy's number. There was nothing… not even a tone. He searched his pocket notebook and found the Walker's number. Miller dialled again. No answer. He let it ring… nothing.

They drove on to within a mile of Bowness to where a police car blocked the road. A constable approached them and the reporter opened the car window.

"Sorry, madam, you'll have to go back," he said. "The road ahead is under water."

"But this man needs to reach his family."

The policeman moved nearer, resting his hand on the roof of the car to peer in at Miller. "I'm sorry, sir, but there's no way in or out of Bowness. The village is virtually isolated until the water recedes."

"What about the rescue helicopters. Have they been in there?" asked Miller.

"I'm afraid not, sir. All our emergency services are working flat out. Every village along the estuary has been severely hit by the flood waters."

The reporter thanked him and quickly reversed away. She turned her car and drove a short distance before turning down a narrow track. "Hang on, it's a bumpy ride but I'll get us close to the village."

"I'm sorry," said Miller;" I don't even know your name, but thanks for helping me. I'm Ben Miller."

"Emma Dixon. I work on the 'Chronicle'," she said, bringing the car to a sudden halt.

A fallen tree lay across the track, and a thicket of brambles and nettles covered the rest.

"Damn it!" cried Emma. "This lane used to lead up to a field just behind the farm." She smiled at Miller. "I had a boyfriend in Bowness a few years ago. We used to…er, do our courting along here."

They left the car and walked to a nearby gate. From here they could see the village, and Miller tried not to imagine what he might find there.

For the first time, he noticed the young woman beside him. She was tall and attractive with short dark hair and a ready smile. Emma had a motherly air about her despite her age… early twenties, he guessed.

"Is that the farm you mentioned, Emma?" he asked, pointing to the eastern slopes.

"Yes. Come on, follow me, Ben. Your things will be okay in the car."

"No, Emma. This is as far as you go. It could be dangerous up there."

"Hey, I'm a big girl now… and a reporter, remember?" she said, waving her camera at him. "Anyway, you get used to this kind of thing."

Miller nodded. "I'm sure you do, but you think you can walk across three meadows in those heels?"

"Oh, goodness me... er, just wait right there," she said, trotting back to the car.

Miller called out that she could leave his clothes, but to bring his briefcase. Before he'd opened the rusted bolt on the gate, she was standing beside him in her gumboots.

The last field was boggy. Miller lost a shoe several times and was caked in mud when they eventually reached the farmhouse. A foot of water was running off the road, flooding the farmyard and pouring through an open door.

"Hello! Is anyone here?" yelled Miller. No-one answered, so he looked inside. A half-eaten sandwich and a mug of cold tea lay on the kitchen table, but again there was no reply to his call. He managed to shut the door, and then began to run as hard as he could up to the road.

On either side of the street men, women and children battled with the flow of water, using anything at hand to block their doorways. His heart was pounding with the effort of running through the knee-deep water, but relief swept over him when he saw Lucy.

She stood in the grounds of a house elevated above the road. He called her name, and when she ran towards him he could see the pain and anguish on her face. Lucy burst into tears as he held her in his arms; her words intangible through the sobs.

A couple had followed Lucy, and the woman offered Miller a weak smile. "You must be Ben?" she said, softly. I'm Lucy's friend, Helen. Come to the house, my husband will explain."

Miller looked to the man beside her.

"Hello, Ben. How on earth did you get here?"

"A reporter brought me across the fields to a farm back there."

Walker offered his hand. "I'm Tom, Alice's father…" At the mention of his daughter's name, his voice faltered. There was a long pause before he said: "Alice and Sarah are missing. There's no hope, Ben. They were at Lucy's when the wave…"

Miller could see tears in the man's eyes, and he put a comforting hand on his shoulder.

A short distance away, Emma Dixon watched them wade back through the water in silence. She thanked the spotty-faced youth at her elbow, who seemed fascinated by the speed of her shorthand as she noted his comments. His information was genuine enough for Emma, as the boy lived in Bowness and went to the same school as Sarah and Alice. He knew the Walker's and Sarah's mum quite well, but not the tall guy with her.

The reporter was pleased with herself for meeting Ben Miller. Whoever he was she would soon find out. He was her 'human interest', and together with the drowned girls and others entombed in their houses… this could be a real scoop for her.

Emma Dixon sighed as she closed her notebook, visualising her name on a front page editorial… "Ben Miller is a lovely guy," she told herself, "but I have a job to do. There's no room for sentiment here."

Up at the house the two couples sat in the kitchen after drying out. Lucy was in a borrowed skirt of Helen's, with Ben wearing a pair of Tom's jeans, tightly belted around his slimmer waistline, and trainers. He held Lucy's hand, and feeling her tremble with grief, the loss of Sarah began to hurt him deeply. First Robert, then his father, and now his lovely daughter…

Helen touched his shoulder, and gave him a mug of tea. Ben asked her: "Can you be sure the girls were in the house?"

"Yes. I spoke to Alice on the phone…" She stopped and sat down, raising a hand to her lips as she began to cry.

Tom put his arm around her. "We rang to see if they were ready for their party," he said. "Then Helen heard Sarah scream. Alice must have dropped the phone when Sarah shouted for her to run."

"Was there anything else?"

Helen was drying her eyes. "Lucy came over then and she heard…"

Ben turned to Lucy. "They must have been in the hall," she said, "because Helen heard Sarah coming down the stairs. I… I just heard Sarah say: 'We have time to hide… Run!' Then the door banged shut."

Miller's thoughts were racing as Walker added: "As you can imagine, Lucy and Helen were hysterical by then. I took the phone from Lucy and kept calling out to the girls. Then after a while I heard this almighty roar and shattering of glass, as though the whole house was caving in. After this, the line was broken."

"I know it's difficult, Tom, but how long would you say it was before you heard that loud noise?"

Tom rubbed his forehead. "I really don't know. A couple of minutes, maybe. Why?"

"There could be a slim chance…"

All three were looking at Ben now, their eyes pleading for any kind of miracle.

"Do you have a detailed map of the village, Tom?"

"Sure, it's upstairs," he said, quickly leaving the room.

Helen cleared the table, and her husband spread out the map. He calculated the information requested by Miller, who then read out what he'd written.

"If you say the water level is twenty yards down from the road junction, this means Lucy's house at the bottom of the hill is about thirty feet under water. The church, however, could be accessible because here the depth is about twelve feet." He looked at Walker. "We need to get down there."

Somewhat confused, Walker said: "But why? The church must be nearly a hundred yards away."

Lucy reluctantly agreed. "It is, Ben… and Alice had hurt her ankle at school yesterday. They would never reach the church in time up that hill."

Miller held up his hand. "You're right… and the girls must have been terrified, but they're also bright and sensible. What Sarah said about having time to hide meant she had somewhere in mind. I think I know where it is."

He turned to Walker. "I'll tell you more later. We have to get inside that church fast. It may not be the answer, but it's our only chance."

"Okay. I'm still a fair swimmer. If we can…" Walker paused. "Wait a minute… the boat! We finished the rowing boat next door. Come on, let's go!"

They all raced to their neighbour's house, and the two brothers quickly opened their shed doors. Miller grabbed a coil of rope and tossed it into the boat, while Walker called two men across the street for some help. They half-carried, half-pushed the boat until it could be launched down the hill in deeper water.

Lucy threw her arms around Miller. "Please, Ben, find our Sarah," she whispered.

The realisation of how much they all depended on him was too emotional for words. He kissed Lucy and held on to her as if it was their last embrace.

A camera clicked several times, and Emma Dixon shouted: "Wait for me! I'm coming with you."

But she was too late. The two men had leapt into the boat and a group of burly Cumbrian lads pushed it out.

Chapter XV

Miller's stomach began to churn as he sensed the depth of water. It was an eerie sight rowing down a street with only the chimneys and rooftops visible on the small cottages. They rounded the bend and among the debris, remains of the lych-gate floated on the surface. As they rowed towards the church, Walker was pleased to see how well it had survived the ferocity of the tidal wave. Even the two stained-glass windows above water level seemed intact, and the apex of the entrance porch was clearly visible. He sighed with relief. There was a way in.

"Over there, Ben, beside the porch," he said.

They manoeuvred the boat and Tom lowered himself over the side. "I'll check out the door first," he said, taking a deep breath before disappearing under the water. When he surfaced again he was gasping for air. "It's okay… we can get in. There's a small window beside the main door, and thankfully I can't see much water inside the church."

He held onto the boat with one hand, brushing water from his face with the other. "The only problem is when we open the main door; the volume of water filling the porch will quickly pitch us inside."

"There is another problem," said Miller. "I can't swim."

"What? You must be crazy! I'll have to go in alone. You row back and get someone else."

"There's no time! You won't even know where to look for the girls without me." Miller picked up the rope and looping it over his head he secured it under his armpits. He tossed the other end to Walker. "Here… grab this. Just pull me where I have to go."

Walker was astonished. He thought Miller was either completely mad or very brave, but it seemed pointless to argue now. He held the boat steady as Miller gripped the side and lowered himself into the water.

"Take a deep breath, Ben, and fill your lungs before you go under," said Walker. "Just try to relax, okay? I'll guide you."

The silence below was deafening to Miller. It seemed as though his eardrums would explode. He had no control of his limbs, drifting away until Walker tugged on the rope. They were at the porch door before Miller opened his eyes, and Walker signalled for them both to push the main door.

For several seconds Miller felt like he was drowning. The memory of someone pulling him up by his hair came back as he found himself sitting with his back against a stone wall. He untied the rope still attached to him, breathing deeply again as he looked around.

To his right, the west windows bowed inwards and water spouted from the small broken segments of glass. Near the pulpit where he'd sat with Reverend Thomas, dust particles drifted through coloured bands of fading light from the stained-glass windows. A few prayer cushions floated past him down the centre aisle, and there was a shoe... the foot inside it bloody and twisted.

"Tom!" he called, heaving himself to his feet. Dazed, he stumbled towards the aisle. Walker lay motionless and partly face down in several inches of water. Miller turned him over, relieved the man was still breathing. He had a nasty cut to his forehead and his left ankle was certainly broken. As the force of water from the porch threw Miller between the pews, it had smashed Walker against them. He was still unconscious when Miller struggled to lift him.

The sheer pain in his ankle roused Walker. He was lying on a pew; his injured foot resting on a cushion with another under his head. There was no sign of Ben.

Miller stood in six inches of water as he searched every drawer and cupboard in the vestry before finding a flashlight. Then he opened the door leading down to the cellar, and water cascaded down the concrete steps after him. He shone the torch slowly left to right across the floor until he saw it... the cover of the well Sarah had mentioned.

Ben checked around its rim; it was rusted in. A nearby open door revealed the boiler room, and in the corner his light picked out a garden fork and spade. Under his breath Miller thanked old George, the gravedigger. He grabbed the tools and set to work on the cover. He jammed the spade all around the edge, the sound echoing in the cellar like claps of thunder. Then as he paused to wipe the sweat from his eyes, he thought he heard Tom. He raised his head, listening more intently.

And there it was again… a faint knocking. But not from Walker… this was below his feet!

"Sarah! Alice!" he shouted, ramming the fork now into the rusted metal with all his strength. At his third attempt the cover buckled as the prongs went clean through. Then he tried again with the spade along the edges… and it moved.

Ben Miller sighed with relief, for as he knelt by the gaping hole in the cellar floor a blast of cold air rushed into his face. He was overwhelmed when the beam of torchlight pierced the musty blackness. The cylindrical shaft was narrow and not deep enough for a well, but it was what he'd prayed for… an escape route for the girls.

In that amazing moment he heard a voice… Sarah's!

"Hold on, Sarah! I'm coming to get you!" he yelled, his heart pounding.

Miller secured the rope to a stone pillar, and then abseiled down into the hole. He found himself in a much larger concrete cylinder, and realised at once it was no ordinary tunnel, but a rare piece of engineering. This was an ingenious and integral part of ancient *Maia* and Hadrian's Wall. He reached out, touching the rough curvature of a Roman aqueduct.

It ran as straight as an arrow, and although crouched over with his knees bent he could still walk, albeit slow and crab-like, along the aqueduct. Even though he couldn't yet see the girls, he never stopped calling words of encouragement to them. Thirty… forty… fifty yards he struggled on through the mud and slime. Then he saw a flash of yellow and red in his torchlight… and two pale but beautiful faces smiling at him. They were huddled together shivering from the cold. "Happy birthday, you two!" was all he could say, and taking them both in his arms was one of the happiest moments of his life.

Back in the cellar, Ben retrieved the rope and led the girls up to the vestry. While they washed away the mud and grime, Miller opened a tall cupboard which held the neatly folded pile of choir robes he'd seen earlier. Sarah and Alice wrapped themselves in them, and the colour slowly began to return to their cheeks.

As Miller washed off his own mud, the door from the chancel opened and water rushed in. Alice gasped at the sight of her father.

Blood still trickled from his temple, but the pain in his eyes turned to tears of happiness as he held his daughter. He looked at Miller. "You're a crazy but courageous sod," he smiled. "How can we ever repay you, Ben?"

"Well just think of a way out of here, and we'll call it even," said Miller.

Unlike a pair of bank robbers who would first plan an escape route, both men had focussed entirely on finding their daughters. Getting in the church was dangerous enough… getting out now seemed impossible.

Their answer came in the sound of shattering glass as the west windows finally crumbled and great torrents of water poured in.

"We'll be buried alive if we go down the cellar," cried Walker. Our only chance is to climb above the top of the porch door and wait for the water to rise."

Sarah nodded. "Yes, and then we can open the main door."

Miller's eyes were fixed on a small wooden cross hanging on the vestry wall. "I have an idea," he said, rushing out into the chancel.

He worked feverously with Sarah and Alice beside him, helping as best they could. Using the existing row of pews against the north wall, they dragged pews across them filling the aisle to form a buttress. Miller then stood on the pew nearest the porch and tossed the coiled rope high over an enormous roof beam. He tied it to the pew's leg, and then slowly hauled upwards until it rested on a ledge in the wall. With the other end wedged against pews in the aisle, it set the desired angle above the door. Miller climbed up, and satisfied it would stand their combined weight, he slid down again.

In the vestry, Walker was making a splint for his ankle. He'd broken two laths from a cupboard shelf and tore strips from a choir robe, but almost passed out with the agony of binding it to his broken ankle. He wiped the sweat from his face before placing his foot to the floor. It felt easier now in the water. He sat in the vicar's chair and waited.

Another fifteen minutes passed, and his negative thoughts began to multiply. What could Ben possibly do to keep them all above the water? Even if they get out, what will they do if the boat's drifted away? It probably has. The girls would make the swim... I might, but Ben can't swim a bloody stroke! Do we leave him to drown in the church? "And where are these damn emergency services?" he said aloud.

"Dad, we're ready," beamed Alice from the doorway. She kissed her father. "Will you be okay?"

"Sure I will, if your uncle Ben lends me his shoulder to lean on."

Miller was at his side now, taking the weight of his injured friend as he hobbled down the aisle. Sarah and Alice were in front, sweeping prayer cushions, church magazines and hymn books away from their path. As they reached the ramp, the three south-facing windows bulged simultaneously before exploding in a shower of glass and lead. The force of water through the far window tore up the pulpit, smashing it to pieces in the transept. They all watched in silence as its remains floated alongside the lectern's broken eagle.

Miller helped Walker to sit astride the pew's seat, and watched as the carpenter began to heave himself up to the top. Alice followed her father while Miller turned to Sarah. She was no longer there.

Sarah waded through water up to her waist now towards the west wall. Before Miller could move she stood between the two widows. With water thundering down on either side, she took a hanging rope in both hands and pulled. The bell never tolled. She tried again, but there was nothing except for the anxious voices calling her back. Sarah let go but grabbed the second rope. This time the bell rang out loud and clear.

Storm clouds gathered over Bowness, and in the fading light villagers braced themselves for more danger. Water levels were starting to rise again as the incoming tide surged across the Solway's wider, and now unrestricted route. In the village streets men were adding more strength to the two dams they'd built. Fashioned mainly from garage doors, supported front and back with an array of ruined furniture, they looked crude but effective. One stood below the school, and the second across the road junction up the hill from the church. It was here where Lucy and Helen stood on a makeshift platform being comforted by neighbours. People had battled through the deluge, and hoped beyond hope the dams would now hold back the tide.

"Have you always lived here, Helen?"

Helen turned to the young woman beside her. "Tom and I got married here seventeen years ago," she smiled.

Emma Dixon made a mental note. "And you, Lucy?"

"I moved here shortly after… but I'm divorced now."

"Oh, I thought Ben Miller was your husband?"

Lucy was reluctant to say anymore. She was grateful to Emma for getting Ben here, but the less she knows the better. "Ben's a dear cousin of mine," she replied.

Emma looked at her, unable to hide her disappointment. "Oh, right," she nodded. "He did say he had family here."

Lucy smiled, inwardly before turning… as everyone else did on hearing the shouts.

"Look out! Here it comes!" yelled someone running up from the school.

The fresh torrent of water had already hit the dam, but their structure held firm. The water level also rose up the hill but settled within a few feet from the second dam. As the cheers subsided into tears and laughter, another sound echoed through the village. Their own church bell was ringing…

Water was rising fast inside the church as its four weary occupants waited. Miller, aware of only one decision he could make, turned to Walker. "It's nearly time for you to take the girls, Tom."

Both Sarah and Alice looked at him. "What do you mean, Ben?" asked Sarah, disbelieving what she'd just heard.

"There's no other way, Sarah. I… I can't swim."

Alice turned to her father. "But we can help him, can't we, dad?"

Before Walker could answer, Ben said, quietly. "Your father helped me in here, Alice. And yes, with a little luck I might reach the outside, but what then? You will never be able to get me any further. There's no sign of rescue outside. We would all drown."

Sarah started to cry. "I'm not leaving you here to die," she sobbed.

Ben put his arms around her, and for one fleeting moment he wanted to tell her she was his daughter... to say how much he loved her. But he said: "Hey... it's your birthday, remember? And your mum's out there waiting for you."

Sarah shook her head, clinging on to him. "No, I can't."

Then Tom spoke softly to her. "It's Ben's wish, Sarah. He doesn't want your mum to lose you as well."

The porch door disappeared as Alice kissed Miller's cheek and jumped into the water. Then Walker embraced him. "I'll never forget what you've done for us, my friend."

Ben smiled as they shook hands. "Be sure to get back safely, Tom." He turned back to Sarah, gently taking her face in his hands. "Come on, sweetheart, it's time to go."

When his daughter looked at him, Ben saw the image of Lucy... the same soft green eyes and blonde hair. He held her once more. "Tell your mum I love her," he whispered.

Sarah nodded, and kissed his cheek. Then suddenly she was in the water beside Alice and Tom. Ben reached down, and for a few precious moments he held Sarah's hand. Then her fingers slipped away and she was gone.

Ben Miller looked around him at the vast expanse of water and shivered. Only half the organ pipes and windows were visible now in the chancel and transept. And water still poured in through the south and west windows. He edged along the ramp as high as he could, hoping for a few minutes more.

His thoughts turned to Robert... his smiling face, and his voice calling him from that frozen lake. And now he could see Lucy… holding out her hands to him; her eyes filled with love. Then Sarah was chasing him from the garden… her laughter echoing around him. Miller found himself smiling. Strangely, he felt no fear of dying, but an overwhelming desire to live as his eyes fixed on something in the water.

The two bell ropes had floated out away from the wall. They were still yards away, but with a good leap I could halve the distance, he thought. No, if I jumped I'd sink like a stone when I hit the water. But a shallow dive would propel me nearer. Come on! You're going to drown anyway. Give it a try…

With his left hand on the wall for support, Miller slowly rose to his feet. The pew moved slightly, its cast iron leg screeching along the ledge. He froze in panic, but it held. Without knowing when or how, the next thing Miller remembered was gulping for air as he broke the surface within a few feet of the ropes.

In sheer desperation he kicked out his feet, forcing his upper body forward. As he did so, he reached out his right hand clutching at the nearest rope. He managed a last breath of air before the swirling waters engulfed him.

The roaring sound above him had faded away when Miller opened his eyes. It was dark and silent. He vaguely felt his leg grazing against the stone font. There was something in his fingers, too… a rope! He held on, then clasping it with both hands he pulled. The rope tightened and he began to haul himself upwards. His lungs were a bursting point as he reached the surface, but the thunderous sound of falling water was music to his ears.

When Tom Walker surfaced in the freezing waters outside, Sarah and Alice were right beside him. There was no sign of the boat. The water had not only risen but was moving towards them. "It's the tide!" he yelled. "Swim as hard as you can."

Sarah and Alice reached the submerged roadway ahead of Walker, who was clearly in trouble. Where the old lych-gate once stood the girls turned back to help him. They guided Walker across to the rooftop of the nearest cottage where he clung on to its chimney. "You go on without me, Alice. I'll be fine here. Just get some help," he gasped.

It was raining when they swam away again as fast as they could. Fifty yards on, side by side, they saw what looked like a blockade up at the junction.Behind it, hopes had been raised by the tolling bell; their mothers' sharing an unshakable belief in the two men they loved.

As darkness fell with the rain over Bowness, a beam of light searched its stricken homes. Villagers shouted and shone torches up at the helicopter as it hovered above them. All eyes were fixed on a man being winched down to them.

The paramedic landed, shouting to be heard over the rotor blades. "Is there anyone injured or stranded here?" he yelled.

Two voices rang out. "Over here! We need help. Please... over here!"

No-one had even noticed Sarah and Alice standing there in the shallow water. The beam of light circled them now and several men were clambering over the dam to help them.

Lucy and Helen cried tears of joy as they hugged their daughters, now wrapped in thick warm blankets. The paramedic signalled to his pilot and a few minutes later, mothers and daughters were all winched on board. As the helicopter lifted again and swept down towards the church, two more arrived in the stricken village.

Ben Miller was exhausted. Only half way up the west wall his strength failed him. So near to the safety of the belfry… yet his hands were numb with cold and barely able to hold on. With his back against the stone wall, he looked across at the second rope Sarah pulled to ring the bell. It was out of reach. He could not remember the last time he prayed, but vowed if the Lord gave him the strength to survive he would…

It is said that in the moments before death all things become clear. Ben Miller never realised this until the rope slipped through his fingers and he was falling…

Less than a hundred yards away, the helicopter hovered over a submerged cottage. Tom Walker smiled, raising a hand to wave as the light focussed on him. On board, Sarah was breaking the news to Lucy about Ben's sacrifice. They were huddled together crying, while Alice and Helen watched anxiously as Tom was lifted to safety.

The medic turned to Helen. "We need to get to the hospital. He's dehydrated and needs surgery on his ankle. I want the girls checked over also. They've been through quite an ordeal."

She nodded, holding Tom's hand. He tried to smile at her but felt a cold swab on his leg, and the needle rendered him unconscious.

Lucy grabbed the medic's arm. "Please… I beg you. Just try the church for me. There's someone trapped inside."

The man looked at her, and then glanced across as the helicopters light raked over the church. He swallowed hard. Nobody can possibly be alive in there, he thought. "I'm really sorry," he said, "but we have to get the girls and this gentleman to Emergency." He patted her hand.

"Two more crews are here, though. Our pilot will send one there to check."

Lucy looked at Sarah, each feeling the others pain and despair as the helicopter climbed and veered away. In seconds the church disappeared and everything in their lives seemed meaningless without Ben.

CUMBRIA

25 YEARS LATER

Chapter XVI

The briefcase Ben Miller had left at the Walker's house on his return from London, contained some remarkable information about the Greek slave, Damon. Many years after the Solway Disaster, Miller's daughter Sarah wrote a book based on her father's life and his research. The publication of 'Fallen Heroes' created a great deal of media attention because at the end of her book Sarah featured her father's *'Dramatis Personae'*. As a result, academics in Roman History conducted an investigation. Arguments raged, but Ben Miller's theory was accepted… and suddenly Damon was no longer the forgotten hero of Rome.

These are Ben Miller's last published words…

DRAMATIS PERSONAE

The following list is not comprehensive but contains a number of prominent survivors from the year 30 BC. Based on examples of historical fact I am now totally convinced, not only of Damon's existence, but his close relationship with these important Roman figures.

MARCUS AGRIPPA… He was the man widely acclaimed as the tactical genius in most of Octavian's victories on land and sea. Agrippa was his general, admiral and lifelong friend. His achievements in Rome's architecture and other fields were unsurpassed in his lifetime. A healthy individual compared to his ailing friend, and yet Agrippa died aged fifty-one. Octavian outlived him by twenty-five years.

GAIUS MAECENAS… A wealthy Patron of the Arts, he was a friend, confidant and political advisor to Octavian. His guidance was paramount to the young Roman's rise to power. Despite their alleged differences in later years, Maecenas bequeathed to Octavian his entire estate.

CORNELIUS GALLUS… A few years after Octavian made him governor of Egypt, Gallus lost thousands of men in a needless campaign against the Nubian Kingdoms. A furious Octavian replaced him as governor, confiscated his estates and banished him from Rome. Exiled in shame after such a brilliant career, Gallus took his own life.

PUBLIUS VERGILIUS MARO… 'Virgil' was arguably Rome's greatest poet. While travelling from Greece to Rome at Octavian's request in 19 BC, he caught a fever and died at Brundisium. His work on the 'Aeneid' was unfinished. Virgil's last wish was for the poem to be destroyed, but Augustus (Octavian) intervened and, much to the relief of poetry lovers throughout the world, he ordered its publication.

OCTAVIA… Sister to Octavian, she was greatly admired and respected in Rome for her humanity and nobility. She epitomised Roman feminine virtues. Octavia had three children with Marcellus, and two daughters with Marc Antony. When he died she even became guardian to his three children with

Cleopatra. Octavia never married again. She died in 11BC and Octavian built numerous temples and buildings to honour her memory.

OCTAVIAN… At the age of thirty-three he was supreme leader of the Roman Empire. Some three years later the Roman Senate honoured him as Caesar Augustus, the first emperor of Rome. His reign brought relative peace to Rome for the first time in two centuries. Known as the Pax Romana - the Roman Peace - it continued long after his death until 180 AD.

Caesar Augustus died in 14 AD. He was seventy-six years old: a remarkable age considering a lifetime of poor health. On his death the Roman Senate declared him a god. Among the many honours bestowed upon him the month of Sextilius was changed to August, and his name Caesar or Augustus was adopted by every subsequent emperor of Rome.

All Roman aristocratic families, particularly someone as prominent as Octavian, would have numerous slaves and bodyguards. Many accompanied their master in times of military conflict. A Roman stone bearing Damon's name can verify this… but I wonder if it will ever be found again?

When a specialist in Roman Nomenclature saw the Latin words from the stone, he concluded that Damon must have been one of Octavian's slaves. He also agreed the slave had died before his master became the emperor Augustus in 27 BC.

In addition to the Roman stone, there are three intriguing references that exist among ancient writings. Two of them are poems.

Qasr Ibrim was once a cliff-top fortress on the edge of the Nile in southern Egypt. More than forty years ago, excavations there revealed numerous Latin papyrus', including fragments of the elegiac poetry of Cornelius Gallus. On another occasion, a single poem was found, and references to Octavian, Antony and

Cleopatra at the Battle of Actium are unmistakable. But more importantly, the poem was written by an unknown Greek - and dated before the conflict! This means the poet must have been someone with intimate knowledge of Octavian's tactical plans. It also speaks of life thereafter in Octavian's favour. The poet's words are his vision of the future Pax Romana.

Secondly, during the period Damon spent in Rome, Virgil was writing the 'Bucolics' - or his 'Eclogues'. After a rather uneventful life the poet came under the patronage of Maecenas, and therefore part of the inner-circle of friends around Octavian.

Virgil honoured them in his poetry. He composed and dedicated the 'Georgics' to Maecenas, and featured Octavian in all three of his major works. He honours his friend Cornelius Gallus in the tenth book of his Eclogues. So... is it any surprise that in his eighth Eclogue, Virgil writes of Damon and his shepherd's flute?

'... The cold shadows of night had scarcely left heaven, the time when dew on young grass is most delicious to the flock; Damon settled to the smooth olivewood and began like this...'

The final source is an agate cup. In 'The Lives of the Twelve Caesars', the Roman historian and biographer Suetonius, writes of Octavian's distinct lack of extravagance following his victory in Alexandria:

'... the only loot he took from the Palace of Ptomelies was a single agate cup...'

Octavian was already a wealthy man without these vast Egyptian treasures... so what prompted him to take a simple agate cup? The only logical explanation is for a memento or a gift.

On the island of Cyprus in 1982, a farmer was planting vines on a ridge in the foothills of the Troodos Mountains. The cup he found was taken to the Cyprus Museum. It was made from agate, of Egyptian origin... and dated to around 30 BC.

I am no expert in ancient history, and hardly a man of importance now in the literary world... but perhaps one day someone will continue my research and give Damon his rightful place in history.

★ ★ ★

The anniversary of the Solway Disaster was always a solemn occasion. Even now, twenty-five years later, people attend memorial services throughout Cumbria.

On this particular April morning a young florist was supervising his staff, arranging flowers in a church. Although this was not his normal undertaking, the church of Bowness-on-Solway meant a great deal to him and his family.

He was a tall, handsome man with black hair and brown eyes, and at the age of twenty-three he already owned two local florists.

An elderly caretaker stood by the entrance door watching him with interest. He twirled a large key in his fingers, waiting to lock up again. There was no impatience in his gesture, merely a little anxiety. He just wanted his church to look its best for the afternoon service.

Almost an hour later, the young man and his female assistants prepared to leave. As he approached the door, he saw the caretaker smiling broadly. "Ah... you approve," said the florist, putting his arm around the old man's shoulder.

"I certainly do, lad. Your mixture of colour is amazing! If we're blessed with a fine day, the sunlight through those stained-glass windows will make the flowers even more beautiful."

The florist was thrilled with the caretaker's words. He turned to his assistants. "Did you hear that girls?" he laughed. "Praise indeed from an expert on beauty." Unashamedly, he quickly planted a kiss on the caretaker's head. "Okay, then. I'll see you later at the service."

They all waved farewell to the old man, whose eyes shone with pride. Back in the porch, he changed his slippers for black leather shoes before locking the door behind him. He walked up the hill, turning right at the junction. A few villagers out in their gardens waved to him as he passed by, and his sprightly step soon brought him home. His wife stood waiting in the doorway of a splendid farmhouse on the eastern slopes of the village. It was fifteen minutes after eleven.

At this time every morning, the editor of the Cumbrian Gazette in Carlisle was drinking her first cup of coffee. She was forty years old: a slim and beautiful woman whose natural flair for journalism and management skills made her, some five years earlier, the first female and youngest editor in the paper's history.

She replaced her empty cup and tucked a wisp of blonde hair behind her ear. As she did so, the gold ring on her finger slipped off. She sighed, and retrieving it from her desk she thought of her husband, John: an army captain now serving in Afghanistan. He was 'unavailable' of course when she'd tried to contact him about her pregnancy. The test was positive enough but she wasn't sure how he'd react.

It had been a hectic few weeks and she looked forward to the afternoon off. Mrs Scott put the ring in her purse and smiled. "At least I know someone who will be overjoyed," she told herself.

The telephone rang beside her. "Hi, Sis!" came the cheerful voice. "Just called to say I love you, babe! Be good and I'll see you in church!"

"You sound well pleased with yourself, Robert. What gives?" she laughed.

"Just got myself another shop in Keswick, but I'll tell you later... must dash."

"Hey! Well done, little brother. I love you, too... Bye."

The caretaker's wish was granted. The sun shone that April afternoon and the church at Bowness looked its very best. Even the vicar, following his memorial tributes, gave praise to their caretaker for his years of duty and devotion to the church and community. But afterwards, while his family waited for him outside chatting to friends, he checked the pews for any left belongings.

Satisfied with his search, the caretaker left the transept and walked towards the porch exit. It was then that he noticed someone behind the font. The man was crouching down, inspecting the two church bells on the floor against the west wall.

"I'm sorry, sir, but I have to lock up now," he said.

The man turned. "Oh, forgive me. I just got carried away."

He was a short, red-faced man with horn-rimmed glasses and traces of grey in his ginger hair. He looked rather overweight for the trendy clothes he wore. "I'm Jack Cooper, a freelance journalist from London," he said.

The caretaker shook his outstretched hand. "A long way to come for a memorial service," he smiled; aware then of a book in Cooper's left hand. He recognised its crimson cover with gold lettering.

"Yes. Too bad my train was delayed. I missed the service after all. But it's well worth the trip just to see this church," he said. "It's truly remarkable, considering what happened here. I... I wondered if you might help me with a couple of questions."

"Well, I only have a few minutes... my family are waiting."

Jack Cooper tapped his fingers on the book. "According to this, the man who drowned in your church was quire a hero. Did you know Ben Miller?"

"Only vaguely... it was a long time ago."

"My mother did. He came to stay at our guest house once in Euston Road," he said, proudly. "I was away at boarding school then so never met him, but my mother knew of him years before. He was the best journalist in Fleet Street, you know? My dear old mum - God rest her soul - collected his articles and news reports. Made me study every one, she did."

Jack Cooper smiled at the memory. "I guess she hoped a sprinkling of his talent would rub off on me. It certainly did on Sarah Miller. Wow! She's gorgeous... and so nice. I was privileged to meet her at a book-signing in London," he said, with the exuberance of a schoolboy. "Look... she signed it right there!"

The old man fidgeted as he watched Cooper, who was now mopping his brow with a large handkerchief which matched his tartan trousers. He thought he would never get away as Cooper went on... "Have you read it yet?"

The caretaker nodded. "Yes. I have, Mister Cooper... it's interesting. She has a vivid imagination... but being a journalist yourself, I'm sure you know the difference between fact and fiction," he said, quietly.

There was no reply. Jack Cooper was looking up at the stained-glass windows above them. "It feels strange standing here in the spot where Mister Miller died with someone else who knew him. Of course I was curious to see this place after reading the book. And no doubt I won't be the last. But I did it for mum as well… a sort of pilgrimage, if you know what I mean?"

"I'm sure your mother would have been very pleased to know that, Jack."

They shook hands again. "Well, thanks for your time, anyway. Very nice meeting you," Cooper smiled. He turned to walk away, but said: "I'd like to pay my respects to Mister Miller, only I couldn't find his grave earlier. Can you tell me where it is?"

"Of course; it's right opposite the porch under a cypress tree."

"Thanks again," said Cooper, cheerfully. "Oh, I never caught your name?"

The old man chuckled. "Folks around here always call me 'Slipper'," he said, pointing down to his feet. "It's a habit I guess… always wear them in church."

When Jack Cooper stepped outside he saw three people standing beside a grave near the cypress tree. He was undecided whether to go and chat with them, when the elderly woman turned and smiled at him. For a moment he thought he recognised her, but realising they were waiting for old 'Slipper', he just waved and headed back down the path.

The caretaker also had a change of heart. He stood beside one of the bell-ropes, his hand gently caressing its rough fibres. Then his fingers tightened around it to pull and ring the bell… but he stopped. The old man smiled as he let go, hearing the sound of a woman's heels on the floor behind him.

"I rang it once… remember?"

Ben Miller turned to look into the soft green eyes of his daughter, Sarah.

She held him tightly… then whispered. "Would you feel really old if you were a grandfather?"

He looked at her with tears in his eyes, and she nodded, kissing his cheek.

Behind her stood his beautiful Lucy and the son he always wanted, Robert. The four of them were now laughing and rejoicing in Sarah's news. But the young florist was intrigued when his father led him across to a bell-rope.

Ben grasped the other. "I've wanted to do this for twenty-five years. And the perfect time is right now!"

Peter Lathe

Epilogue

Only Ben Miller knows where he found the strength to haul himself out of the water and climb that same rope again all those years ago. It was almost four hours later when a helicopter rescued him from the belfry. Since that day he dedicated himself to the church.

He would be the first to admit that 'someone on high' sent him there to find his daughter. The book about Roman Britain he'd borrowed from the study at Lucy's house gave him a vital clue. Remnants of the concrete 'dog kennel' Sarah told him about that day in the garden was certainly Roman. They were used as inspection chambers for Roman engineers cleaning or repairing their aqueducts.

These chambers were set seventy-five metres apart, meaning the next one in line was somewhere in the church. Miller remembered pointing out to Lucy a part of Sarah's report which mentioned a 'well' in the church's cellar. He gambled with his life to find her ... but won.

With the money from his father's sizeable estate, he both financed and supervised the church's restoration. Apart from the exact replicas made of the south and west stained-glass windows, he used local workmen. Among them was his great friend Tom Walker, who hand-carved the lectern's eagle. Builders converted the weakened bell tower into a bell-cote, and both 'dog kennel' shafts were filled in without trace. The Roman aqueduct was returned once more to ancient *Maia*.

Meanwhile, Ben and Lucy moved into a new home with their daughter Sarah. They bought the old farmhouse Miller had reached across the fields on that fateful afternoon. He gifted the unwanted pastures to villagers and local farmers, keeping just enough for a few hens and goats, and a lush green paddock for Sarah's pony.

The restoration work was completed in the summer of 1988. Its re-opening celebration was blessed with the wedding of Ben and Lucy Miller. Records show bridesmaids, Sarah Miller and Alice Walker with Tom Walker as best man. This was followed eight months later by the christening of a baby boy... one, Robert Miller.

Both the Miller children graduated with honours from university, before Sarah met and later married John Scott, a young army officer.

They were extremely happy years for the family, endorsed by a community which respected and upheld Ben Miller's request for anonymity. Church officials wanted to install plaques and such in honour of his generosity, but Ben politely refused. He was delighted, however, to become caretaker. And so, over the years, his amazing courage and dedication to the church was remembered in a single word... 'Slipper'. As far as anyone knew, Ben Miller died on April 4th 1987.

On his second day as caretaker, Ben was sweeping the church's cellar floor when he noticed some sacking against a wall in the boiler room. He turned on the light and crouched down for a closer look. The sacking was rotten and came away in his hand to reveal a headstone.

On the top in a sealed plastic sleeve was an envelope. He stood, holding it up to the light and read a card inside:

'Reverend Thomas,
I guess this must be for someone dear to your heart. I hope our work pleases you, and be sure old George is careful with it!
Many thanks… Henry Armstrong'

Ben Miller smiled. He realised long ago that Reverend Thomas and George were good men. There was no mysterious plot by the church, as he'd first imagined. They just wanted to protect their heritage. The Roman stone belonged to *Maia…* not some distant museum.

Ben reached out and touched the stone. He knew exactly where to place it… beside a cypress tree near the grave of a young woman named Emma Dixon.

The reporter's story never made the front pages, for on the evening of April 5th 1987 she was killed in a car crash. All her documents and photographs of Ben Miller were destroyed in the flames.

Such tragedies affect many families at one time or another. And even as Sarah celebrated the news of her pregnancy with her loved ones in the church, a telegram was being prepared. It would inform Sarah that her husband, Captain John Scott, had been killed in action.

The headstone standing beneath the cypress tree is admired by many visitors to the church. The shiny black marble has gold lettering, bordered with a colourful inlay of wild flowers. The words are those of Reverend Thomas...

Silent he lies near Hadrian's Wall,
Long after Roman eagles fall
On ancient ramparts of winters' gone,
Where heroes turn to flowers...
Every one.

Its inscription bears no name, but in reality it immortalises a Greek slave they called Damon.